Bolan scanned the room for other signs of danger

Although the sniper attempt had failed, he wasn't about to let down his guard. Someone was determined to kill the Mexican president.

The room was in pandemonium. Many of the governors sat, frozen in fear. The federal protection team had sealed off the exits. Maybe now Bolan could get some answers.

As he turned to the unconscious hit man at his feet, the Executioner smiled.

Finally someone to interrogate.

MACK BOLAN ®
The Executioner

DON PENDLETON'S
EXECUTIONER®
THE
WARNING SHOT

BOOK 1

THE BORDER FIRE TRILOGY

A GOLD EAGLE BOOK FROM
WORLDWIDE®

TORONTO • NEW YORK • LONDON
AMSTERDAM • PARIS • SYDNEY • HAMBURG
STOCKHOLM • ATHENS • TOKYO • MILAN
MADRID • WARSAW • BUDAPEST • AUCKLAND

First edition October 1999
ISBN 0-373-64250-4

Special thanks and acknowledgment to
Jerry VanCook for his contribution to this work.

WARNING SHOT

Poor Mexico, so far from God and so close to the United States.

—Porfirio Diaz

To maintain a position of power you need respect from your people. Once that is lost, so is the power.

—Mack Bolan

Dedicated to the memory of Colonel Rex Applegate.

PROLOGUE

Chicken bones were strewn haphazardly across the dirty wooden floor. Animal hides covered the walls. The heads of animals, some savage like jaguars and wild boars, others domestic such as cats and dogs, were mounted on the walls, creating a macabre sort of wallpaper. All of the animals, whether wild or tame, bore one thing in common. Their open mouths and bared teeth bespoke a helpless terror rather than the ferocity usually found in the trophies of the hunter.

They had died in sacrifice rather than combat.

Here and there, ancient blood stains covered the threadbare couches and chairs. Equally stained were the blades of the daggers lying randomly on the splintered coffee table and lamp stands. Some stone, others of brass and steel, the weapons seemed to retain an aura of the barbarous acts they had performed in the past—and a promise to do so again.

To the man or woman unlucky enough to enter the room, the sight immediately conjured up images of witchcraft, sorcery, necromancy. But the visual atrocities throughout the room were nothing compared to the stench.

The room reeked of sweat, mescal, marijuana and putrefying blood. The blended fetor somehow raped, rather than simply assaulted, the sinuses. So strong was the rankness that it hung almost tangibly in the air, implying that anyone who crossed the threshold could reach out and break off a piece—if he dared. But if the sights within the room paled in comparison to the smell, the smell paled equally to the uneasiness the room inspired. One couldn't enter without falling victim to an anxiety that bespoke horrendous acts of violence, inconceivable torture of the flesh, and unthinkable sins against God and man.

The old woman seated in the armchair watched the man walk through the door. He was an exception, she knew, as she was also. So too, were her sons and the other men and women she employed. Rather than being repelled by the sights, smells and aura of the room, they fed off it, gathered sustenance from it; indeed, it was their life's blood.

"Buenas noches," said the old woman as the man took a seat on the couch across from her.

The man didn't speak for several seconds. He seemed fascinated by a brass dagger on the coffee table in front of him. He picked it up, studied it intently, then set it down again. "Tell me what's good about it," he finally said in Spanish.

His voice, as always, sounded odd to the old woman. His locution was excellent, but the pronunciation was so strange that she couldn't place the accent. She studied the man's face; she had barely been able to see the lips move behind the thick beard as he spoke. "Most things are on schedule," she said.

"Most is not good enough," the man with the beard said. *"All things* must go as planned if we are to be successful."

The old woman nodded uneasily. Her magic was strong. But it wasn't as strong as the worldly power this man wielded; a power that would prove beneficial to her in the days to come. If she remained valuable to him. She watched him closely, careful that her face didn't betray her inner anxiety, for he, alone among men, could bring fear to her heart. He had come to her months ago for help, and she had supplied it, killing many of his enemies and erasing many of his problems. But one problem, a major problem, she had been unable to solve.

Emilio Romero. The world-famous Mexican investigative reporter couldn't be bought off and had gone into hiding, sending his stories of government corruption to American newspapers and magazines.

"Has he been located?" the man asked.

The old woman shook her head. "Not yet. But it's only a matter of time."

The man's eyes narrowed slightly—the first sign of emotion he had exhibited since entering the room. "Time," he said, "is a commodity that is in short supply. Romero is close to the truth. Each day, each hour, each second brings him closer."

"He will be found," the old woman said, lacing her fingers in her lap. She stared across the coffee table. "My son Santiago has advised me that—"

Her words were cut off by the sudden ring of the aged black rotary phone on the end table next to her. Slowly, she unfolded her hands and extended an emaciated arm to the instrument. Her bony fingers curled around the receiver and lifted it to her ear. "Yes," she said. She listened intently for a few moments, the fear in her heart dissipating with each word. "Bring him here," she said when the voice on the other end had finished speaking. "Now." Then she hung up the receiver.

The sputtering of an aging vehicle's engine sounded outside the house. A few moments after that the door to the room burst open. Two burly men dressed in white peasant shirts and linen trousers dragged a bloody and beaten form through the entrance. The old woman smiled, looking from her two sons and the stranger to the bearded man on the couch. Roberto and Santiago dumped the bound and gagged man unceremoniously onto his face next to the coffee table. They looked to the man with the beard, smiles of triumph on their faces.

Santiago bent forward, removing the gag from the prisoner's mouth.

"Get him on his feet," ordered the man with the beard.

Emilio Romero staggered as he was hauled to a standing position, finally resting all his weight on his left foot. The old woman glanced at his right knee and saw the rip in his slacks. Blood had stained the formerly navy-blue material a wet black, and a stark white color—bone—could be glimpsed through the tear. The old woman's eyes moved to the blunt side of the machetes in the belts of both her sons. Half-dried blood still covered the wide blades. They had wisely used the unsharpened edges to subdue the man, and their foresight made her smile with pride.

A wicked smile broke out across the face of the man on the couch, the hairs of his mustache parting to reveal slick wet lips. "Señor Romero," he said. "At last we have the pleasure of meeting face to face."

Romero groaned as Santiago and Roberto cut the ropes from his wrists. The two brothers stepped back, taking positions directly behind him. The reporter brought his hands stiffly to the front of his body, rubbing his bleeding wrists in agony. Then a fierce light seemed to invade his eyes, and he stared at the man on the couch. "I have the story," he said, his strong voice contradicting the condition of his body. "The *whole* story. And it is on its way to *The Washington Post.*"

The bearded man's eyebrows rose in mock surprise. "Is it?" he said. He reached into the inner pocket of his white sport jacket and pulled out a thickly stuffed envelope. It bore the stampings of the Mexican postal service. "Could this be it?" he asked and laughed.

The light in Romero's eyes evaporated in defeat. The bearded man knew there was no need to inquire about other copies of the manuscript.

Yet a small portion of Romero's former determination remained, enough for him to say, "If I can learn the truth, so can others. You will never succeed. If there is truly a God in heaven, he will never allow it."

The man on the couch threw back his head and cackled wildly. "The older I become, the more I learn, and the more I realize how little we all know." He covered his mouth and coughed. "But of one thing I am certain." His eyes narrowed again and he stared in hatred at the battered form in front of him. "There is no God in heaven," he said in almost a whisper.

"If there was, He would never allow one such as myself on His earth." His eyes moved from Romero to Roberto and Santiago. He nodded.

Roberto reached quickly around Romero and drew the razor edge of his machete across the reporter's throat. A geyser of blood shot forth and the man on the couch held up his hand in defense and moved slightly to the side as blood flew his way.

Santiago stepped forward, bringing his own machete down on the crown of Romero's head. The blade sunk deeply into the skull with a sickening splintering sound, wedging itself firmly in the bone. Santiago held onto the handle as Romero collapsed to the floor, then pried it from the man's head with another stomach-curdling crunch. The reporter gasped, the sound muffled by the scarlet fluid trickling from the gaping wound in his throat.

The gurgling ended as Santiago and Roberto fell upon him in an orgy of flashing silver blades and flying crimson.

1

He had seen men stabbed, shot and beaten to death. He had seen brains, blood and bone fly through the air like sleet in a hurricane. Much of the time he had been responsible for the carnage himself—so often, in fact, it had earned him a nickname.

The Executioner.

But Mack Bolan had never killed a man needlessly; never without just cause. Every life he had ended over the years had been taken because there was no other recourse. The men he had killed—various criminals, terrorists, spies and assassins—had been wolves preying on the weak and innocent.

Yes, Bolan had seen his share of killing over the years. But he had rarely seen anything that sickened him like what he was witnessing that morning.

Bolan made his way through the tangled brush toward the wetland in the clearing below. The barks and snarls of pit bulls, mixed with the frantic squeals of a four-hundred-pound boar, met his ears. Next to him, moving quickly but with a look of hesitancy covering his bearded face, walked Don Juan de Fierro Blanco, president of Mexico. The president was dressed in carefully pressed khaki slacks and a matching bush vest from Banana Republic. A Mexican-style clip-point Bowie knife with a ten-inch blade hung from his brown leather Eddie Bauer belt. A canvas safari hat, ringed by a leopard-patterned band, sat atop his head—L.L. Bean.

As they neared the edge of the pool of water Bolan saw that

the dogs had cornered the boar against a ten-foot embankment. General Antonio de Razon, Fierro Blanco's chief military advisor, stepped in to grasp his president gently by the elbow. "Wait for the catch dogs," he warned. "Then when you go in, make it swift. Up and under the belly—the guide will show you where. Pump the blade, then step away."

The president nodded nervously. A trickle of sweat ran down his cheek, then off his chin.

Behind him, Bolan heard more anxious barking as the catch dogs were released from the back of one of the pickups. A moment later, five more pit bulls, larger than the dogs who had tracked their prey, burst down the grassy slope and into the muddy pool.

For a moment the boar was lost within a maelstrom of churning water. Then, as the turbulence died down, Bolan saw the animal again. The bay dogs had moved back to allow their fiercer cousins room to work. Two of the pit bulls lunged forward, their massive teeth sinking into the flesh around the boar's ears. A third moved in, clamping his jaws over the pig's snout between the tusks as the final two dogs tried to maneuver behind the already helpless animal.

"Now?" Fierro Blanco asked, his voice shaking with fear.

Razon shook his head. The sunlight streaming through the trees made the general's red beard shine, calling to Bolan's mind the many Irish mercenaries who had fought in the Mexican Revolution, who then settled and married local women. Razon had been the first to kill a hog that morning in a spectacle almost as disgusting as this one was turning out to be. The dogs had trapped what looked to be a cross between a Russian boar and feral pig among some rocks. The hog had broken a leg in the initial battle, fighting on valiantly using three legs until he had finally been taken to ground by the pit bulls. Razon had waddled in on his thick tree-trunk legs in the gaudy full-dress uniform Bolan could only suppose he must wear for all occasions. While the pit bulls pinned the hog to the ground, the general had cut the animal's throat.

"Now? Should I do it now?" Fierro Blanco asked again. The sweat rolling off his face had soaked his beard, creating a wet, oily appearance.

"No, not yet," Razon said. "It's still too dangerous, *el presidente*. Wait until the guide instructs you." He nodded toward the short grey-haired hunt guide on Fierro Blanco's other side. As he did, the boar gave a mighty heave of his neck and threw the pit bull from its snout into the air.

The dog yelped as he disappeared beneath the surface of the water. Then another of the guides, Tomas, if Bolan remembered correctly, suddenly appeared on top of the embankment directly above the boar and dogs. He uncoiled a lasso and dropped the loop over the head of the boar. Two other guides joined him, tugging on the rope until the hog's head stretched high into the air.

Now the dog who had been thrown moved back in. The other two pit bulls joined the pair on the boar's ears, chomping down on the animal's flanks. Together, with the help of the hangman's noose and the three trawling guides overhead, they maneuvered the boar's head into the muddy bank and safely away from Fierro Blanco.

"Now," the guide said. He took the Mexican president's upper arm and escorted him out into the water.

By now the hog had been chased several miles, then had fought the dogs for another half hour. He hung almost motionless, exhausted, his only movement the shaking of his body as his lungs gasped for oxygen. The guide rested his left hand on the mud-soaked fur covering the animal's back. With the fingers of his right hand, he tapped the hog's underbelly. "Here, sir," he said. "Do it quickly now, before the mighty beast regains his strength."

Fierro Blanco's hand shook as he drew the Bowie knife from

its Kydex sheath. With a high-pitched snarl, he thrust the ten-inch blade into the hog's belly.

Even from where he stood, Bolan could see that the thrust had missed the spot pointed out by the guide. The boar let out an almost human scream. Finding new strength, he wrestled against the five pit bulls and the noose. Blood poured from the wound in his side as he continued to struggle and squeal.

Fierro Blanco jumped back, the water splashing around his feet.

"Here," the guide said, taking Fierro Blanco's knife hand and guiding the point of the Bowie to the spot he had indicated earlier. He grasped the president's wrist firmly. Then, with a sudden thrust, he helped the man insert the blade, then pump the steel up and down inside the hog.

This time, a stream of red shot forth, jettisoning across the water to the mud next to the tiny reservoir. A huge pool of bright crimson began to form on the wet earth. The boar twitched as his life's blood poured out of him, before his squealing pleas for life finally halted.

"Bravo, *el presidente!*" Razon cried out, clapping his hands.

"Bravo!" the guides joined in to congratulate their leader.

Bolan turned away, his eyes falling on Tomas as the guide made his way down the side of the short cliff to the water, the rope still in his hand. Tomas, alone, wasn't smiling and cheering. He stared at Don Juan de Fierro Blanco, his face blank but his eyes betraying the hatred in his soul, and Bolan wondered if Tomas was the only member of the hunting party other than himself who understood the hypocrisy of the whole ordeal.

He wasn't. As the soldier turned back to see the guide help Fierro Blanco out of the water, Captain Juanito Oliverez moved in next to him. The captain, who served as one of the president's bodyguards, couldn't hide his displeasure as Tomas did. Shaking his head, the captain turned to look into Bolan's eyes. "There is something very dishonorable about this," he whispered in a low voice so only Bolan could hear. "Something I can't adequately describe. I have always loved hunting. But I'm now very confused.''

Bolan nodded. ''The dishonor isn't in the hunting,'' he said. ''And it's not in the kill itself. The dishonor comes from pretending that this is some death-defying act of heroism. In reality, it's no different than shooting the thing with a scoped rifle from a hundred yards. Or leading it through the slaughterhouse line toward the hot-dog grinder.''

Oliverez frowned for a moment, then nodded. His right hand fell to rest on the butt of the Government Model .45 pistol holstered at his side. ''Yes,'' he said. ''You have put into words what I could only understand in hazy thought.''

''The dishonor is just beginning,'' Bolan added as Fierro Blanco stepped out of the water. ''The stories of what happened are about to start growing.''

As if to add the period at the end of the Executioner's sentence, Fierro Blanco resheathed his bloody knife and looked up. The fear was gone now from his face, and he beamed widely. ''General Razon!'' he barked. ''You have made arrangements with the taxidermist?''

''Yes, sir,'' Razon smiled, bowing slightly. ''And the meat processor.''

''I don't care about the meat,'' Fierro Blanco scoffed. ''Take it, leave it to rot, it doesn't matter. But be sure the head and shoulders are mounted properly.''

Tomas and the other guides dragged the boar out of the water and dropped him next to the president's blood-soaked pant legs. Bolan noticed once more that Tomas's eyes flared in anger as he watched Fierro Blanco, but being closer now, the guide quickly turned away so the Mexican leader wouldn't see. The president dropped to one knee, grabbing the snout of the dead animal and shaking it. ''Ah, so you are not as tough as you thought, eh, piggy?'' he said. A crude laugh belched from his lips as he rose back to his feet. ''General,'' he shouted.

"These tusks are too small. Make sure the taxidermist fits the trophy with larger ones. The biggest he can find."

"Yes, sir," Razon nodded.

"Madre de Dios," Captain Juanito Oliverez muttered under his breath at Bolan's side. "I'm ashamed to even witness such a spectacle."

The Executioner could only nod.

Presidential aides now came down the slope from the road carrying clean clothing, towels, water cans and soap. Fierro Blanco, the smug smile of the conquering warrior still covering his face, excused himself and disappeared with the men into the trees.

Bolan followed the Mexican president with Oliverez trailing silently behind. Watching over the man was his job, after all, regardless how unpleasant that job was turning out to be.

Mexico was in turmoil, and that turmoil was already spilling across the border into the United States. Two major revolutionary groups, the *Partido Revolucionario Marxista* around Mexico City, and the *Cuidadano para Democracia Mexicana Legitima* in the North, were running rampant, kidnapping government officials and prominent businessmen, upsetting polling locations with gunfire and planting bombs in government buildings. Narco-traffickers were having a field day. Top government and police officials had been bought off and drugs were crossing the border into the U.S. at a higher rate than ever before. Assassinations, looking suspiciously government-sanctioned, of journalists, politicians and indeed anyone suspected of opposing the Fierro Blanco administration, were committed almost daily—several bodies had even turned up buried on land owned by the Mexican president.

Some of the president's top officials had already been indicted, and the president himself was being investigated. One attempt on the president's life by the *Marxistas* had already been made, and Mexican Intelligence agents—if they could be trusted—suspected more were in the planning stages.

Which was the Executioner's reason for being in Mexico. Fierro Blanco, denying any wrongdoing and no longer knowing just who he could trust, had made an unprecedented move and appealed to Washington for help. But the request, combined with the quickly escalating situation in Mexico, had left the U.S. President in his own quandary. It was time to recertify Mexico as cooperating with anti-drug efforts. If Fierro Blanco turned out to be on the take, it would be political suicide for his American counterpart. On the other hand, illegal aliens were now crossing the border to avoid the violence in Mexico on an average of one million a month, turning American cities along the border into hotbeds of violence. The U.S. economy was suffering, with union members picketing the influx of cheap labor, and their demonstrations, more often than not, turning into full-fledged riots.

Perhaps the most dramatic problem was the outbreak of gang violence in cities like San Diego, Phoenix, Santa Fe and Houston. The ease with which marijuana, cocaine and heroin were reaching the U.S. had brought down street prices radically. In order to raise profit margins once more, the various Mexican drug cartels were attempting to eliminate competition. That meant eliminating each other, and their weapons of choice were Uzis, AK-47s and explosives. On American soil.

The President indeed had a problem: He would be damned if he recertified Mexico and Fierro Blanco turned out to be corrupt, and he would be just as damned if he didn't and the violence in America continued. So the Commander-in-Chief had appealed to the men and women to whom he always looked when conventional means of dealing with problems proved ineffectual.

The operatives of Stony Man Farm.

Bolan thought briefly of Stony Man's other counterterrorist teams as Fierro Blanco's entourage stopped in a clearing and began helping the president undress and wash the mud and blood from his body. Able Team was in Alaska, in the middle of an operation designed to shut down a gigantic Russian Mafia drug pipeline that ran across the Bering Strait into Canada and the U.S. Phoenix Force was tied up in Iran, where the same crazed zealots who had taken the American Embassy hostage years before were suspected of planning an invasion of the Persian Gulf in order to take control of oil prices.

Fierro Blanco finished washing and began to dry off as Bolan scanned the surrounding brush for any sign of snipers or other attack. Since Able Team and Phoenix Force were otherwise disposed, he had come to Mexico alone. As usual, he carried U.S. Department of Justice credentials under the name of ''Mike Belasko.'' Ostensibly, he was serving as a presidential bodyguard, and a temporary federal commission had been issued him as well. But his real mission was to learn the truth about Don Juan de Fierro Blanco. Was the Mexican president involved in narcotics, murder and other nefarious acts? Or was he simply an unknowing and innocent pawn in someone else's plan?

Fierro Blanco finished drying and stepped into fresh khaki slacks, a short-sleeved safari jacket and new boots. He glanced at the mud-spattered hat on the ground but one of his aides was a step ahead of him, shoving a clean white pith helmet into his hands. When he saw another of the men starting to take away his knife, he shook his head violently. ''No,'' he said. ''I will carry it the rest of the day, regardless of its condition. Then, perhaps, I shall have it mounted next to the boar. It's a weapon of honor now, like *Coloda*, the sword carried by El Cid when he drove the Moors from Spain.'' He took the knife from the man and stared, transfixed, at the bloody blade. ''Truly, as the Japanese say, this sword has a soul.''

Bolan turned away again. The Mexican president's unusual accent—the aggregate of various European finishing schools and universities—seemed somehow to heighten the fraudulence of his words.

Fierro Blanco now strutted back toward the road. Bolan and

Oliverez fell in beside him with the other men behind them. "So, Belasko," the president said. "The day is still young. I know you declined earlier...but would you like the next pig to be yours?"

The Executioner forced a smile. "My job is to watch over you, Mr. President," he said. "I can't do that and stab pigs at the same time." The vague meaning underneath was lost somewhere between Fierro Blanco's ego and brain.

Razon, Oliverez and Tomas were already in the pickup when the president arrived. The boar had been beheaded. The rest of the carcass lay rotting in the sun next to the vehicle. The dogs and two of the guides waited in other idling trucks.

"Captain Oliverez," Fierro Blanco said as Tomas reached to help him up into one of the seats in the rear of the pickup. "The next hog is yours, if you have the courage. Señor Belasko doesn't feel up to it." He smiled a sneer of superiority.

Oliverez looked down at the bed of the pickup. "I must beg off, Mr. President," he said. "For the same reason as our American friend. My duty is to protect you, *patron*. I can't allow...*pleasure*...to come before that."

Fierro Blanco chuckled. It was clear that he believed Oliverez's reason for declining was fear. He tapped on the rear windshield of the truck. The guide turned, and stuck his head out the window. The president said, "Return to the lodge. With the exception of General Razon, it appears I'm surrounded by cowards this morning."

Bolan pulled himself up into the truck and took the seat across from Tomas. Again, he saw the contempt in the hunting guide's eyes. But this time, there was something different. Something he couldn't put a finger on. He knew only that his battle senses, learned in war and honed to a razor's edge over the years, had gone on red alert.

The guide started the engine and they took off down the road. The president reached into an ice chest, popped the cap off a beer and settled back to enjoy his adrenaline high. After a few minutes, his eyes closed and a deep guttural snoring sputtered from his lips.

Bolan watched Tomas, still trying to figure out what it was about the man that caused him to take notice. His answer came almost too late.

As the vehicles pulled onto the gravel drive in front of the hunting lodge, Bolan saw Tomas move his hand to his side. The pickup stopped, and Fierro Blanco stood. Raising his hands high over his head, he stretched like the awakening lion he believed himself to be.

The realization of what was about to happen hit the Executioner just as Tomas made his move. With a sudden jerk, the guide produced a seven-inch dagger from behind his back and lunged toward Fierro Blanco's exposed abdomen.

Bolan shot forward, his arm extended between the two men. With the weapon an inch from Fierro Blanco's sternum, the Executioner's open palm caught Tomas's wrist and forced the weapon to the side. The guide's momentum drove him on, and the point of the dagger embedded itself in the wooden backrest of the seat next to the president.

The Executioner's own momentum lifted him onto his feet. His shoulder struck Fierro Blanco in the ribs, flipping the man up and over the side of the truck. As Tomas jerked his dagger from the wood, Bolan moved in, hoping to take the man alive for interrogation.

It wasn't to be.

Bolan reached out, grabbing the wrist that held the dagger. He twisted sharply, hearing bone snap. The dagger fell to the bed of the pickup but at the same moment an explosion roared behind the Executioner. Half of Tomas's face disintegrated. The would-be presidential assassin flew back against the cab of the truck, then slithered to the floor.

Bolan turned to see Captain Juanito Oliverez gripping the Government Model .45 revolver. A thin trail of smoke drifted up from the barrel.

President Don Juan de Fierro Blanco stood beside the pickup. The president of Mexico looked at the semiheaded body slumped against the cab.

El presidente's bloodless face no longer looked like that of the conquering warrior.

SCOTT HIX KNEW that it made no difference how high he turned the air conditioner. It would still be hot in his office. That was because Tijuana was hot.

Hix stood behind his desk and stared down at the invoices awaiting his initials. His secretary had been trying to coerce him into signing them for two days now, ever since he'd returned from Los Angeles, but his mind wasn't on the task. His heart never had been in it. The fact that Baja Import and Export, the company he had started after being discharged form the U.S. Army, had turned into a multimillion-dollar business was due to one thing and one thing alone: luck. He had been in the right place at the right time and Baja had grown on its own, in spite if his lack of interest.

Moving away from the desk, Hix walked to the wet bar against the wall and looked at the half full bottle of Old Bushmill's Single Malt Irish Whiskey. In front of it, a clean tumbler and a bottle of club soda beckoned. He glanced at his watch. No. Still too early.

Hix took a seat in the stuffed armchair that faced his desk and stared at the wall behind it. The framed pictures brought a smile to his face, reminding him of a more exciting, if less affluent, period in his life. Looking back at him, he saw Colonel Rex Applegate in the first picture. The former World War II Office of Strategic Services close-combat expert sat behind three of the books he had written. Next to him was a chart displaying an Applegate-Fairbairn fighting knife. Schematics of the various components explained the blade, cross guard and the carefully weighted handle. But it was the colonel's eyes that kept drawing him back. Even in his eighties, those eyes bore out from the picture with the intensity of a true warrior. Hix read the inscription for perhaps the millionth time: *To Scott Hix, Cordially, Rex Applegate.*

He smiled for the first time in days. His uncle, a Korean war vet, had been a big fan of Applegate's point-shooting system and had taught Hix the art when he was five years old. He still remembered Uncle Gene lining up the little green army men on the mantle over the fireplace, then handing him the dart gun.

"Just point it like you would your finger," Uncle Gene had said.

"But it's not a real gun," Hix remembered protesting.

Uncle Gene had laughed. "They aren't real soldiers either, Scotty. But the principle is the same. Try it."

Now Hix broke into a low chuckle. He had practiced hour upon hour. Shooting, reloading the dart gun and shooting again until he could knock the tiny figures off the mantle nearly every time. It had been the best firearms training he had ever experienced, and had prepared him to resist some of the sillier "modern" techniques the army wanted him to teach after he'd become a close-quarters combat expert himself.

The chuckle ran its course and Hix stared a moment longer at the picture. The bottom line was, along with British Captains W.E. Fairbairn and Anthony Sykes, Colonel Applegate had been the pioneer of close-quarters combat, both armed and unarmed. So, after hearing a million and one stories about the man from his uncle, Hix had grown up holding Rex Applegate in the same category as other childhood heros; some real like Babe Ruth, George Foreman, Audy Murphy and Eddie Rickenbacker, others actors like Roy Rogers, Clint Eastwood and Arnold Schwartzenegger. As a kid, they had all been lumped together in that hazy world in which fact and fiction become one. But as he grew older, Hix had realized the difference. Ruth and Foreman had been real—sports legends. Rickenbacker was a war hero, and Murphy had been both. These were the guys that the actor-heros portrayed. With Hix's natural inclination toward close-quarters combat, Rex Applegate was definitely the real thing. While Hix had never been able to bring himself to tell the colonel in so many words and probably never would, getting to know, becoming a friend to and regularly corresponding with Colonel Applegate had been highlights of his life.

The memory of his trip to Los Angeles returned suddenly, chasing the happy memories from Hix's mind. He saw an image of his father hooked to the kidney dialysis machine, looking small and gray and lonely. Frank Hix had taken on that look immediately after Scott's mother died, almost four years ago now. The elder Hix hadn't been the type to commit suicide or take to the bottle. But neither had he proved the type to start a new life. Instead, he had retreated somewhere into himself shortly after the funeral. He still talked and smiled and occasionally even laughed. But to anyone who knew him well, it was obviously an act. Frank Hix just wasn't there any more. Kidney failure had given him an excuse to retreat even farther, and now he lived from one dialysis treatment to the next, sleeping as much as possible in between. His life had ended along with Hix's mother's, and since that day he'd just been doing his time like a convict sentenced to life.

Hix moved back to his desk, sat and crossed his legs. The empty knowledge that he didn't really know his own father overcame him, bringing with it the black, almost overpowering wave of depression that always accompanied that realization. It wasn't that he hadn't tried; he knew he had. Perhaps his father had tried too, in his own way. But they had been so different, with so little in common, that when they talked it seemed that they came from separate planets.

He remembered what he'd been like in his early teenage years—wild, reckless and rebellious; always in search of new adventure to relieve the boredom of middle-class life—and he knew what he'd gotten from his father was exactly, if not less than, what he deserved.

But Hix suspected that his father felt the same way. He suspected that Frank Hix believed he had gotten less than he deserved in a son. The younger Hix had never shown any inclination to enter the family business. What he had grown to be, however, was a damn fine soldier and a well-respected close-quarters combat instructor assigned to Army Intelligence—neither of which his father seemed to recognize, respect or understand. Frank Hix had called the Army a phase his son would outgrow. And when Hix had finally resigned his commission to try to be what his father wanted, Frank Hix had breathed a sigh of relief that the phase had passed. It hadn't. Three years of renting apartments and trying to look interested when a tenant's toilet overflowed had nearly driven him to stick a shotgun in his mouth. That's when the fighting had returned—this time with words rather than fists. But the words hurt both men more than any black eye or broken nose Scott Hix had gotten as a teenager. Hix's mother had done her best to act as a buffer, and when she died Hix realized she had also been the emotional epoxy that bonded his father and him together. Once she was gone, so was the bond.

Hix glanced toward the Old Bushmill's bottle again when the phone suddenly buzzed on his desk. He reached out and pressed the receiver to his ear. "Yes, Conchita?"

The secretary seemed hesitant. "Señor Hix," she said. "Señor Quartel is on the line."

A genuine smile now broke across Hix's face. His former fraternity brother and best friend, Ronnie Quartel, had been a drama major at UCLA. Then, after a decade of bit parts and commercials, he'd suddenly become the newest Hollywood action-adventure superstar. Quartel had surpassed names like Van Damme and Chan, and was now at the top of the box office with Schwartzenegger and Stallone. Quartel's love for Hispanic women was legendary, and he visited Hix in Tijuana between almost every film.

Still smiling, Hix said, "Put him through, Conchita."

A series of clicks sounded in his ear, and then Ronnie Quartel came on the line. "*Buenos dias,* Mexican pimp," he said.

"You say *buenas tardes* in the afternoon, Ronnie," Hix replied, "and your Mexican pimp is exactly what I'm beginning to feel like. Can't you find any women in Hollywood to sleep with?"

"They're standing in line," Quartel said laughing. "But I thought I'd bring them down for you."

In the background, Hix heard several girlish giggles. "Is that him?" a voice purred.

"I've told these girls about my friend who's a real live Gulf War hero," Quartel went on. "They can't wait to get their hands on you."

Hix paused. His visit to L.A. hadn't exactly left him in the mood for the wild parties Quartel's visits always spawned, and he was tempted to make up an excuse. On the other hand, maybe that was exactly the kind of diversion he needed right now. "When are you coming?" he asked.

"We should wrap tomorrow morning," Quartel said. "See you tomorrow night." The actor cleared his throat. "Is Martina still around?"

"Got married," Hix said. "But I'm sure I can wrangle some girls that will meet with your approval."

"At least she'll have the memory of sleeping with Hollywood's number-one box office attraction," Quartel said chuckling.

"That ought to make Sly and Arnold shake in their boots," Hix said. "Never let it be said Hollywood changed you, Ronnie. You were just as arrogant in college doing all those old Thornton Wilder plays."

Quartel said, "Adios!" He paused. "Did I at least say that right?"

Hix laughed. "See you tomorrow." He hung up and looked back to the stack of invoices. The brief conversation had raised his spirits a little, and he didn't want to dampen them again with drudgery. The invoices could wait until tomorrow, too. He stood up, walked to the bar, lifted the Old Bushmill's bottle, then set it back down. No, there would be more than enough drinking—another thing better left until tomorrow.

Returning to his desk, Hix slid open the upper right-hand drawer and reached inside until he had found what he was looking for. He then unbuttoned his khaki shirt. The little .32 caliber Seecamp went into the pocket on his Bianchi belly-band holster, and he rebuttoned the shirt. Looking into the drawer once more, he lifted the custom-made Applegate-Fairbairn fighting knife, a gift from the colonel himself. A moment later it had disappeared into his right front pocket, partially extended through the carefully tailored hole at the bottom. He had learned that trick from W. E. Fairbairn's book, *Get Tough,* and it had worked well for him over the years when a concealed carry was necessary.

And that was becoming more and more the norm in Mexico these days. The *Cuidadano para Democracia Mexicana Legitima* was growing stronger all the time in Mexico's northern states. Accidentally stumbling into one of their outbreaks of violence was always a possibility, as was meeting up with one of the border bandits or other criminals the current unrest in the country was spawning.

Hix closed the drawer. He opened the door to his office and tried to walk past Conchita's desk while her head was still buried in the open file cabinet. He didn't make it.

"Señor Hix!" the secretary said, mildly put out. "Those invoices must be—"

Hix didn't break stride. "Tomorrow, Conchita," he said as he hurried out of the office. "First thing, I promise." He opened the door and stepped out into the Tijuana heat.

THE EXECUTIONER'S EYES opened suddenly, and he found himself staring at the luminous hands of his wristwatch. 0245 hours. His shift outside the presidential suite began in thirty minutes.

Bolan rose from the bed in the small sleeping quarters that had been assigned to him within Mexico's presidential mansion, known as *Los Pinos*—The Pines. He dressed quickly, donning a navy blue sport shirt, matching slacks, and athletic shoes.

The soldier paused in front of the mirror. He had considered wearing one of the blacksuits—the skintight combat uniforms issued to the operatives of Stony Man Farm for night work—then discarded the idea. While part of the early morning hours would be spent in clandestine activity, his approach to the site would have to be in the open. He needed something dark—something that wouldn't reflect light—but also something that wouldn't look out of place within *Los Pinos*. The dull non-reflective navy blue would work almost as well as black, and would be far less obvious.

Sliding the sound-suppressed 9 mm Beretta 93-R machine pistol into its shoulder rig, he shrugged into the harness and snapped the retainer around the belt at his waist. The big .44 Magnum Desert Eagle loaded with 240-grain hollowpoint ammo went into the hip holster on his right side. A Gerber Applegate-Fairbairn Combat Folding Knife, its 4.5-inch spear-point blade honed to a razor's edge on both sides, carried in a horizontal Kydex sheath on his belt, completed his arsenal for the night shift.

Opening the door, Bolan stepped into the hall and walked toward the presidential suite. He had dozed off and on for three hours, trying during his waking moments to come up with a plan that would get him inside the suite occupied by Fierro Blanco and his wife, Josefa. The president's private study, he knew, lay just off the master bedroom, and seemed the most likely place to find evidence of the Mexican leader's honesty or dishonesty. But Bolan still needed to come up with a way to get inside. And all of his plotting throughout the night had gone unrewarded.

In addition to the other guards scattered throughout *Los Pinos*, two men working staggered shifts were always stationed just outside the door to the suite. When Bolan had left earlier to sleep, Oliverez and another bodyguard, Sergeant Felipe Gomez, had been on duty. The Executioner was scheduled to replace Oliverez, joining Gomez during the last hour and a half of the sergeant's shift. Ninety minutes after that, Gomez would be replaced with another guard who would help the Executioner finish his tour, and then Bolan would return to his room for another catnap before arising to accompany Fierro Blanco during his day.

The soldier listened to the ancient wooden floor of the hallway creak beneath his feet as he walked. The problem, regardless of who the guard might be, was that there would always be another man with him. And the Executioner hadn't yet devised a plan to distract that man long enough to enter the suite and search the study.

Turning a corner, Bolan saw Oliverez and Gomez. Gomez leaned against the wall, his eyes closed in sleep or thought. He didn't appear to notice the Executioner's approach. Oliverez, however, who stood directly across from the sergeant against the railing that circled the staircase leading to the floor below, had already turned toward the corner by the time Bolan appeared. The captain's hand fell automatically to the same .45 pistol he'd used to kill the would-be assassin earlier that day.

Bolan smiled, both in greeting and silent gratitude that Oliverez wouldn't be his partner that night. The captain had already proved to be an alert, conscientious executive protection specialist, and any chance the Executioner had of entering the suite grew even slimmer if he was on duty. Bolan shifted his gaze to Gomez. The man still hadn't stirred.

Oliverez returned the Executioner's smile. "Good morn-

ing,'' he said in heavily accented English. ''It's good to see
you. I'm tired.''

Bolan nodded. ''Take off,'' he said.

Oliverez hooked a thumb toward Gomez. ''Perhaps you will
have better luck keeping this idiot more awake then I have
had,'' he said. ''On the other hand, his slumber has also been
something of a blessing. He's infatuated with one of the kitchen
staff…a Maria something or other. He speaks of nothing else
when awake, and is probably dreaming of her even now.'' He
turned to Gomez. ''See! Look at him!''

Bolan followed Oliverez's look and saw the blissful grin
covering Gomez's face.

''It's enough to make one vomit,'' the captain said. His right
foot shot out, striking Gomez in the shin. ''Awaken!'' he cried
out.

The dreamy look on the sergeant's face changed to one of
pain. His eyes opened as one hand fell to his shin. ''Maria?''
he said, trying to get his bearings.

''No,'' Oliverez said. ''It's only me, not your blessed Maria.
Wake up! You disgrace all of Mexico in front of our American
friend!''

Gomez rubbed his eyes, then offered Bolan his hand.

The Executioner shook it. Oliverez shook his head in disgust.
He nodded goodbye to the Executioner and disappeared down
the same hallway from which Bolan had come.

Sergeant Gomez not only appeared awake now, he seemed
fully alert. His attention, however, seemed to have little if anything to do with guarding the man and woman on the other
side of the door. His eyes began an ongoing circuit of nervous
darts, jumping from his watch to the hallway to Bolan, then
starting the process all over again. At first, soldier wondered if
the man might be an alcoholic in need of a drink. But that
didn't prove to be the case.

The Executioner spent the next twenty minutes watching
Gomez out of the corner of his eye, wondering how he could

get the man away from the door long enough to enter Fierro Blanco's study. Even as incompetent as Gomez appeared, it didn't seem possible. Then, the answer to both the sergeant's anxiety and the solution to the Executioner's dilemma presented itself in the form of a pale white face that suddenly peeked around the hall corner.

Maria was mildly attractive. Light-skinned for an Hispanic, with bleached blond hair and soft brown eyes. She was dressed in the white uniform the kitchen staff wore, and appeared reserved about showing herself. The Executioner could understand that. No one besides the presidential protection team was allowed on this floor of the mansion at this hour of night. Being caught here would be grounds for dismissal—or worse.

"Maria..." Gomez breathily whispered. He stared at the woman still half hidden by the corner, then his frightened eyes suddenly shot back to Bolan. "Señor Belasko," he said. "I—"

Bolan had never believed in relying on luck. But when coincidence did present itself, he always took advantage of it. And he had no intention of wasting this opportunity. Grinning broadly, he said, "Gomez, relax. I know she's not supposed to be here. But I won't report you. Hey, what can she hurt?"

The apprehension on Gomez's face was replaced by mild shock, then extreme gratitude. "Belasko," he said, shaking his head in disbelief, "you are a true friend."

"Had you doubted that, Gomez?"

"No...well, perhaps. We have all wondered why you were brought here by the president. And we wondered what you would be like...being a gringo, I mean...."

The Executioner turned back to the corner and waved the woman forward. She moved shyly into view, gradually quickening her pace as her confidence grew. Finally, she flew into Gomez's arms. The sergeant gripped her as if she might get away, pressing his lips to her's.

Bolan cleared his throat and the sergeant broke the kiss. "Gomez," the Executioner said. "Believe me, I understand.

I've been in love myself. Go find a place where you two can be alone. It doesn't take both of us to hold up this door.'' He nodded toward the presidential suite.

With what appeared to take a tremendous act of will, Gomez moved his right hand away from Maria long enough to grasp Bolan's. ''If you ever need anything...''

''Go,'' Bolan said, cutting him off. ''I'll look after things here. Just be back in time for the shift change.''

As soon as they were out of sight, the Executioner turned back to the president's door. He pressed an ear against the wood but could hear nothing inside. That came as no surprise. The fact that Oliverez and Gomez had both spoken in normal voices rather than whispers meant Fierro Blanco's bedroom must be well within the suite.

Pulling a set of picks from his pocket, the Executioner worked the door's simple tumbler system quickly. The lock was old, and designed more to remind the guards not to burst in unexpectedly than to stop anyone intent on entering. A series of clicks sounded softly in the early morning hours. A moment later, the door swung open.

Bolan entered the suite and closed the door behind him. He waited patiently, letting his eyes grow accustomed to the darker surroundings. When they did, he saw that he was in a living room elaborately furnished with antique divans, tables, chairs and other heirlooms from Mexico's past. On the far side of the room, he saw an open door.

The Executioner crept forward slowly, staying close to one wall to minimize the creaking of the ancient wood beneath his feet. It would be impossible for anyone awake not to hear the noise, but old mansions like *Los Pinos* were continually settling; their occupants grew accustomed to such strange nighttime noises. He moved on, taking a step, then stopping. Taking two or three or four steps next, but never the same number in a row. He wanted to avoid creating a pattern of noise that might be recognized as footsteps.

Blanco than he had before, which meant tomorrow night
ould have to find a way into the president's primary office
e floor below. That, he knew, would prove as difficult if
more so, than entering the study. And tomorrow night, luck,
e form of a starry-eyed and horny bodyguard, wasn't likely
e in his corner.

Bolan glanced at his watch. He had fifteen minutes before
shift change. He had to return to his post. He moved to the
or and switched off the light. He had made it back to the
trance to the bedroom when he heard the voice.

"Juan!" Josefa de Blanco whispered hoarsely. "There is
omeone here!"

The president grunted sleepily.

"Juan!" her voice said more urgently now. "Juan, wake
up!"

The Executioner heard the rustling of bedsheets and covers.
Then Fierro Blanco mumbled, "What is it?"

"I heard something!"

Fierro Blanco sighed. "You are always hearing something,"
he mumbled. "This is an old house. Old houses make noise.
Please, go back to sleep."

"No! This was real. There is someone in your study!"

The president, fully awake now, formed his words more
clearly. "And how would they have gotten in, Josefa?" he
asked. "We have guards everywhere. We're the most well-
protected man and wife in Mexico." He sounded as if he were
speaking to a slow-thinking child.

"Don't speak to me like that!" Josefa spit. "There is some-
ne in your study, I tell you. Or perhaps in one of the closets
ck there. Go check!"

Fierro Blanco sighed again, and the Executioner heard the
springs creak. He glanced from the closet to the storage
, then to the closed study door behind him. Getting caught
would at the very least mean the abortion of his mission

Passing through the open door, Bolan found another short
hallway. Yet another door—closed this time—stood at the end.
He moved forward once more and this time he could hear the
sounds of two people snoring on the other side. One snore
boomed like a loud, rolling kettle drum. The other was softer,
more feminine.

The Executioner twisted the knob.

The door opened slowly, squeaking softly. But Fierro Blanco
and his wife must indeed have been used to the noises of the
old mansion because neither set of snores halted or changed
cadence. The bedroom was semilit with moonlight streaming
through the windows, and Bolan saw the Mexican president
lying on his back in the king-size bed, the covers thrown off.
Fierro Blanco wore only pajama bottoms. Next to him, wearing
a plaid flannel nightgown, slept Mexico's first lady. Josefa de
Fierro Blanco's hair had been rolled into curlers the size of
fruit juice cans, and white skin cream covered her face, reflect-
ing the rays of the moon like a mirror.

As he closed the door behind him, Bolan was amused to see
he'd been wrong in his assumption that the loud snores came
from Fierro Blanco. It was Josefa who was threatening to bring
down the mansion walls, with the heroic hog-killer beside her
responsible for the dainty little sounds.

The soldier took a few seconds to examine his surroundings.
Embellished ornately, the room bordered on uncouth. Bolan
couldn't help thinking of Mexico's millions of starving men,
women and children; many of whom could be fed for a year
with the sale of just one of the solid-gold lamps on the night-
stands by the bed. On the other hand, the U.S. had its share of
poverty these days. He supposed the same could be said of the
White House.

In any case, the elaborate excesses of *Los Pinos's* interior
decorators weren't Bolan's immediate problem. He continued
to scout the room. Beyond the bed, to the side, he saw a dressing area with two full-length mirrors facing each other. The

effect was the creation of twin tunnels that grew smaller and smaller, extending into infinity. Beyond the mirrors, a dressing table had been built into the wall. Doors stood on both sides of the table, and the one to the right was half open revealing hanging dresses, skirts and blouses. The other door was closed. The bathroom, he presumed.

Neither of those doors interested the Executioner. It was the one just to the side of the bed—two feet from President Fierro Blanco's sleeping head—that caught his eye. It had to lead to the study.

Bolan moved slowly across the room past the foot of the bed, his eyes on the sleeping forms and his ears attuned to the snoring. The floor in the bedroom was carpeted, unlike the bare wood in much of the mansion, and a silent prayer of thanks floated up from his soul. The creaking beneath his feet was at least muffled. Reaching the dark opening, the soldier found a short step up. He moved into a small anteroom, took a final look over his shoulder at Fierro Blanco and his wife, then moved deeper into the recess. From the pocket of his shirt he unclipped a small Mini-Mag flashlight, cupped the beam with his left hand and twisted it on.

A soft glow emerged from the bulb, turning his fingers red.

Using only enough light to get his bearings, Bolan saw another large walk-in closet to his right. Inside, he could see a rack bearing a variety of men's shoes. Hanging from the bars were Mexican military uniforms, two dozen well-tailored suits and row after row of shirts. He switched the beam to the other side of the anteroom and saw a shorter door, worked in under an overhang in the ceiling. A simple latch held the door in place, and when he bent to open it, he saw suitcases and other luggage piled from the floor to the short waist-high ceiling.

The soldier turned the beam straight ahead and found the study. The door was open.

Bolan moved slowly again, the wood beneath his feet squeaking with each step. Entering the room, he turned back

for a moment. If he closed the door behind him on the overhead light, the soft glow at the bottom visible from where the president slept. He did so, a later the room was illuminated. Before him, he desk, arranged so that anyone sitting behind it cou door. Wooden filing cabinets, couches and chairs tered around the rest of the room. Hunting trophie thing from bobcat to elephant—covered the walls, an between the snarling heads were plaques, photogra other honors Fierro Blanco had received throughout hi Hardly a square inch of the cedar walls was visible ben self-accolade, and Bolan couldn't help wondering where Blanco would find room for the boar he had killed th before.

The Executioner worked quickly. Starting at his right, made his way around the room, searching filing cabinets, shelves and finally the desk itself. He wasn't sure what he was looking for—anything that might prove that Fierro Blanco was either dirty or innocent of corruption. A locked drawer at the bottom of the desk fell to his picks, and in it he did find evidence of dirt—but not the kind he needed. *El Presidente,* it appeared, had a penchant for bondage, and several pornographic magazines catering to this fetish lay beneath a copy of *Sports Illustrated.*

Closing the drawer again, Bolan surveyed the walls. H started over, moving counterclockwise once more and checki behind the animal mounts, photos, certificates and plaq Once more, he found nothing; no safes or hollowed area pulled back the Persian carpet in the middle of the flo again came up with nothing. The couches and cha searched beneath, around and under, then unzipped t ions to look inside—proved equally fruitless.

Satisfied that he had examined the room thorough satisfied with the results, the soldier killed the l turned to the anteroom. He knew no more about to learn the truth about Fierro Blanco. More likely, he'd find himself in a Mexican prison.

He made his decision swiftly, turning and opening the study door again as quietly as possible. With any luck, Fierro Blanco would check the closets first since they were on the way, giving him more time.

The door closed again behind him, the soldier heard the sound of bare feet on the wood in the anteroom. He turned quickly toward the desk. It offered his only chance. Sliding as silently as possible across the floor, he circled behind the desk, jerked out the chair and ducked into the opening.

He had just pulled the chair back in when he heard the study door open. The overhead light switched on.

Josefa de Fierro Blanco's voice drifted in through the opening. "Have you found him yet?"

"No," Fierro Blanco said wearily. His voice lowered and Bolan heard a series of Mexican oaths under the man's breath.

"Check behind the desk!" she ordered.

Bolan stiffened. The mission was now compromised. His only chance would be to incapacitate the president and his wife, escape the mansion and get out of Mexico before the two were found. He shook his head in anger.

Failure was unacceptable to the Executioner.

"I have already checked there," Fierro Blanco said in a condescending singsong voice. "There is no one here. I'm coming back to bed now."

A moment later the light went off and the door closed.

Still under the desk, Bolan's eyes shot to his watch. The green hands told him he had less than ten minutes before Gomez was relieved. The lovesick man would be back anytime now—if he wasn't already. And if the sergeant saw him leaving the presidential suite, it wouldn't be any easier to explain than being caught in the study.

Bolan moved swiftly now, trying to estimate just how much noise the two people would attribute to normal house sounds and pushing the edge of that estimation. Back in anteroom, he heard no snoring. Dropping to his hands and knees, he peered around the corner into the bedroom.

His face was less than two feet from Fierro Blanco's. The man's eyes were closed, and his chest moved rhythmically up and down. Bolan stretched farther. Just beyond the sleeping president, he saw Mexico's first lady. Not only was she awake, she was sitting up in bed.

Bolan moved back again, considering his options. He could try to get out one of the windows in the study, then make his way back into the mansion. But the time that would take made him cast aside the idea. Besides, the chance of doing that without one of the many guards spotting him was zero.

He was still thinking when he heard the bedsprings creak again. Pressing his back against the wall of the anteroom, he saw a shadowy form glide swiftly across the opening. Then the first lady's reflection could be seen momentarily in the mirror as she opened the door to the bathroom. She switched on the light and closed the door behind her.

The Executioner knew it would be his last chance. With even less regard for noise now, he rose to his feet and hurried across the bedroom toward the door. He heard a toilet flush as he opened it, and took one last glance over his shoulder toward the bed as he slipped through. Fierro Blanco was still dead to the world.

Bolan hurried down the hall. He reached the final door and twisted the knob. There was no sense stopping to take time to wonder if Gomez was already there. There was nothing the Executioner could do about it if he was.

Stepping into the hall, Bolan was relieved to see it vacant. He closed the door behind him again, then leaned against the wall, drawing in a deep breath of relief.

He was exhaling when Gomez appeared around the corner. His hair was a mass of tangles, his clothing in disarray and a series of hickeys started high on his neck and formed a trail out of sight beneath the collar of his white shirt.

His face bore the stupid, lopsided grin of the totally satiated idiot.

Gomez thanked Bolan again, then leaned against the wall, eyes closed, in the same position the Executioner had found him in earlier.

A moment later, the door to the presidential suite opened. A weary-looking president stuck his head into the hallway. "Is everything all right?" he asked.

Bolan nodded. "Of course," he said.

Fierro Blanco yawned. "Josefa thought she heard noises in the study. Now she swears she saw someone dart out of the bedroom when she left the bathroom a few moments ago." He paused for another yawn, then said, "The old woman is crazy," and closed the door again.

Gomez's replacement, a Lieutenant Sanchez, came on duty a few minutes later.

Felipe Gomez staggered off to recuperate.

2

General Avia Portilla ran his fingers through his beard and watched the droplets of sweat sparkle to the ground in the bright mountain sunlight. He wiped his hand across the already stained cotton khaki BDU pants, then looked up again to stare out over the mountains surrounding him.

A rush of pride and political fervor surged through the *Partido Revolucionario Marxista* leader's chest. Not far from there, close to a century before, Emiliano Zapata had led his band of bandits-cum-revolutionaries in an agrarian revolt against the rich hacienda owners who had enslaved the peasants. The Mexicans of those days had practiced a system known as *latifundismo,* which had been passed down to them from the former Spanish rulers. *Latifundismo* had been a despicable procedure in which wealthy men had stolen the land, then set themselves up as feudal lords, living off the toil of the commoners.

The pride in Portilla's heart faded but the ardor remained. He looked down, spitting into the dirt next to his boots. Nothing had improved since those days of sacrifice by men like Zapata and Pancho Villa. Not really. Oh, the names of the rulers changed every so often. But it seemed to make no difference who held the power in Mexico, the rich always took advantage of the poor. Revolutionaries, once they gained control, turned into the same selfish bastards they had replaced. Their philosophies, once pure, were gradually tainted by greed until they themselves became the monsters they had fought against.

Portilla shook his head as he heard the transport truck pulling up behind him. Would the coming revolution turn out any different than those of the past? Would Mexico's power and wealth finally be wrested from the hands of the few and given to the masses, or would the names of the players at the top of the roster simply change again? Portilla knew his own motives were pure. But what of the other leaders of the movement? What of the man who issued his orders and what of the mysterious man, whom he had never met, who lay somewhere behind it all?

The revolutionary general took a moment to reflect upon the situation. The *Marxistas* had been failing for lack of funds. Then suddenly, a Mexican government official had approached him with a proposition. Another man—it wasn't made clear whether he too was part of the current Mexican regime—was willing to finance the PRM's activities. This man also had contacts that could provide weapons and other equipment. There were no strings attached.

Portilla felt the light nausea of anxiety sweep through his belly. He had taken the offer, since the alternative would have meant the abandonment of the PRM within weeks. But he knew better than to take his contact's words to heart. There were always strings attached; they just didn't always show up at the beginning.

Behind him, the *Marxista* leader heard the truck pull to a halt. He turned to see it standing next to the tiny shack that served as his headquarters. A tall lanky man, his middle-aged face still bearing the pock-marked scars of youthful acne, dropped down from the passenger's seat of the vehicle.

Colonel Francisco Paz walked forward carrying the leather swagger stick that was as much a part of him as his arms, legs, hands or head. An involuntary scowl spread across Portilla's face. The swagger stick was an offensive affectation of Paz's. It brought to Portilla's mind—he wasn't sure exactly why—images of the rulers he so hated. Perhaps that was because swagger sticks appeared to serve no utilitarian purpose. Oh, one made of wood or steel could at least serve as a weapon of sorts. But leather? The simple fact was, it made him want to throw up every time Paz appeared.

As the colonel neared, Portilla saw the frown on the scarred face. He wondered what the cause of the colonel's distress might be. Paz had taken a PRM attachment to pick up a truckload of rocket-propelled grenades stolen by Marxist sympathizers on active duty within the Mexican army. Although Portilla's government contact had made the arrangements, the general knew the deal had been orchestrated by the "mystery man." At least the arrangement was proving beneficial so far, taking care of one of the shortcomings common to a movement such as the PRM: They knew there were sympathizers within the army but had no contact with them. The rocket-propelled grenades came to them as a result of the new intelligence network the mystery man provided. Portilla didn't know exactly how he would put them to use yet, but the opportunity to acquire them had arisen, and he saw no sense in letting it slip by. Even with good connections, Portilla knew a revolutionary army never had enough weapons. They had to take advantage of every opportunity that arose.

Colonel Paz stopped three feet in front of his commander and threw up a hand in salute. Portilla nodded in return. "You don't look happy, Francisco," he said.

The colonel's eyes fell to the ground. "I don't bring good news."

Now it was Portilla's turn to frown. He assumed something had gone wrong with the pickup of the RPGs but before he could inquire, several men began unloading boxes from the rear of the truck. The boxes were clearly marked. The grenades were there.

Altering his question to a more general query, he said simply, "What is it then?"

Paz looked up from his boots. "The attempt on the president failed, General Portilla."

The PRM leader felt the pit of his stomach tighten. The anger spread upward into his chest, tightening his neck, then flushing his face with blood. He started to speak but found himself unable to choke forward any words. Taking a few seconds to gather control of himself, he finally spoke through clenched teeth. "Tell me about it."

Paz shrugged. "Tomas was with the president," he said. "He had replaced one of the guides for the pig hunt as planned." He paused. "But you already know that. Tomas had planned to kill Fierro Blanco during the commotion that ensued during the last kill of the day—when the others would be tired and the president's own men, having encountered no problems until then, would have let down their guards." He cleared his throat, then went on. "But the trip was cut short. In desperation, Tomas drew his dagger at an inopportune moment."

Portilla waited for him to go on. When it became obvious that prompting was necessary, he said, "Explain."

"Fierro Blanco's new gringo bodyguard stepped between the two men to divert Tomas's thrust."

Portilla's thick bushy eyebrows lowered. He had heard of the big American Fierro Blanco had added to his protection team. There were rumors that he came from the CIA. "Was Tomas taken into custody then?" he asked.

Paz shook his head. "He was shot. Oliverez, I believe."

Portilla spit again into the dirt. He knew this Juanito Oliverez; knew him well. The PRM had attempted to buy Oliverez's loyalty on several occasions. When that had failed, the captain's life had been threatened. The threats had gone unheeded, and when an anonymous phone call had implied that Oliverez's family could be at risk, the captain had actually broken into laughter and suggested the *Marxistas* do their homework before they issued such stupid warnings.

Oliverez was an orphan. He was unmarried and didn't even have a girlfriend.

Portilla turned his attention to the men unloading the truck. Perhaps the RPGs could be used to kill Fierro Blanco. Right now, however, that was a moot point. While they had the rockets, they had no launcher. The general scratched his beard again. That seemed to be the way of things—always something missing. Some small but vital item of equipment was always left off of the list that went to the mystery man, or some essential bit of intelligence information never drifted down from him to the *Marxistas*. Sometimes Portilla even wondered if this mysterious benefactor might not, in reality, only be creating the illusion of assistance while actually sabotaging their efforts.

Turning his attention back to Paz, Portilla said, "The president is scheduled to speak tomorrow at the Bosque Chapultepec. Who's our best sniper?"

Paz took the khaki cap from his head and ran his fingers through his damp hair. "Lopez," he said. "Without question. But he is in Monterrey. You sent him to—"

"I know that!" Portilla snapped. "Who is next in line?"

"Guttierez."

"How accurate is he?"

Paz shrugged.

Portilla frowned. "We have no time to summon Lopez. Take Guttierez and as many men as you need to set it up. I want the president dead tomorrow. In the meantime, I have my own plan..." He caught himself and stopped in midsentence.

Paz waited a moment, then said, "Yes?"

The PRM leader shook his head. "Never mind," he said. "It doesn't concern you. Go now."

Paz snapped to attention, saluted and hurried away.

Portilla walked swiftly to the front door of his headquarters and twisted the knob. He cursed under his breath, finding it locked. There was really no need for a lock in this hidden mountain compound, and a simple push-button snap device was all that guarded the door. He often inadvertently activated it on his way out. He reached into his pocket for his keys, then cursed again. In his mind, he saw the key ring in the middle of his desk.

The leader of the PRM turned and started around the building toward the back entrance that was always open. As he turned the corner, the scowl on his face suddenly became a wide smile. The locked front door was nothing but a minor nuisance but it served as an efficient metaphor for the plan he had in mind to eliminate Don Juan de Fierro Blanco. Guttierez's attack would serve as the front door to the operation. If that door turned out to be "unlocked" and the sniper's bullet was successful, fine.

If not, Portilla grinned as he entered his headquarters from the rear, it didn't matter. His backup plan was bound to work. If Guttierez failed, Avia Portilla would simply "go through the back door," as he was doing now.

THE BOSQUE DE CHAPULTEPEC was Mexico City's finest park, and it was set just west of Mexico City's finest street, *Paseo del la Reforma.* Modern buildings lined both sides of the *Paseo,* yet a stone's throw away could be found the heart of an age gone by. Historical monuments drew attention to the important intersections along the avenue, and the street itself linked the old city to the new.

Bolan watched the workers put the finishing touches on the platform next to the statue honoring Simon Bolivar. He glanced over his shoulder to where Don Juan de Fierro Blanco still sat in the back of his armored limousine surrounded by Oliverez and other federal bodyguards. The Executioner had already scouted the speech site for any sign of trouble, paying special attention to the areas around the stage where a bomb could be hidden. Other members of the president's protection team had investigated the grounds farther back, using techniques they had learned from the U.S. Secret Service. Again utilizing the

Secret Service's lead, the guards had stationed two-man countersniper teams throughout the park. One man would stand by with a high-powered rifle while his partner scanned the grounds with binoculars.

Looking beyond the barricades set up farther into the park, the Executioner saw the hundreds of people already gathered and being held at bay by Mexican police. The officers all carried M-16s with bayonets affixed for crowd control—an image that would have been unacceptable in the U.S. The sight brought to his mind an old joke about the difference between the way American police handled hostage situations compared to their neighbors to the south. The story went that American officers made contact with the hostage taker and said, "Sir, we have your mother and sister here. They'd like to talk to you." Mexican cops made contact, then simply said, "Señor, we have your mother and sister."

Bolan glanced up at the surrounding buildings for perhaps the thousandth time. He would have preferred reconning for snipers himself but the simple fact was he couldn't be in two places at one time. He would have to rely on the professionalism of the other members of the protection team.

And hope none of them had been bought off.

The sounds of car doors opening behind the Executioner caused him to turn, glancing simultaneously at his watch. It was time. He watched Fierro Blanco exit the limo surrounded by guards. They stayed tight, shielding the president from harm as they made their way toward the platform. Bolan fell in with them, his eyes skirting back and forth for anything out of place, anything unusual. Now wasn't the danger time, however. The president was too well insulated by human flesh. But when he took his place behind the podium, he would stand alone. In full sight, and possibly "sights," of anyone who had outwitted the police troubleshooters.

Fierro Blanco waved and smiled as he mounted the steps to the stage, then took a chair directly behind the podium. Bolan dropped into the chair to his right as he'd been requested to do by the president. Oliverez took the seat on the man's other side. The request had obviously angered some of the other members of the protection team. It had been all too obvious that Bolan and Oliverez were the only men Fierro Blanco completely trusted.

The police holding back the people now moved the barriers to the sides. By now the crowd had grown from hundreds to thousands, and they flocked forward amid the usual din of noise at such gatherings. But all crowds have a collective personality. Some are happy, some are sad. If the unified "voice" Bolan heard in the rumblings was any indicator, this crowd was angry.

General Antonio de Razon, again in full-dress uniform, waddled to the podium and began his introduction of Fierro Blanco. For a moment, Bolan watched the fat man's thick beard bob up and down as he spoke, before he continued to scout the immediate area, as well as squint into the distance for any sign of trouble. He didn't know what he was looking for; perhaps a furtive movement or the shimmer of sunlight off a rifle scope. He would only know it if he saw it.

Fierro Blanco took the speaker's stand amid scant cheers and abundant boos. It was all too clear that while he might still have the support of a few people, most had turned against him. Bolan saw a glimmer of action in the corner of his eye and watched three burly police officers club one of the hecklers over the head with their nightsticks, then pick him up off the ground and lead him toward a nearby paddy wagon. Some of the other naysayers quieted. But not all. There were too many of them, not enough police, and they knew it.

The president waited for the crowd to calm, then began to speak. He hadn't finished the first sentence when the shot rang out.

Most of the men on the stage hit the ground. Bolan and Oliverez both lunged for Fierro Blanco, pulling him to the floor of the platform. A stunned silence fell over the crowd, broken

by a second shot. As the two men shielded the president with
their bodies a rural police officer dived onto the stage and
joined them. A third round struck the wood an inch from Bolan's head. The Executioner spun onto his back, still keeping
Fierro Blanco beneath him. The big .44 Magnum Desert Eagle
leapt into his hand as he glanced past the now-screaming throng
of people in front of the stage. The rounds hadn't been fired
from close range, and they hadn't come from a pistol. They
were rifle rounds, from a sniper somewhere in the distance.

Almost a full minute went by. When no more shots were
fired, the other guards on the stage suddenly threw themselves
forward onto Fierro Blanco. Bolan looked at one man in disgust
as he rolled back to check the president. Fierro Blanco was
shaken but appeared unhurt. There was no blood on him or the
platform around him. Climbing to his feet, the Executioner
watched the members of the protection team jockey for position
in Fierro Blanco's field of vision. Now that the threat had
passed, each man wanted to be remembered as being there to
give his life for his leader.

The soldier held the Desert Eagle in front of him as he
watched the crowd begin dispersing. Most were happy to flee
on their own. Frustrated Mexican police officers clubbed and
herded into movement those who had frozen. Bolan walked to
the podium and stared down at the wood planks. One round
had drilled through the stand and into the platform below. He
squatted, trying to follow the angle of trajectory with his eyes.
It was impossible to pinpoint a location with the naked eye.
The sniper might not have been the best shot in the world but
he had chosen his stand wisely. Any of several tall buildings
in Bolan's view could have hidden a rifleman. It wouldn't be
until the discarded weapon was found or the angle of trajectory
could be calculated mathematically that the exact site would be
discovered. All of which meant the shooter had plenty of time
to escape. Bolan suspected he was already long gone even now.

Rising again, the Executioner turned back to Fierro Blanco

and the others. "Surround the president," he ordered. "Keep close on the way back to the limo."

The blood had drained from Fierro Blanco's face as Bolan helped him back to his feet. He stared up at the soldier and tried to speak. The words came out like a frog croaking. He gulped, rubbed his neck, then whispered, "Water...does anyone have any water?"

The police officer who had joined the others on stage when the shooting broke out hurriedly stepped forward, jerking a canteen from his belt. "Here, *el presidente*," he said.

Fierro Blanco took the canteen from the man's hand and unscrewed the cap. He held it to his lips.

The Executioner didn't know what tipped him off. It might have been something he saw in the cop's eyes or manner. Perhaps his sixth sense, honed to near perfection over the years, picked up something else. It didn't matter. Before he himself even knew what he was doing, Bolan had reached forward and slapped the canteen away from Fierro Blanco's lips.

Don Juan de Fierro Blanco stared at the Executioner, his eyes startled and his cheeks still filled with water.

Bolan didn't hesitate. He slapped the president's cheeks. The other guards—even Oliverez—gasped in shock. As the liquid shot from Fierro Blanco's mouth, Bolan smelled the distinct odor of bitter almonds. Turning he saw the cop making his way down the steps of the platform. "Grab him!" he ordered, but Oliverez had already recovered from the dismay of seeing the president slapped and put two and two together. The captain dived headfirst down the steps and tackled the policeman. Several other members of the team leapt after him. After a brief struggle, the cop was handcuffed.

Fierro Blanco had been too flustered at being slapped to notice what transpired with the policeman. His face now turned red in anger. "What's the meaning of this!" he screamed at the top of his lungs. Then he saw the commotion at the bottom of the steps and the realization of what had happened seemed to come over him all at once. His color drained once more. *"Madre de Dios...."* he whispered under his breath.

Bolan stepped forward and took the man by the arm. "Did you swallow any of it?" he asked.

Fierro Blanco shook his head. "No...I don't think so...." he said uncertainly. "What was it?"

"Arsenic," Bolan said. "Strong taste but under the circumstances they figured you'd drink fast before it got to you. They were almost right." He did a quick 360-degree recon of the area, then said, "Come, Mr. President. Let's get you out of here before something else happens. It would be wise to get to the hospital for observation, just in case."

With no further ado, the soldier hurried the Mexican president back to the limousine.

DAVID MCCARTER DUCKED behind the outcropping of rocks long enough to let the 7.62 mm NATO rounds of the Iranian Revolutionary Guardsmen zip by. Not far away, he heard more gunfire as additional IRG tried to pin down the rest of Phoenix Force. He was about to lean back around the barrier and return fire when the cellular phone in the breast pocket of his camouflage BDU shirt suddenly vibrated. He flipped the switch on his belt, deactivating the radio microphone in front of his face to avoid interference, and pulled the phone from his shirt.

The Phoenix Force leader had no doubt who would be on the other end. Stony Man Farm alone had this number.

A chuckle escaped from McCarter's lips as he had a quick mental flash of Barbara Price, Stony Man's mission controller, opening the conversation with, "Did I call at a bad time?" A bad time to call for most men meant the spaghetti on the stove was boiling over, or someone had just rung their doorbell or they were having an argument with their wife. For the Farm's operatives, however, it usually meant they were in the process of being shot at.

The Phoenix Force leader shifted the weight of the Heckler

& Koch MP-5 submachine gun to his right hand, his index finger just outside the trigger guard. "Yes, Barb?" he said as he pressed the answer button. As he did, another burst of fire struck the rocks between him and his assailants.

There was a brief pause on the other end of the line. Then Price said, "Sounds like you're busy."

McCarter, a former British SAS officer, chuckled again. "Not the exact words I'd expected but close."

"I'll be brief," Price said.

McCarter leaned around the rocks and fired a quick 3-round burst toward where his attackers had taken cover in a grove of scraggly trees. "Yes, quite," he said, his Cockney accent conveying the message with typical British understated humor.

"What's your situation?" Price asked.

"About six klicks south of Bandar Abbas," McCarter answered, ducking back around the rocks to avoid the return fire. A head appeared above the rocks ten yards to his side and the Phoenix Force leader swung his weapon that way. He lowered it again as he watched Calvin James release two more 3-round bursts from his own submachine gun then drop again. "Ran across a squadron of these IRG chappies outside Bandar Abbas and we've been playing hide-and-seek ever since."

McCarter knew Barbara Price well enough to pick up on the concern in her voice. To the uninitiated, it sounded like the epitome of calm professionalism. "I've got Charlie Mott hovering just outside in international waters," she said. "Is there a place where he could set down?"

Running footsteps sounded on the other side of the rocks. McCarter lifted the barrel of the MP-5 with his free hand just in time for an IRG corporal to run into it. The man's belly worked like a sound suppressor as three more 9 mm hollow point slugs shot from the German-made subgun and blew out his back. McCarter waited as he fell, glanced at the dead eyes to make certain the kamikaze was no longer a threat, then turned back to the phone.

"Pardon the interruption," he said. "No, I don't know of any place Mott could land without being met by a large reception party of very unhappy Shiites."

Price laughed briefly. "I'll overlook your mispronunciation of that last word. What do you suggest?"

McCarter glanced around the rock again, satisfied himself that the rest of the men in the trees were content to stay where they were for the time being, then said, "Our best bet is to make our way to the sea. Charlie flying an amphibian?"

"No."

"Well, see if he can come up with one. It'll be a few hours before we can rendezvous with him anyway."

"Affirmative," Price said. "We should be able to work a deal with Saudi Arabia. I'll get back to you to work out the coordinates as soon as I know anything."

McCarter hung up. Flipping the radio switch again, he spoke into the headset mike. "Phoenix One to Two through Five," he said. "Come in Phoenix and state your position."

One by one, Calvin James, Rafael Encizo, Gary Manning and Thomas Jackson Hawkins all called in. McCarter already knew where James was, and the other three members of Phoenix Force were close by.

"Prepare to move out," McCarter said. "We'll assemble just south of these rocks."

"Where are we heading?" Jackson wanted to know.

McCarter took a second to answer. He knew why Price wanted them out of there, and it wasn't only for their own safety. The situation must be heating up fast in Mexico, and with Able Team still tied up in Alaska, Mack Bolan was the only operative on the scene.

Well, things were getting hot here in Iran, too, McCarter thought as he twisted into position to fire another volley at the men in the trees. Unless all of the intelligence information the West had was wrong, Iran was preparing to invade both Oman and the United Arab Emirates in order to take control of the

Strait of Hormuz. If it was successful, it would effectively control the entire Persian Gulf and could pretty well set world oil prices to suit itself.

Phoenix Force had been sent to recon the region and get the inside scoop. They had some of it, but not all of it. McCarter couldn't afford to go to Mexico yet.

The Phoenix Force leader watched the men in the trees slowly making their way backward in retreat. Or was it a ploy while others circled the rocks? He didn't know, and it didn't matter. Either way, the time to move out was now.

"Let's go!" McCarter said into the face mike. Firing a final burst of 9 mms slugs, he turned and began making his way through the rocks.

No, he couldn't afford to leave the Mideast right now. On the other hand, he didn't like the idea of Bolan trying to take on the entire problem in Mexico on his own. But if the Phoenix Force leader could help the big guy, he intended to do it.

A bullet ricochetted off the stones at his side and McCarter swivelled, firing from the hip, and dropping an Iranian Revolutionary Guardsman who had followed him into the rocks. The man's bottom lip fell in shock beneath his bushy mustache as the trio of 9 mms bullets formed a triangle just below the red scarf at his throat.

The Phoenix Force leader turned, climbed over a steep slope, then dropped into a narrow passage between the rocks. An idea had just occurred to him, an idea that might not completely solve both the problems in Iran and Mexico, but would go a long way toward it. He still had in-country recon work ahead of him here. But it wouldn't take all five of the warriors of Phoenix Force to pull it off.

INFILTRATING FIERRO BLANCO'S study off the man's bedroom hadn't been easy. Getting into the main office of the president would be even harder. But even if he did, there was a further complication.

One of the cardinal rules of undercover and other covert assignments was that the clandestine operative "always had a story and a reason to be there." Had Bolan been discovered inside the president's sleeping quarters, his story would have been that he had been on duty in the hall, heard suspicious noises inside and had come to investigate. His reason for doing so quietly would have been the wisdom of assessing the situation before making his presence known.

Weak? Certainly. But at least it was something.

If he were caught inside the president's official office, he would have nothing.

Bolan turned the corner of the hallway on the floor below Fierro Blanco's suite and saw the two guards outside the door. He had met them earlier, along with the rest of the protection team; Mario Estaban and Antonio Ruiz. He walked casually their way, nodding a hello. They nodded back. Stopping in front of them, he said, "All is well?"

Both men nodded again. "What of the president?" Estaban, the taller of the two men, asked.

The Executioner looked up at the ceiling toward the president's quarters. "Asleep," he said. "Didn't swallow any of the poison, but they pumped his stomach to make sure. He's worn-out from the experience. His doctor is there, watching him."

Ruiz, shorter and broad-shouldered, shook his head and mumbled under his breath. *"Madre de Dios,"* he said. "What is our country coming to?"

Estaban continued his questions. "What about the cop?" he asked. "Did you learn anything from the traitorous bastard?"

"Only what I knew already," the Executioner said. He had interrogated the rural cop while the president was being examined and had been disappointed at how little information the man could provide. He had been paid the relatively small sum of a thousand U.S. dollars to poison Fierro Blanco. "The cops are underpaid and open to corruption."

Like most federal guards, Estaban had little but contempt for his rural counterparts. "They should all be shot," he said.

"I'm sure this one will be," Bolan said. "I'm going to catch forty winks."

Both men raised their eyebrows. "Señor?" Ruiz said.

The Executioner smiled. "Gringo expression," he said. "Means I'm going to get some sleep."

Bolan turned, walked back to his sleeping quarters and opened the door. The hair-thin strip of brown "door-colored" paper he had wedged into the jam at ankle level fluttered almost invisibly to the floor. He picked it up. Good. No one had been in his room. Hurrying to the bed, he pulled out a cellular phone and scrambling device from between the mattress and box spring. He attached the two instruments, then tapped in a number.

A second later, an Israeli-accented voice said, "Yes, Striker."

"What's your location?" Bolan inquired.

"I'm about a block and a half away. Have I been cleared at the gate?"

"That's affirmative," the Executioner said. "I talked to them an hour ago. Your password is 'frog.'"

The Israeli voice on the other end suddenly took on a French accent. "How racist of you, old friend."

Bolan chuckled. Yakov Katzenelenbogen, former Phoenix Force leader and now in semiretirement as an advisor to Stony Man Farm, was a French Jew. He and the Executioner had fought the good fight together for many years, and knew each other well. "The boys at the gate picked it, not me," the Executioner said. "In any case, they've been told you're delivering a new washer and dryer and picking up two worn-out units."

Katzenelenbogen, better known simply as Katz, said, "How convenient, since I just happen to have two appropriate boxes on hand."

"After you get through the gate, come to the delivery entrance. Don't sweat it if one of the guards decides to escort you. I told them I'd meet you there."

"See you in a minute or two," Katz said.

The Executioner smiled as he cut the line and put back the phone under his pillow. He moved to the door, replaced the strip of brown paper and made his way to the elevator at the end of the hallway. He encountered only two of *Los Pinos'* staff going about their late-night duties as he made his way through the mansion to the delivery entrance. Both men recognized him—he had been introduced to the entire staff upon arrival—and nodded greetings without questioning glances or wondering stares as to why he was there. He had the run of the mansion, with the exception of Fierro Blanco's private suite and the only other room in which he held interest—the office.

Bolan frowned as he cut through the kitchen to the delivery area. He still had no reason to be in the president's office alone at this time of night. And he wasn't going to find one. He'd have to take a completely different approach to his soft probe of Fierro Blanco's desk. Which was why he'd called Stony Man Farm and requested Katz.

The delivery van, bearing the trademark of a Mexico City appliance dealer, pulled to a halt as the Executioner opened the mansion's back door. He watched one of the gate guards drop from the passenger's seat, nod to Katz and start back on foot toward the front gate. He wondered how their conversation had gone. While the former Phoenix Force leader was fluent in French, Hebrew, English and Russian, his Spanish was limited. His dark complexion might pass him off as Hispanic but his words never would.

Bolan walked to the van as Katz rolled down the window. *"Buenas noches,"* the French Israeli said.

The soldier smiled. However he'd pulled it off, Katz had been successful in maintaining his cover as a deliveryman.

"Boxes in back?" Bolan asked.

Katz nodded as he opened the door and dropped to the pavement. He circled the van and inserted a key in the rear door. A moment later, he reached in and pulled out a two-wheeled dolly.

The Executioner took a quick recon of the area to make sure there were no curious eyes, then reached in and lifted the empty container. He was surprised to find it slightly heavier than he'd expected. Glancing at the writing on the sides of the cardboard, he saw that it was marked as the dryer. He placed it on the dolly. "What's in it?" he asked.

Katz smiled. "I built a plywood frame around the inside," he said. "We don't want our cargo shifting and giving us away."

Bolan nodded. He pulled out a second dolly, loaded the washer box onto it and turned toward the entrance.

The soldier led the way through the mansion to the large utility room where the laundry was done. The area was deserted, and they set the boxes against a bare wall. "The problem is getting from here to the office upstairs," Bolan said, turning to Katz. "Anybody who sees us is going to raise an eyebrow."

"Any suggestions?"

"Yeah," said the Executioner. "Pray."

"In French or Hebrew?" Katz asked, grinning. "I've been Catholic and Jewish, you know."

Bolan smiled as he turned and led the way out of the utility room. "Take your pick," he said. "I understand it all goes to the same place."

The two men walked swiftly to the elevator. As they rode the car upward, Katz reached into the pocket of his coveralls and produced two hypodermic needles. "One for me," he said, palming the syringe much like an assassin hiding a knife, "and one for you." He handed the second needle to the Executioner.

Bolan took the syringe. "What is it?" he asked.

"Demerol," Katz said as the doors opened and they stepped into the hallway.

Bolan led the way again, rounding the corner to the president's office at a casual stroll. He kept the syringe out of sight behind his leg as he approached the two men. "Ruiz, Estaban," he said as he drew within arm's length of the two guards. "I'd like you to meet an old friend of mine." Without further ado, he reached up, grabbed Ruiz by the back of the neck and jerked him forward. The needle easily penetrated the thin fabric of the man's suit jacket and entered his upper arm.

Out of the corner of his eye, the Executioner saw that Katz had plunged his own syringe into Estaban's shoulder. Both men stood motionless for a moment with astounded eyes. Before they could recover and respond, the drug had entered their systems and they collapsed forward into Bolan's and Katz's arms.

"This is the touchy part," Bolan said. "If anybody sees us now, there'll be no explaining."

Katz nodded as they dragged the two limp forms quickly down the hall to the elevator and pushed the button. They held their breaths, praying silently that the car would be empty when it reached their floor. They didn't exhale until the doors had rolled open and the two guards were safely inside, headed down.

"So far so good," Katz said.

The guards's dragging feet made soft noises across the carpet as Bolan and Katz towed them toward the corner of the hall that led to the laundry room. They made the turn unseen and continued on. Once inside, Bolan could shut the door behind them while they loaded the sleeping men into the boxes. From there on in, it should be simple. No one would question the president's personal guard and a jumpsuit-clad workman hauling an old washer and dryer out of the building.

They were three feet from the laundry door when a pretty young woman wearing a black-and-white maid's pinafore turned the corner behind them and came to a halt.

Bolan let Ruiz slide to the floor and turned to see the woman's open mouth and frightened eyes. She didn't know what exactly she was seeing. She just knew it wasn't right.

The Executioner saw her vocal chords contract as she prepared to scream. Sliding across the carpet, he shot one hand behind her neck, the other covered her mouth a half-second before the call for help went out. Pulling her close, he felt her lips tremble beneath his hand as he whispered, "*Señorita*, we don't want to hurt you."

The maid looked up at the Executioner, her dark eyes clearly flashing doubt. Bolan glanced at Katz, who was already moving forward. From his coveralls he produced a third syringe and plunged it into the woman's tricep. She jerked slightly in the Executioner's arms, then her eyes closed and she became as lifeless as Ruiz and Estaban.

Lifting the beautiful young maid over his shoulder, Bolan hurried her into the laundry room and stretched her out on the tile. Katz was at his heels with Estaban. Together, they pulled Ruiz through the doorway and closed the door.

"I almost didn't bring a spare," Katz said, looking down at the syringe which was still in his hand. "I'm glad I did." Then his eyes moved toward the washer and dryer boxes against the wall. "But we have no extra box."

Bolan shook his head. "We'll have to make do," he said. Grabbing Estaban under the arms while Katz grasped the man's ankles, they lifted the guard up and into the empty cardboard box. Katz pulled a roll of duct tape from his coveralls and secured the top.

Ruiz, though heavier, was more compact. As soon as he was inside, Bolan began arranging his arms and legs to conserve room. The movement caused the guard to stir but his eyes didn't open. "The dose was strong—it'll keep him out for hours," Katz said, answering the Executioner's unasked question.

When Ruiz was as far at the bottom as he was going to go,

Bolan and Katz lifted the young maid. She settled into the box faceup on top of the guard, her short skirt rising to reveal black panties beneath.

Katz raised an eyebrow and smiled. "My, my," he said, "at my age, it's nice to be reminded occasionally I'm still alive."

The Executioner chuckled as he pulled the skirt down over the girl's legs, folded her arms into the box as best he could and stepped back. A good two inches of the woman still extended above the top of the box. And she couldn't be jammed down any farther.

Bolan scanned the laundry room looking for another suitable container. There wasn't one. Disgustedly, he said, "We'll have to take them like this, Katz. We'll leave the flaps up on the side. That'll cover most of her. As long as nobody gets too near or looks too close…" He let his words trail, knowing Katz understood.

The two men from Stony Man Farm lifted the boxes onto their dollies, opened the door and started down the hall toward the rear exit once more. Footsteps sounded in the distance, gradually growing closer as they neared the service entrance. Bolan was about to open the door when a voice said, "Belasko?" He turned to see Oliverez, wearing his pistol belt over a pair of baggy black sweatpants and a T-shirt. His coarse black hair was a mass of tangles and he looked like a victim of insomnia.

The Executioner kept his body between the captain and the open box as he maneuvered the dolly against the wall. Then, as Oliverez started forward, Bolan looked at Katz. "I'm sorry I can't help you further, friend," he said. "But I see I have business to which I must attend." He moved swiftly away and met Oliverez as the man started down the hall toward them..

"What are you doing?" the captain asked, his voice betraying no suspicion—just curiosity.

Bolan kept his body in front of the shorter man, hearing Katz open the service door behind him as he answered. "Guy's delivering a new washer and dryer," he said. "Sent him by himself. I wasn't doing anything so I thought I'd give him a hand."

Oliverez nodded. "It's the kind of thing I myself would do," he said. "But few others who work here would lower themselves. Perhaps it's not right but the caste system is stronger in Mexico than in your country. It always has been and always will be."

Bolan shrugged again. "It doesn't have to be," he said. "Mexico could have a true democracy." By now he had heard Katz wheel one of the dollies—he presumed the Stony Man advisor would have chosen the one with the open top first—through the door.

Oliverez chuckled. "You sound like you might support the revolutionists in the north," he said.

"The *Cuidadano para Democracia Mexicana Legitima?*" the Executioner asked, still stalling for time.

"Yes," the captain said. "The CDML."

Bolan returned the smile. "I can support their ideas—not their actions in trying to implement them."

"As can I," Oliverez nodded. "I believe in democracy. True democracy. But murder, bombings, kidnappings...the slaughter of innocent women and children to achieve it? Never."

Behind him, Bolan heard Katz return and begin wheeling out the second dolly. He turned to see that it was, as he'd suspected, the sealed container holding Estaban.

"I didn't mean to take you from your good deed," Oliverez said. "Perhaps we both can help the poor man." He moved past Bolan and down the hall.

Bolan followed. They exited the back door and reached the van just as Katz was lifting the box into the rear door. Glancing over the two shorter men's heads, the Executioner saw the first box shoved up against the back of the driver's seat. Rags, a tool box and other items had been piled on top of the maid's sleeping body to camouflage it. It looked like the box was simply overflowing with miscellaneous junk.

Oliverez helped Katz shove the box the rest of the way in and closed the door for him. The former Phoenix Force leader bowed at the waist. *"Muchos gracias, patron,"* he said in a passable accent.

"Simply capitan will do," Oliverez replied. "I'm not your *patron,* and no other man is either."

A puzzled look filmed Katz's eyes. Bolan almost laughed. He was playing the part of the ignorant peasant who couldn't fathom a world without feudal-like masters and serfs. Bowing again, Katz opened the door of the van and slid behind the wheel.

Bolan and Oliverez walked back into the mansion together. "You see what I mean?" the captain said as they passed the laundry room. "This old man has lived his whole life under someone's thumb. He can't even understand that he should have no *patron.*" He threw up his hands in disgust. "I had hoped a walk would help me sleep. Now I'm afraid I'll be up all night thinking about this."

The big American shook his head. "You're doing what you can," he said. "You can't change it all overnight."

"No," said Oliverez. "I can't. But I can't help wanting to." He stopped and extended his hand. "I'll see you in the morning, Belasko. I'm going to try to rest again now."

"Good luck," the soldier said. He watched Oliverez disappear around a corner.

Bolan took the stairs this time, coming out next to the elevator. He hurried down the deserted hall to Fierro Blanco's office, pulled the pick set from his pocket and opened the lock.

A moment later, he was inside. As he waited for his eyes to grow accustomed to the darkness, he thought of the two men and the woman in the back of the van. They wouldn't be missed until tomorrow when their shifts changed. It would be assumed that the men had deserted; considering Mexico's state of affairs such desertions were becoming more and more frequent, even among trusted officials. As for Ruiz, Estaban and the maid themselves, when they woke up in a few hours, they would be at Stony Man Farm. They would be kept secured there, and would probably live better during their stay at the Farm than they did at home. When all of this was over, they'd be drugged again and returned to Mexico. A cover story for their disappearances would be invented depending on who was in charge when the mission was over. They would never know exactly where they'd been, or what had happened. But Stony Man would tie up the loose ends.

A brief wave of sorrow filled the soldier as his eyes cleared and he saw that he was in the outer office of Fierro Blanco's secretary. Not all of the loose ends could be covered. There was little that could be done if Estaban and Ruiz had wives and families that would worry about them. The young maid had worn no wedding ring but she might well have a boyfriend or fiancé. Even if she didn't, she would have parents, brothers, sisters...

Bolan pushed the distracting and unproductive thoughts from his mind. There was nothing that could be done about some things; such were the fortunes of war. The missing trio would return to their families as soon as this mission was over, no sooner, and there was no way he could change that.

But it was another good reason to move with the utmost speed. The Executioner moved from the door toward the office of Don Juan de Fierro Blanco.

3

The men were dirty; the whores, ugly. And the Cantina Celito Lindo itself wasn't much, either.

Roaches scurried across the cracked concrete floor and ran steeplechases over the bottles of lukewarm beer, glasses and ashtrays on the tables. The acrid odor of body sweat, alcohol, tobacco, marijuana, urine, vomit and cooking grease mixed with the cheap perfume and natural musk of the *señoritas*-for-hire. Broken table legs were the rule rather than the exception.

A couple—a Hispanic woman and her boyfriend, a tall gringo biker with a three-day stubble of beard—looked as if they'd just stepped off the set of *Mad Max*. The rest of the human refuge in the cantina might well have made up the cast of *Night of the Living Dead*.

Calvin James led Rafael Encizo through the open door out of the burning warmth of the Mexican sun and into the staggeringly stale heat of the shadowy bar. Both men scanned the room for signs of danger as they made their way to a corner table.

The eyes of the patrons were on the two Phoenix Force warriors as they cut through the crowd. Both James and Encizo wore torn, faded jeans and soiled T-shirts. Their last shower had been half a world away in southern Iran. They had dressed down for the meeting, knowing Bolan had set it up among the denizens of Mexico City's worst barrio to avoid being spotted by anyone who knew him. But they hadn't dressed down far enough, James thought, as he pulled a ramshackle chair away from the table.

James sat, careful not to break the rickety chair. David McCarter had decided he could spare no more than two of his team until the Iran problem stabilized, and had picked him and Encizo because both were fluent in Spanish. Encizo, being Cuban, could also pass as a native Mexican if need be. And while it hadn't been said in so many words, Calvin James suspected that speaking Spanish wasn't the only reason he had been chosen, either.

The black Phoenix Force warrior felt the hilt of the custom-made fighting knife dig into his back as he leaned against the back of the chair. He had grown up on the streets of Chicago's South Side, a tough kid who had learned to use a blade in order to survive. Navy SEAL training had refined his technique but it had been his own motivation that carried his skills even beyond that. Each year, he attended knife seminars given by Combat Technologies in Walla Walla, Washington, where he practiced with some of the world's foremost bladesmen.

James was an expert knife fighter. He had studied the techniques of Applegate, Fairbairn, Biddle and Styles, as well as the Eastern arts of tanto-jitsu and Filipino kali and arness. He had made each style his own, blending them all into his personal system of attack and defense.

James inhaled a lungful of smoky stagnant air. He knew his prowess with the blade was the other reason McCarter had chosen to send him to assist Bolan in Mexico. Guns made noise. Knives didn't. And silent killing might well be called upon during the Executioner's clandestine mission.

Shifting in his chair, James moved the knife to a more comfortable position. Known as the "Crossada," it was a cross between a traditional Bowie knife and an Arkansas Toothpick. The Crossada normally sported a twelve-inch blade but John "Cowboy" Kissinger, Stony Man Farm's Chief Armorer, had reground James's model to ten inches to aid concealment.

Encizo took the chair across from James, twisting it sideways so his back would be against the wall. James watched his friend make a more in-depth survey of the patrons and then shook his head. Encizo also shook his head. "Not a great advertisement for my people, is it?" he whispered across the table.

James grinned. "We're in Mexico," he said. "You're Cuban."

"I meant Hispanics in general," Encizo whispered back.

James chuckled. "These maggots hardly represent Hispanics in general," he said.

The appearance of Bolan in the cantina's doorway returned James and Encizo to a serious mood. He wore blue jeans, a black shirt and combat boots. His eyes skirted the room much as theirs had done upon entering before they fell on the corner table. James saw the American biker give the stranger the once-over as Bolan walked toward them.

A moment later, the Executioner had pulled out the third chair at the table and sat. With Encizo and James having taken the chairs against the wall, Bolan was forced to sit with his back to the crowd and the door. He made no big deal of it, although James knew it was not the seat he would have chosen himself. And the Phoenix Force warrior felt a brief swell of pride that the big guy would trust him to watch his back.

"Glad to see the doorman let you pass," Encizo said. "We were afraid this might be one of those joints where only the rich and famous get in."

Bolan smiled. "So I'm not rich and famous?" he asked.

"You're sure not rich," Encizo said. "And you're not even famous under your current alias."

"I've taken you to worse places than this."

"And no doubt will again," James nodded. "So, what's the scoop, Striker?"

He saw Bolan turn and circle the room with his eyes one final time before he spoke. He seemed to halt his inspection momentarily on the American biker and his darker-skinned girlfriend, then turned back to the table.

"I've been through Fierro Blanco's office and private study," the Executioner said. "So far, I haven't found a thing to lead me to believe he's dirty." He paused, then added, "Then again, I haven't found a thing to prove he isn't, either."

"What about all the assassination attempts?" Encizo asked. "They wouldn't be trying to kill their own man, would they?"

"Depends on which *they* you mean, Rafe," Bolan said. "Mexico has so many dissenting factions. At one end of the spectrum are the Marxists—the PRM. At the other end are the Citizens for Legitimate Mexican Democracy based in the north. In between, you've got probably fifty smaller, lesser known revolutionary groups. Fierro Blanco could be tied into any, all or none of them. If he's clean, they may all want him dead. If he's dirty, the groups he isn't aligned with may be behind the attempts, and if he's being paid off by them all, and any of them have found out, they'll be angry that the man's trying to burn the candle at both ends." He paused, then said, "Then again, there's always the chance that the assassinations are being staged by *el presidente* himself as a cover—to make him look innocent. None of them have been particularly professional with the exception of the poisoning."

The waitress appeared again, and silence fell over the three Stony Man warriors. Bolan nodded at the beer in front of Encizo and the woman turned on her heels and left.

"The poisoning doesn't sound like a setup," James said. "Didn't he swallow some of it?"

"No, but he had it in his mouth. I got to him just in time."

"Still…" James said.

The Executioner nodded again. "Yeah, I know. If he set it up himself he was cutting it real close. What was he going to do if nobody stopped him? Stand there with his cheeks puffed out until we caught on?"

"He could have spit it out," Encizo said. "Arsenic mixed

with water has a strong taste. If nobody saved him, he could
have claimed he noticed the taste.''

"I thought of that," Bolan said. "And it's a possibility. But
he'd have been taking the chance of absorbing enough through
his mouth to get mighty sick. No, I don't think so. Call it a
hunch if you want but I watched the man. My gut feeling was
he didn't know anything about it.''

James and Encizo nodded. Bolan's sixth sense was legendary
among the Stony Man troops, and an Executioner hunch was
second only to a documented fact from multiple sources.

"Of course that doesn't tell us whether or not the other attempts were his doing," James said. "So we're back to square
one.''

"There's an old military expression for a situation like this,"
Encizo said.

"Yeah," James agreed. "And the first word is 'cluster.'''

The waitress brought Bolan's beer and another brief break
in the conversation. As soon as she was out of earshot again,
the big guy said, "That's it from my end. Fill me in on your
briefing stateside.''

James took a sip of beer and set the bottle down, causing
the table to wobble. When he glanced back up, he saw the
leather-clad biker in his peripheral vision. The man seemed to
be trying to lean closer to him, Encizo and Bolan. Probably
thought they were DEA agents. James looked into the Executioner's eyes. "We were only at the Farm long enough to refuel
and pack fresh gear. Brognola briefed us as we went. But the
bottom line is, the Mexican problem isn't just lapping over the
border anymore. The dam's broke and it's crossing like a tidal
wave.''

Bolan's eyebrows rose slightly, encouraging him to go on.

"You already know how illegal immigrant traffic has increased. Our President has sent eighty thousand troops to help
the Border Patrol. They stretch from Brownsville to San Diego
and there still aren't enough men to stop them. *Bandidos* have

always operated south of the border—immigrants bring their valuables with them—but now they're crossing into Texas, New Mexico, Arizona and California to catch the ones who've gotten away. The immigrants lucky enough to make it into the cities are causing such a tremendous population explosion that there've already been tuberculosis outbreaks in El Paso and Nogales.'' He paused to catch his breath, then continued. ''Somebody set off a car bomb in Los Angeles yesterday morning. The *Times* got a letter from the *Legitimas* claiming responsibility. But the FBI thinks it was really one of the drug cartels—that the letter was a phony to take the heat off them and put it on the CDML.''

''And put even more drugs on the streets than ever,'' Bolan predicted.

''It's as if it's doubling every day,'' Encizo added. ''Which has brought prices down to where every first grader can afford to buy crack out of his lunch money. It's even too easy to smuggle right now for the cartels. Their profit margins are down. To raise prices again they've got to eliminate each other, and it's already starting. Turf wars are in full swing in San Diego, Phoenix and Albuquerque. There were five gang-style murders in Houston last night that the cops think are tied to it. Four of the bodies were Hispanic and one was a known Mexicali Cartel enforcer.''

''Any action being taken?'' Bolan asked.

''They've formed a joint DEA-Military task force to send out in addition to the troops with the Border Patrol,'' James said. ''There are rumors of a new underground tunnel between Sonora and Arizona, and the task force is supposed to find it.'' He shook his head. ''The way the Man in the White House has cut military spending, I hope nothing happens anywhere else. There's about to be a full-scale drug war in the southwest the likes of which the U.S. has never seen. Before it's over, we'll have committed so many troops to it that we'll be like ducks in a shooting gallery to the rest of the world.''

Bolan drummed his fingers on the table next to his beer bottle. James could see the man's mind at work in the expression on his face. Across the room, the American biker and his girlfriend stood and kissed. She jerked back suddenly, giggling and rubbing the stubble on his face that must have spiked her. He fondled one of her breasts for a moment, then the woman left through the front door. The biker sat.

Finally, the Executioner said, "Any intel as to whether or not the Mexican government itself is behind the drug smuggling?"

James shrugged. "Impossible to know. At least some of the government has been bought off. But Mexico's always been like that. As to whether or not the dirty money goes all the way to the top—to your new ward—they don't know anymore stateside than you do."

Bolan quit drumming his fingers. "Okay guys," he said. "The way I see it, we're fighting on at least three fronts already. We've got the right-wing *Legitimas* in the north and the left-wing *Marxistas* down here. But both groups are spreading all over Mexico, and they're moving fast. Then we've got the drug cartels—which are really about a dozen fronts, if you want to break them down." He tipped his beer and swallowed what remained. "I had a little undercover work for you here in Mexico City but that's going to have to wait. The dope going into the U.S., and the violence it's bringing innocent citizens at home, concerns me more right now than what's here."

James nodded. "If I were a betting man, I'd bet Rafe and I are on our way back to take over the joint task force."

"You'd win that bet," Bolan said. "Get hold of Brognola. He can set it up through the President."

"You got it," James said. "Anything you want us to do before we leave?"

The Executioner nodded. "Yeah, there is. Let's find out why the dirtbag whose girlfriend just left seems so interested in us."

Few things could shock Calvin James when it came to the

abilities of Mack Bolan. But this time, he had to admit that even he was surprised. As far as he could tell, Bolan had seen the American once when he entered the cantina, then again only when he had turned around. Since then, the soldier hadn't been in a position to catch the man looking at them like James had done. He had definitely not been able to see the woman leave. Yet, somehow, he *knew*.

Calvin James felt a grin break across his face. Mack Bolan was the very heart and soul of Stony Man Farm. Little things like this were the reason why.

SMOKE ROSE FROM the gun barrel. The man holding it took a step back from the body at his feet, and gazed into the sunset.

"That's a wrap!" the director called out.

Ronnie Quartel broke his gaze and turned to the director, Tom Domnick. A wild grin appeared under his handlebar mustache. The gunslinger raised the .45 Colt pistol to his lips, blew the last of the smoke from the barrel, and said, "Well, thank God for small wonders. Boys and girls, it's party time!"

A cheer went up from the rest of the cast and crew.

Quartel shoved the pistol into the holster of his Buscadero rig and ripped the hot bandanna from his throat. He reached up, pulled the white Stetson from his head and sent it flying across the set like a Frisbee. In the corner of his eye, he saw one of the makeup girls catch it and hold it to her breasts like she'd just caught the bridal bouquet at a wedding. Quartel turned toward the woman. Tall and slim with raven-black tresses. Nice chest, and legs that stretched all the way from Earth to the moon. Had he nailed her sometime during the shoot? He couldn't remember.

Striding toward his motor home just off the set, Quartel unbuckled the gun belt as he walked. He stretched it out to his side, confident that the unseen hand of one of the crew would take it from him. He wasn't disappointed.

By the time he reached the vehicle, four of the women in

the movie—three extras and a bit part—had fallen in behind him. All four were blondes and built like they'd fall forward if one ounce of pressure were applied to the back of their heads. Just the way his old buddy Scotty-boy had always liked them. At UCLA it had been the cheerleader types Hix went for. Well, these little blond movie starlets were just slightly older versions of cheerleaders. They all were what he and Hix had called the "essential three Bs" of college: blonde, big-boobed and brainless.

Quartel felt a frown come over him as he waited for another faceless member of the crew to open the door to his motor home for him. That was how Hix used to like them, anyway. He wasn't sure about his old friend anymore—couldn't tell exactly what he liked these days. Hix had been acting strange lately. Not himself. Probably just the same old crap with his old man.

The movie star mounted the steps to his motor home with the same grace he demonstrated when he vaulted onto a horse. He moved to the bar in the living room, unbuckling his chaps as he waited while the crew member holding his gun belt set it down on the couch and poured him three fingers of Jose Cuervo Gold tequila. He tried to remember the boy's name as he tossed the chaps next to the Buscadero rig but couldn't. The kid was just another of Hollywood's thousands of wanna-be stars, so he said simply, "Thanks, kid."

The young man beamed as if he'd just won the lottery.

The gaggle of giggling blondes had followed him into the living room too, and he saw now that they all carried overnight cases. "What you got in your bags there, girls?" he asked, then raised the glass to his lips and downed half of the tequila.

"Well," tittered one—Quartel thought her name was Tara Something-or-Other— "clothes and makeup, of course."

The tequila burned its way down Quartel's throat and warmed his stomach. He gave the girls one of his award winning smiles and said, "The makeup I can understand. But why the clothes?"

He was met by four blank stares.

Quartel was wondering where his drink-mixer had gone when Tom Domnick stuck his head inside the door. "You be ready a month from now, Ronnie," the director said in the voice of an overworked mother. "I don't want you showing up on set overweight with a thirty-day hangover."

Quartel laughed good-naturedly. Domnick was directing his next picture, too. "I'll be a lean, mean, fighting machine Tommy-boy," he said. "What is it I'm playing again?"

Domnick sighed. "A cop, Ronnie. It's a cop movie. You've got the script."

"Oh yeah. Now I remember. Good part." He had no idea if it was or not. His agent had advised him to take it, and since the man hadn't led him astray yet, he had signed the contract without even opening the script.

Domnick evidently knew this, or suspected as much. "At least read the damn thing while you're off," he said. "Believe it or not, there are some of us who don't get a kick out of twiddling out thumbs around the set while you sit in here trying to learn your lines." His eyes rolled around the motor home, then stopped on the chaps and gun belt on the couch. "Want me to send someone to pick those up?" he asked.

"Nah," Quartel said. "I'll take them along. Give them to the *señorita* I like the best."

"That's a gun in that holster, Ronnie," Domnick said. Again, he sounded much like a mother whose patience was being tried by an unruly child. "Not a prop gun. It's loaded with blanks but it's a real gun. You're going to Mexico, and the Mexican government is having its problems these days, in case you haven't bothered to pick up a newspaper. They don't smile on bringing guns into the country."

Quartel laughed again. "You don't know my buddy Hix," he said. "Hell, Tommy-boy, Hix *owns* Tijuana. Besides, they always recognize me at the border. Worst thing that ever happens is I get stuck signing autographs to Captain Pedro This and Sergeant Pancho That. Don't sweat it.''

Domnick closed his eyes and blew air through his closed lips, making them flutter. ''Suit yourself, Mr. Megastar. A few days in a Mexican jail might do you some good anyway. Bring you down to reality.''

Quartel grinned. ''It'll never happen, buddy. Like I said, you don't know Hix.''

The director nodded. ''Well, at least we've got a month to get you out.'' What looked like a forced smile came over his face. ''Have a good time.''

''We fully intend to,'' Quartel said as Domnick ducked back out of the motor home. ''Right girls?'' He was answered with another round of cheerful giggles.

The boy who had carted in his gear finally realized his glass was empty and poured him another three fingers. While he waited, Quartel looked through the window and saw Normandi West. The assistant director was on her way to her car. She looked tired after the long weeks of shooting.

Quartel picked up his glass, his eyes glued on West. He'd tried several times to get into those tight cutoff jeans he saw her wearing now. He'd been unsuccessful. She wasn't his type, really—he usually preferred Hispanic women, which explained his frequent trips to visit Hix—but West was an exception. She was blonde but a very different kind of blonde than the ones who had followed him to his motor home. She had a brain to go along with her beautiful face and body—a damn good one, too. And the woman had class with a capital *C*. So what was it about West that made him want her so bad? Quartel hadn't asked himself that question until now but he knew the answer immediately. The fact that she didn't want him turned him on. Normandi West wasn't impressed by who he was. Not in the least. So she was one hell of a challenge.

On impulse, Quartel set down his tequila and vaulted down

the steps of the motor home. He jogged across the set, catching up to the assistant director just as she stuck the key into the door of her Toyota.

"Hey, my baby!" Quartel said.

West looked up with eyes more green than her shirt and smiled. "Ronnie, I'm not a baby. And if I was, I wouldn't be yours."

Quartel forced a smile as he felt his tequila-enhanced temper start to rise. He had never learned to handle rejection very smoothly. He simply hadn't encountered enough of it throughout his life to practice very much. "Okay, sorry about that. Didn't mean anything by it."

West laughed. "I know you didn't, Ronnie. I'm sorry. I just can't resist when you leave yourself that wide open. What can I do for you?"

Quartel leered dramatically up and down her body. "Well, now that you ask..."

"Be serious," West said.

Quartel let the leer return to a friendly smile. That was something he had practiced. "Well, for one thing you can tell me what it is you don't like about me."

West's smile was genuine. "But I do like you, Ronnie. You're a lot of fun to hang out with. I just don't want to sleep with you. Those two things don't always go hand in hand, you know." She laughed again.

"Come to Mexico with me," Quartel blurted out.

The woman chuckled, a deep hearty sound that came from her chest. "What, and fight you off all weekend in a country that probably wouldn't prosecute you if you raped me? I don't think so."

"Come on, Normandi. You know I'm not the type for that."

Normandi West nodded her head. "I know, and I'm sorry again," she said. "I didn't mean that. But I don't want to have to counter advances the whole time, either."

"You won't have to," Quartel said, his confidence building

again. Her tone of voice had held an ever-so-slight waver that time. A tiny "maybe" had crept through. "I'll tell you what," he said. "When we get there, I'll give you one chance to go to bed with me. But I've got to warn you, if you turn me down, you won't get another opportunity." His voice changed to that of Sheriff Jake Bass, the character he had played in the movie. "Nobody gets a second chance with Jake Bass," he said, quoting a weak line he sincerely hoped would be edited from the film.

West's laughter was like music this time.

"Come on, Norm," Quartel pressed. "Do something impulsive for once in your life. We'll have fun."

She glanced into her Toyota, then back. "I was going to the mountains for a few days. I've got a bag packed…"

"So grab it."

"I can't leave my car here."

"I'll send that kid who follows me with the tequila bottle to take it home for you."

"You drive a hard bargain, Sheriff," West said.

"Is that a 'yes?'"

West opened the car door, pulled a purse and an overnight bag off the passenger's seat, and closed the door again. "It's a yes."

Quartel grabbed the bag and car keys from her before she could change her mind, circled an arm around her waist, and they started back toward the motor home. "We're gonna have a hot time in the old town tonight," he said.

"Not too hot," West said, opening her purse. "Unless you force the issue." She pulled out a small cannister of pepper spray and held it up for Quartel to see.

Both Ronnie Quartel and Normandi West laughed again as they walked to the motor home. It had been a joke, after all. But Quartel knew there was a hidden meaning in the humor.

"Well, maybe you'll like my buddy Hix," the Hollywood

star said as he stepped back to let the assistant director up the steps.

"If he's anything like you, I probably will," West said. "But that doesn't mean I'll sleep with him, either."

Quartel bounded up into the living room after her and stopped just inside the room. He handed her keys to the Tequila Kid and sent him to take care of the Toyota. Then, turning to the blondes spread out across the couches and chairs, he said, "Children, we have a new student joining the class today. One of the rarest creatures on Earth, a blonde with a brain."

The four starlets feigned pouts. West punched him lightly in the stomach and said, "Behave yourself."

"No fun in that," Ronnie Quartel said. He lifted the tequila bottle off the bar as he passed and hurried through the motor home to the driver's seat. A strange feeling hit him as he sat behind the wheel. He knew he wasn't going to be nailing Normandi West on this trip. Probably never would. But he was still glad to have her along.

A little confused, Quartel took a quick chug of tequila straight from the bottle—cowboy style—then started the engine. "Girls—and Normandi—" he called over his shoulder. "Let's go to Mexico."

THE CANTINA CINCA was slightly better than the *Celito Lindo*. Maybe half the roaches and at least a few of the patrons had seen a bathtub during the past year. Beyond that, it was pretty much the same.

Bolan slid into one of the fraying fake-leather booths against the wall while James and Encizo took the bench across from him. He smiled inwardly as he watched the little Cuban turn slightly so he could watch the room in the reflection of a cracked window that looked like it led to a storage area. Together, he and Hal Brognola, a high-ranking U.S. Department of Justice official and Stony Man Farm's Director of Sensitive Operations, had handpicked each of the men who made up

Phoenix Force and Able Team. They had come from top military units all over the free world. With the exception of Able Team's leader, Carl Lyons, of course. Lyons had been an LAPD detective who had, strangely enough, spent a good deal of his career trying to track the man known as the Executioner. Of course Brognola, as a Justice Department agent, had been trying to do the same thing during the early years when Bolan had been engaged in his one-man war against the Mafia. It was funny how things had worked out. Brognola and Lyons had finally realized that Bolan was on their side, wanting nothing more than to make the streets of America safe, as they did. Stony Man Farm had eventually been formed, complete with a crack computer staff, armory and other divisions. Over the years, together they had fought criminals, terrorists, dictators and madmen.

Bolan was proud of the men sitting across from him. They were the best of the best. And he was glad they were with him.

"So," James said, glancing up into the window himself. "See any sign of our *Mad Max* buddy?"

"Not yet," the Executioner said. "Give him a minute or two. He doesn't want to be too obvious."

"You think he's a pro?" Encizo asked. "He's not acting like one."

"Semipro," Bolan answered. "Contract scumbag. For who, I don't know. Maybe the *Legitimas,* maybe the *Marxistas.* Maybe somebody else. He might even be from Fierro Blanco's office. What I want to know is how he got onto us."

"How did you spot him?" James asked. "I mean, I was sitting where I could see him watching us. You weren't. When did you peg him?"

"When I walked in the door," Bolan said simply.

This time, it was an elderly Mexican man wearing brown slacks and a chewing tobacco-stained white shirt who came over to take their order. *"Cerveza, por favor,"* the Executioner told him, holding up three fingers. As soon as the man was gone again, he said, "I had noticed the guy's clothes and leathers were dirty. Looked like they'd been lying in the mud all night."

James frowned. "Yeah?"

"His skin was clean. The two don't go together."

Calvin James nodded. He looked as if he wanted to slap himself on the forehead. He had probably noticed the same thing unconsciously, and something had told him the man was "wrong." But he hadn't put it together the way Bolan had.

Bolan was about to speak again when he saw James glance up into the reflection. "You won't believe this," he said.

The Executioner looked up. Coming through the door was the man they had watched earlier. Wearing the kind of lightweight white suits gringos always wore in movies set in Mexico, he also had on the thick black sunglasses actors playing such parts seemed to favor. Beneath the glasses was a long drooping Zapata-style mustache. Other than that, the man was clean-shaven.

"Well, that explains what took him so long," Encizo said, looking at the new arrival. "He had to go shave to complete his junior G-man disguise."

"This is pretty pathetic," James said, nodding slightly. "He might as well have just put on one of those Groucho sets with the glasses, nose and mustache all rolled into one. Who in the world do you think this clown is?"

Bolan shrugged. "I don't know, but I'd like to find out." He watched the man take a stool at the bar as the old Mexican brought their beer. "Let's drink up. Then you take off, Calvin. Turn left on the street, go a block or so and find a place to jump him. Rafe and I'll wait a few minutes, then leave too. Try to pick your spot close to an alley or someplace else where we can question him. If you have to go farther than a block, stay on this street so we don't lose you."

James frowned, his dark chiseled features narrowing. "You don't think he'll see through it?"

"A guy who'd wear *that* disguise?" Encizo said. "He couldn't see through a clean window."

Bolan took a swig of the lukewarm *cerveza* and continued to watch the man in the white suit in his peripheral vision. The guy had it easy this time. He could stare into the mirror behind the bar and see their table. But he was even making himself obvious while doing that.

A few minutes later, James downed the beer at the bottom of his bottle and looked at his watch. "Gotta go guys," he said slightly louder than necessary, as if two beers wasn't all he'd had that night. "See you later." He turned and strode out of the bar with the purposeful gait of the half-drunk.

The man in the white suit watched him go, frowning slightly. Then his eyes returned to Bolan and Encizo.

Five minutes later, Encizo whispered, "You know, he might just be a mugger."

The Executioner shrugged again. "If he is, he's going to a lot more trouble than your average street punk. I've never known one yet who carried his own wardrobe department with him." He killed the rest of his beer and reached into his pocket, pulling out several peso coins and dropping them onto the table. "What do you say we find out?"

Encizo grinned. The two men stood and left the bar.

CALVIN JAMES LOST his semidrunk stride two steps left of the door. His eyes squinted into the afternoon sun. He grinned, realizing they would have adjusted to the light by the time Bolan and Encizo left the bar. But the eyes of the man following the Executioner and his fellow Phoenix Force warriors, wouldn't have.

Walking swiftly down the sidewalk, James took in the surroundings. The people in this part of Mexico City were poor. And the ones along this block of cantinas would be drunk if they had enough money. Even if they weren't, they would be accustomed to violence. Seeing a gringo jerked off the street wasn't likely to be any big deal to them. And even if it was, calling the police wasn't standard procedure. Like the down-trodden in all parts of the world, counting on cops wouldn't be high on their list of priorities.

James came to the end of the block. He hadn't passed an alley or even a doorway that looked suitable. Crossing the intersecting street, he moved past more low-rent beer dives. He watched a whore argue prices with a potential customer. They were both angry, and he shook his head as they finally came to some agreement and entered the front door of a fleabag hotel.

The knife expert shook his head. He had never understood such things. Screaming furiously into the face of a complete stranger one moment, then having sex with her the next, had never fit into his format for lovemaking.

Ahead, James suddenly saw exactly what he needed. And exactly what he didn't.

A narrow alleyway led off the sidewalk between another cantina and an abandoned building. As he drew closer, he saw an open door to the empty structure. The alley provided a perfect place to hide, and in a few quick steps they'd have the American inside the building and out of sight. They could interrogate him at their leisure from that point.

The only problem was the Mexican cop standing at the entrance to the alley.

James slowed his pace as he formulated his simple plan. Dreadfully underpaid regardless of the government in power, Mexico's local police officers had always been famous for graft. It was, however, considered rude to be too blatant about the subject. Smiling widely, he walked up to the uniformed man and said, "Good evening, sir."

The man eyed him suspiciously. "Good evening," he mumbled.

"Sir," James said, "some friends of mine have some business we must conduct. This alley would be the perfect spot. Would it be possible for us to use it?"

The man's suspicious eyes narrowed further. No doubt he suspected a drug deal was about to go down, and he was trying to determine just how much money he could get out of James. "Perhaps," he said.

"We wouldn't expect to use the area for free, of course," James said. "We would like to *rent* the space. Do you know the owner by any chance?"

"Yes," said the officer, all suspicion suddenly leaving his face. He smiled—he was now on familiar ground. "The owner is a very good friend of mine."

"Do you know what he would charge us, by any chance?" James asked.

"I would guess about twenty-five dollars American," said the cop.

James nodded, reached into his pocket and pulled out a hundred-dollar bill. "I have nothing smaller," he said. "But we may need the area all afternoon. Could you possibly give this to your friend with our thanks?"

The officer's eyes grew wide. He nodded as he took the bill. "It will be my pleasure," he said.

"Thank you," James said, smiling again. "If we don't meet again, please remember me as one who appreciates your help."

The cop nodded. "Have a nice stay in Mexico," he said and walked off, disappearing around the corner.

James wasted no time. Ducking into the alley, he saw an abundance of windblown trash carpeting the dirty bricks beneath his feet. The alley wasn't really an alley, he saw now. Just an indent of sorts between the two buildings for utility meters, trash cans and a variety of other odds and ends. Stacked against a corner where the two structures met were several old and tattered bullfighting posters. Roughly three feet wide by five high, they weren't a perfect cover by any means. But they would work.

James grabbed the poster closest to him and pulled it to the corner next to the street. Pressing his back against the wall of the cantina, he crouched behind the thin cardboard and positioned it at an angle in front of him. He reminded himself that the pupils of the man leaving the other cantina wouldn't have contracted to deal with the sun by the time he reached the area. Even if they had, he would have only a microsecond to see James behind the poster. Not fast enough for the man to escape.

It was siesta time now, and there was little traffic along the street. James had been in position no more than a minute or two when he heard two sets of footsteps coming along the sidewalk. A second later, Bolan and Encizo passed. James watched Bolan's eyes flicker toward him but his face remained forward. The knife expert smiled. The Executioner had seen him. Bolan and Encizo continued walking past the abandoned building.

James glanced at the open door to the vacated premises. He figured he could reach out, grab the man as he walked by, employ whatever lock technique presented itself and have his prey into the building in about three seconds. And there was no one on the streets to see any of it happen.

Ten seconds later, James heard another set of steps. He relaxed his muscles, focusing his attention on the sidewalk just past the corner, ready to spring. The steps drew closer.

The white suit appeared blurry as the man passed. James tossed the poster to the side and lunged forward, catching the gringo by the wrist and twisting it behind his back. He was reaching up for the man's hair with the other hand when he saw a flicker of movement to his side. A split second later, a body bumped into his. Turning his head, James saw the uniform and the surprised look on the face of the man wearing it. The Phoenix Force warrior cursed silently under his breath.

He had taken care of the cop standing in front of the alleyway. But he hadn't counted on another one being inside the cantina and appearing at the most inopportune moment possible.

The cop reacted quickly, taking a step back. His hand fell

to the butt of the pistol in the holster on his belt. James glanced quickly over his shoulder and saw that Bolan and Encizo had turned down the block. They had been forced to continue walking to set the trap, and were now too far away to help. With no other choice, James dropped the arm of the man in the white suit and dived toward the officer.

The cop's gun had just come out of the holster when James's right hook caught him in the jaw. The man's head snapped back. The revolver went flying as the man's eyes rolled back and he slumped to the ground.

James turned back to the gringo to see that he, too, was now drawing a gun. The grips of a 1911-Government Model pistol were in his right hand and the barrel was sliding out of the white cotton slacks.

Still at close range, James opted for the Crossada rather than the Beretta 92, also tucked under his T-shirt. If there was a second cop in the vicinity, there might well be a third, or more, and the last thing he needed was a gunshot that brought them running. Besides, they wanted the gringo alive for questioning. And there was still a chance to make that happen.

That chance evaporated quickly.

The American, who had been so stupid in his surveillance and choice of disguises, now showed a rare moment of intelligence and took a step backward, away from the big blade, as his gun came out. He raised the pistol to chest level. Forced to take one more step to close the distance now, James lost the precious time advantage he needed.

As the barrel drew level with his sternum, James stepped to the side out of the center line. At the same time, he twisted his wrist down into a vicious back cut. The move had been the specialty of none other than James Bowie—the technique the American frontiersman and Alamo hero had used more frequently than any other knife-fighting maneuver—and the one that had made him the single most famous blade fighter in history. The back cut was almost a forgotten art in the twentieth

Century, but Calvin James had studied Bowie's style in addition to the other western and eastern disciplines. He understood the deadly efficiency of this movement and understood it and its variations well. And now he called upon it.

The Crossada's heavy ten-inch blade sliced down through the cuff of the gringo's white suit. It journeyed through skin, muscle, tendons and bone, then reversed that order and cut the other side of the cuff. The gringo's hand fell to the sidewalk still gripping the Government Model pistol.

The man looked up, his mouth open in shock. He raised the stub of his arm to his unbelieving eyes, and just stared. Blood shot from the severed limb as he fell on his back to the pavement.

James saw that death would take place in less than two minutes. He jerked a bandanna from his pocket, grasped both ends and twirled it into a tourniquet. He was about to drop to one knee when what felt like a freight train suddenly hit his side, sending him sprawling. The Mexican cop he had thought was unconscious tumbled on top of him, a nightstick raised over his head.

As the club descended, James slid sideways, scraping two layers of skin off his back against the rough concrete. He reached out, letting the nightstick catch itself in the bandanna, then twisted and jerked.

The wooden baton flew out of the cop's hand.

The Phoenix Force warrior rose at the waist, looping the bandanna around the back of the officer's neck. Falling back again, he used his weight to pull the man's forehead down into the pavement.

This time, the cop was out for the count.

James crawled to the gringo, wrapping the bandanna around the man's upper arm. He heard running footsteps and looked up to see Bolan and Encizo grind to a halt. Bolan held the giant Desert Eagle in one hand. Encizo carried a Beretta identical to James's.

The knife expert used the hilt of the Crossada to twist the tourniquet, knowing full well his effort was fruitless. Too much time had elapsed while he wrestled with the police officer. "The cop came out and—"

"We saw," the Executioner said, dropping next to him. He grabbed the gringo by the hair and lifted his head. "Who are you?" he demanded. "Who hired you?"

The man tried to answer but only gibberish came out of his mouth.

Bolan slapped him lightly across the face. "Don't die!" he said. "Tell me! Who hired you?"

Again the man's mouth opened. But now he wasn't even able to babble. And when his mouth closed again this time, his eyes followed.

James sensed stirring to his side and turned to see the Mexican cop waking. He and Bolan rose to their feet. The knife expert shook his head. "If he hadn't come out of the bar—"

"I know," the big guy said. His hard eyes fell on the man in the uniform. Then he looked up one end of the street and down the other. "Let's get out of here. We can't kill him, and the first thing he'll do is radio for backup."

A minute later, Calvin James, Rafael Encizo and the man known as the Executioner had disappeared into the Mexico City barrio.

4

The knives, forks and spoons were of the finest Mexican silver. The china place settings, wine glasses and other tableware were of equal quality. And the clothes on the men seated around the table, the governors of the states of Mexico, were no less resplendent.

Bolan sat at the head table next to the podium. Like he'd done in the president's bedroom two nights before, he couldn't help contrasting Mexico's rich to their poor. The men and women he had seen at the *Celito Lindo* and Cantina Cinco earlier in the day could have worked all their lives and never be able to afford the fork he was holding right now.

Fierro Blanco sat to Bolan's left. As he had done at the speech in the park, Mexico's president had positioned the Executioner on his right side with Captain Juanito Oliverez covering the other flank. Four more federal bodyguards sat along the table just past Oliverez.

On the other side of the podium was General Antonio de Razon. The general seemed to be the president's personal lapdog, accompanying him everywhere he went. The Executioner wondered when the man had time to run the army. The general was dressed in the same gaudy uniform he always wore, but if there was any difference, it seemed that Razon had managed to squeeze even more medals and gold braid onto the fabric that covered his portly body.

Bolan looked over the tables as the governors ate. It had been announced that the meal would consist of the boar *el presidente* himself had killed, and indeed the men were now dining on pork. But the Executioner remembered the remains of the slaughtered animal being left to rot by the side of the road. Had someone returned later to retrieve and butcher the pig? He didn't think so. He had taken a good look at the boar Fierro Blanco had so clumsily stabbed, and it had been at least six years old. The Executioner had killed similar animals a time or two himself when in wilderness survival situations, and the meat had made jerky seem tender by comparison. The flesh the leaders of the Mexican states now ate had come from well-fed, well-tended young pigs, not some aging boar who had survived off what he could scavenge from the wilds.

Don Juan de Fierro Blanco's hypocrisy, it seemed, knew no bounds. But did hypocrisy, and all of the president's other less-than-desirable traits, also mean the man was a dishonest public official? The Executioner still didn't know.

Bolan continued to scan the room as he waited for the men to finish eating and the president's speech to begin. The waiters, dressed in elegant tuxedos, moved about the tables filling wine glasses and dealing with assorted minor problems as they came up. The soldier watched the governor from Jalisco at the table closest to the speaker's stand drop his spoon. A young dark-skinned man with a towel over his forearm produced a clean utensil almost before it hit the floor. Near the center of the room, a tall slender waiter was using his towel to mop wine spilled by the overturned glass of the governor of Chiapas. Everything, so far, was going smoothly and as planned.

When it appeared that most of the men had finished the main course, the servants began bringing out some sort of flaming dessert. Bolan declined when the waiter serving the head table brought it. He continued to watch the room. He had seen no signs of danger, and indeed the men at the meeting were all governors of the various states. To think any of them might attempt an assassination—at least personally—bordered on nonsensical. One of them might well have personal reasons to want Fierro Blanco dead but they weren't the type of men to do it themselves.

The Executioner had spoken to Oliverez about the waiters and other personnel. All had been carefully investigated before being hired, and none had been on the president's payroll for less than two years. Maybe, Bolan thought, we can have a simple little function without anybody trying to kill anyone else for once.

Feeling a presence behind him, Bolan turned to see the waiter moving along the line with a water pitcher. He nodded toward his empty glass and turned back to the room just as General Antonio de Razon grasped his knees with his hands and pushed his bulk off the chair. The general waddled importantly to the podium and tapped the microphone. The buzzing sound of the governors's collective voices gradually diminished to silence.

"Esteemed leaders," Razon began. "Governors of the great states of the Republic of Mexico, I welcome you." He paused for the sparse polite applause that followed, then went on. "Today, we are privileged to listen to our esteemed president, Don Juan de Fierro Blanco. It is with great respect and esteem and without further ado, that I present him now." Razon turned toward the president's seat and bowed.

As Fierro Blanco rose to an applause only slightly more enthusiastic than that which had followed Razon's welcome, Bolan couldn't help wondering where the general had taken his public speaking lessons, and if he might not have only recently added the word "esteem" to his vocabulary.

Fierro Blanco walked to the podium while the waiter—Bolan was surprised to see that the tall slender man who had mopped the wine earlier had now taken over the head table—hurried along, filling their glasses one final time before the speech. The soldier was reminded of the fact that the president had refused to drink anything during the meal, and had exchanged his plate with one served to a federal bodyguard. It was an old trick that

Pancho Villa had used almost a century before. But was the man really still concerned with poisoning? Or was it all for show?

The president rested his hands on the edges of the platform. His face bore a painful expression—but one that looked well thought out, practiced, then manufactured. He let the room fall once more into silence, then waited a few more moments for effect before beginning. "My friends," he began in a hushed voice. "I will not lie to you, nor would you believe me if I did. All great nations experience peaks and valleys in their majesty. All experience periods of peace and prosperity. All experience periods of conflict and trial. But what no great nation in history has ever experienced is failure. Failure does not come until a great nation is no longer great. And I tell you my brothers, my fellow leaders, my friends…" his voice had gradually risen in both pitch and volume, and now he paused a moment, "…the Republic of Mexico is still the great nation it has been since 1910!" Now, Fierro Blanco not only paused but stopped speaking, obviously waiting for the applause he assumed would follow.

It didn't.

After several embarrassingly silent seconds, the president picked up where he had left off. "No one will argue that we are experiencing a period of turmoil," he said, a bead of sweat breaking out on his forehead and dropping down his cheek. "But let us look at each obstacle as a challenge, and let us look at each separately." He began breaking Mexico's current problems into categories.

As he spoke, Bolan continued to search the room. His job wasn't to listen to Fierro Blanco's "state of the nation" address; it was to make sure the man didn't get killed while he delivered it. He watched the faces and hands of the governors. Some were bored. Some were frustrated. Others appeared angry. But all of the faces kept quiet, and regardless of what other emotions the soldier read in the lines and shadows of their features, all were apprehensive.

Like Bolan himself, none of the Mexican governors knew for sure whether Fierro Blanco was dirty or not. None of them knew for sure whether or not he was responsible for the murders of political opponents and the journalists who had written against him. But all of them knew one thing with complete certainty: If Don Juan de Fierro Blanco was the monster some reported him to be, he wouldn't likely hesitate to order the assassination of a Mexican governor who got too far out of line.

All but one, it appeared.

As he concluded his speech, Governor Hector Torrez of Sonora suddenly rose to his feet. *"El Presidente,"* he said in a slow congenial voice. "Might I ask one quick question?"

Fierro Blanco stared across the room to where the man stood near the rear. He hadn't called for questions, and indeed his outline for the speech, given to the governors in advance, didn't include a question and answer session. The meeting had been planned as a one-way propaganda session without chance for rebuttal. But now he had little choice. "Of course, Governor Torrez," he said. "Please ask."

"You have outlined many reforms that we need," Torrez said. "But each will take time. Have you given any thought as to how we are to survive while these reforms are being put into place?" He drew a deep breath, then said in a sterner voice. "We are overrun with corruption. Drug cartels are the real government. The people are starving, and even as we speak, the President of the United States is about to decline his recertification that we are cooperating with his country's drug efforts." Now he took a breath, and when he spoke again his voice was angry rather than stern. "What you are proposing is ludicrous! It's too little too late! This nation is crumbling, falling apart at the seams, and you, Don Juan de Fierro Blanco, are to blame!"

Now the silence that fell over the room made the former ones sound like a carnival. Some of the other governors' mouths dropped open in shock. Others showed small grins of satisfaction that someone had found the courage to voice words they dared only think. Most continued to sit wooden-faced, awaiting the next development in the minidrama unfolding around them.

The Executioner doubted that what happened next was what they expected.

Fierro Blanco stood speechless, his face red with both anger and embarrassment. As Bolan watched, he caught a glimpse of black slacks and white jacket out of the corner of his eye, and saw the waiter—the tall thin man again—moving along the table with the wine carafe. The Executioner wondered briefly who had trained him; it was unheard of to distract anyone when the president was speaking. Then he saw the hand beneath the towel, caught a brief glimpse of steel, and knew the answer.

What the waiter was about to do hadn't been learned in any school for domestics.

Before Fierro Blanco could respond to the accusation, the towel over the waiter's arm fell to the floor. A small stainless steel Derringer appeared two feet from the back of the president's head. Bolan watched the waiter's thumb move to the safety as he dived out of his seat.

Nervousness caused the waiter to fumble the safety, which was all that saved President Don Juan de Fierro Blanco.

Bolan's arm reached the man just as the safety came down. Close now, he could see that the weapon was an American Derringer DA 38. A relatively new firearm, the small gun was manufactured in .38 Special, .357 Magnum and .40 S&W calibers. But it made little difference which chambering the waiter now held. At the distance at which he stood, even a relatively light .38 load would blow off the back of Fierro Blanco's head and send his face out over the governors in the audience.

Over the hush that still filled the room, the Executioner heard a soft grinding sound as the double-action trigger moved backward. With no time to disarm the would-be assassin, he did the next best thing. The palm of his right hand struck the man on the wrist, diverting the aim of the weapon from the president. The deadly little Derringer boomed with a roar worthy of Bolan's own Desert Eagle as the bullet blasted out of the short barrel.

Bolan heard a scream as he brought his left hand down in a looping punch that caught the waiter on the cheek. The man held on to the pistol as he sprawled to a sitting position on the floor. He lifted the gun toward the Executioner, a strange, distant look covering his face.

Using the momentum he had already established to continue moving, Bolan stepped in and brought his right foot around in a crescent kick. The inside of his shoe caught the man's wrist this time, and he heard a faint crack as bone broke. This time, it was the waiter who screamed. A second round fired as the gun went flying from his hand.

Without hesitating, the Executioner stepped onto his right foot and lifted his left. The other shoe shot out in a front snap kick that caught the assassin under the chin. The man's head shot backward. He closed his eyes and fell to his side.

Bolan had already drawn the Desert Eagle, and now he pivoted, scouting the room for other signs of danger. The sniper had been only the first of a two-part attempt last time, and he wasn't about to let down his guard. Not yet.

The room was in pandemonium. Many of the governors stood or sat, frozen in place. Others had at least the foresight to take cover under the tables. One man—the governor of Morelos if the Executioner remembered correctly—sat on the floor with crazed eyes, the waiter's first wild shot having taken him high in the shoulder.

The federal protection team was now joined by reinforcements from outside the room, and together the men sealed off the exits. Bolan scowled at the scene before him, then turned back to the unconscious man at his feet. Slowly, the scowl turned to a grim smile.

The assassination attempts just kept coming. But he finally had what he'd been wanting ever since his plane landed in Mexico City.

A live assassin who was about to experience some very special interrogation—Executioner style.

JAMES PAID THE CABBIE who had brought them from the airport, and got out. He heard Encizo's footsteps behind him as he entered the building and followed the hastily made signs that pointed toward the offices that were being set up as headquarters for the U.S. Army-Drug Enforcement Administration task force. He had spoken to Stony Man Farm during the Grimaldi-flown flight from Mexico City, and learned that he and Encizo were to contact a Special Agent Nelson as soon as they arrived.

After a series of turns, the Phoenix Force warriors saw the arrow directing them into a suite of offices. Another cardboard sign read Operation Border Lord. They stepped in to see men in coveralls installing phone lines while other workers set up new computers to go with the three already in place. James was about to ask someone where he could find Nelson when he caught a glimpse of a burly man speaking to one of the workers across the room.

James couldn't help but smile. Winston "Pug" Nelson hadn't always been a DEA agent. In fact, he must have gone from Navy retirement into narcotics work sometime during the years since Calvin James had been a SEAL. Although they had never been with the same team, James had known the man from training and a couple of joint assignments. As he watched Nelson now, the Phoenix Force soldier saw him turn toward the door and was reminded of how the man got the name Pug. The former SEAL had once been the Navy's light-heavyweight champion, although rumor had it that his nose—which looked

like something that belonged on a Pekinese—had come more
from barroom brawls than fighting in the ring.

Nelson turned and caught sight of James. The DEA man
frowned for a second, then chuckled as he recognized his ex-
SEAL friend. He stopped what he was telling the workman in
midsentence and made his way through the crowded office like
a tailback on his way to the goal line. Stopping two feet in
front of James, he said, "*You're* one of the top-secret big-time
mystery guys I just got the call about?"

"I'm afraid so, Pug. Who called you?"

Nelson shrugged. "One of those top DEA assholes I usually
try to hide from," he said. "Assistant Deputy This-or-That of
That-'n-This. You know, one of those guys who rises through
the ranks without ever buying dope or getting their hands
dirty."

James thought of the men and women who made up Stony
Man Farm. All of them had paid their dues; they had street
experience long before they came to the Farm. "Nobody
climbs that way anymore," he said. "At least not where I work
now."

"And exactly where is that?" Nelson smiled, his smashed
nose seeming to spread even wider. "I couldn't get jack out
of the suit who called. He just said the orders came all the way
from the White House."

James returned the smile. Stony Man Farm was America's
best kept secret. Besides Hal Brognola at the Justice Department, the President of the United States was the only other
government official who even knew of its existence. "Did this
'suit' tell you to ask questions?" he said.

"Actually, he told me not to."

James shrugged his shoulders in response. "I'd tell you if I
could, Pug," he said. "But I can't."

Nelson's face took on a new scowl, but it was one of puz-
zlement rather than displeasure. "Secrets, huh? Even between
former SEAL buddies? Never thought I'd see the day."

James laughed. "And I never thought I'd see the day when you hit below the belt like that," he said. "A former champ like you ought to know better."

Now Nelson laughed, too. "Okay," he said. "If the White House wants to bring in the spooks on this, what do I care?"

James offered a knowing smile in response. If Nelson wanted to think he and Encizo were with the CIA, it was fine with him. At least it would keep the former fighter from continually trying to find out where the Stony Man warriors did work.

Nelson took a step back and James saw now that he had put on a few pounds since his days with the teams. He wasn't fat by any means, but neither did he look ready to go through the SEAL's hell week all over again, either. He'd be fighting heavyweight instead of light-heavy if he were in the ring these days.

"So, are you going to introduce me?" Nelson glanced to Encizo.

James nodded, then made the introductions. "Want to show us around, Pug?" he asked. "I'd like to get started."

Nelson turned back toward the room. "Honeycutt!" he yelled above the bedlam of banging hammers and power saws. "Take over and see that this mess gets set up!"

A sandy-haired man wearing eyeglasses stuck his head up from behind a computer monitor. "Aye-aye, Captain," he said.

"Wise Air Force sissy," Nelson muttered under his breath. "All right, let's go." He pushed between James and Encizo and led the way into the hall. The men from Stony Man Farm followed, and a few minutes later they were cruising through the streets of El Paso in a huge Chevrolet Suburban.

Nelson kept up a constant monologue as they drove, pointing toward city parks, vacant lots and other areas where Mexican men, women and children were camped out in tents and inside cardboard boxes. "There's just too many to process back," he said, shaking his head. "The jails are already overflowing with the ones that break the law. That's violent law. If they keep to themselves, or just steal and don't hurt anybody, they're safe from prosecution for all practical purposes.''

"What's the dope situation?" Encizo asked, leaning forward from the backseat.

Nelson snorted. But before he could answer, a Hispanic man wearing a bloody white T-shirt suddenly stepped in front of the Suburban. The fed slammed on the brake and honked the horn at the same time. Neither the horn or the squeal of rubber had much effect on the man. He turned and looked at the windshield with vacant eyes, gave it an imbecilic grin and floated across the street.

Nelson let out his breath in a whoosh. "That answer your question?" he asked.

They reached the outskirts of El Paso and moved into the sandy rural area. Nelson cut down a dirt road. They passed several groups of illegal aliens walking north, their belongings packed in boxes, blankets—anything they could find that would carry their loads. "There are eighty thousand troops along here already," Nelson said. "They still can't stop it."

They drove to the Rio Grande river and James saw a small rickety bridge. A fence had once stood in front of it but it had been torn down. The soldier was slightly surprised when Nelson didn't even slow as he neared the bridge. "The situation has turned the border area into a no-man's-land," he said. "We penetrate up to five or ten miles, no one says a damn thing. The Mexicans do the same thing on our side."

A small military convoy appeared just over a rise as they moved on. The soldiers had stopped a group of immigrants heading for the border, and were instructing them to turn back. Nelson pulled to a halt next to a jeep, and flashed his DEA credentials at a captain. The man nodded and the former boxer drove on.

"What are these rumors about a drug tunnel?" Encizo asked.

Nelson opened the glove compartment and pulled out a cardboard package of cheap cigars. He unwrapped the plastic from one and stuck it in his mouth. He punched in the cigarette lighter on the dash as he answered. "There is one—it's more than just rumor—I'm convinced of that. But damned if I know where it is."

"No snitches?" James asked. He knew that even with all of their new high-tech gear, the DEA, and every other drug organization, still relied more on informants than equipment.

"Not yet," Nelson said, biting down on the cigar as he lit it. "But I just got here myself. Give me time."

A mile or so later, they topped another ridge and saw two groups of soon-to-be illegals. The first, comprised of roughly a dozen men, women and children, was less than a hundred yards away. Nelson slowed the Suburban and drew up to a man walking out front.

James squinted into the sun through the windshield as the man walked confidently forward. Often called *coyotes,* such men made a living as guides, leading illegals across the border. This one, who now stopped next to Nelson's window, looked half peasant and half bandit.

Nelson rolled down his window. "Turn back," he said.

"Turn back?" the man asked with false surprise. "Why?"

"Because you don't have visas or permits and these people with you damn sure aren't American citizens," the former SEAL growled.

"But señor," the coyote said, his unshaven face twisting into a leer. "If I'm not mistaken, we are in Mexico."

"Where are you going?" Nelson asked.

The leer didn't fade. "We're looking for a nice place to have a picnic," he said.

"You come across the border, and I see you, I'll personally shoot your ass," Nelson said. "You got that?"

The leer faded only slightly. *"Comprende,"* the coyote said. "We have no intentions of crossing the border."

Nelson pulled the Suburban away in a whirlwind of sand and dirt.

While he'd been talking to the coyote, James had seen several vehicles approach the second group heading toward the border. Approximately a half mile in the distance, the people appeared to have stopped. Now, as the Suburban started that way, several gunshots suddenly rang out.

Nelson floored the gas pedal and the big vehicle shot forward in another storm of desert sand. As the people in the distance grew larger, James saw some of them jump back into the pickups and cars that had just arrived and start south again.

A moment later, the Suburban slid to a halt. Nelson drew a SIG-Saur 9 mm pistol from his belt and jumped out. James and Encizo followed, their Berettas leading the way.

Several men and one woman were down. Other women and kids stood wailing in panic.

"Bandidos," Nelson said, surveying the scene. James saw his eyes travel up toward the escaping vehicles. The Phoenix Force warrior heard a moan and dropped to one knee next to a wounded man in his early twenties. Blood poured from a gut shot and another in the man's upper chest. A froth of red misted from his mouth each time he exhaled. He tried to speak but James couldn't make out the words.

The soldier leaned closer. "What?"

"My...wife..." the man groaned in Spanish.

James glanced to the woman on the ground nearby. Dead.

The dying man surprised him when he said, "No...not... her..."

"Who, then?" James asked. "The other women are all okay."

The man on the ground shook his head, the movement bringing a round of blood-spraying coughs. He moaned again, then said, "They...took her."

Nelson and Encizo had joined him now. "Let's go," Encizo said. He turned to Nelson. "You can radio back for medical help."

Nelson shook his head. "Negative," he said. "They'll be

deep into the country before we can catch up. If we can catch them at all.''

James turned to him. ''We can't just let them take her,'' he said. ''You know what they'll do to her.''

An older woman stepped out of the crowd of weeping women and crossed herself. ''Señors,'' she said. ''The bandits were led by Victorio Vega. They will sell the woman into slavery...'' She paused to cross herself again. ''*After* they have defiled her in unspeakable ways.''

James saw Nelson look up at the horizon again, off to where the vehicles had already become tiny specks. ''That name—Victorio Vega—mean anything to you?'' he asked.

''He was mentioned in the intel briefs,'' Nelson said. ''Small-time bandit. Robs people crossing the border...'' His voice trailed off as if he was still thinking about something.

''We've got to go get her,'' Encizo said. ''If you won't come, at least let us use the Suburban.''

''I've got direct orders,'' Nelson said. ''If I penetrate over the ten miles, I'm history with the DEA.'' He held up a hand when James tried to speak. ''Giving you the Suburban would violate policy, too.''

James stared at the man. ''Are you the same Pug Nelson I remember?'' he asked.

There was another long silence, then Nelson spun on the balls of his feet. The former SEAL sprinted to the Suburban and jumped behind the wheel. James and Encizo were only a step behind.

Nelson jerked the radio mike from the dashboard and held it to his mouth. A few seconds later, medical help for the wounded was on its way from El Paso. The Suburban spun its wheels once more as they took off after the bandits.

''What the hell,'' Nelson said, turning to James as the dirt flew up the sides of the big vehicle. ''I'm already retired from the Navy, right? What do I need with another pension coming in?''

The former Navy SEAL grinned the same way James had seen him do a dozen times in the ring—just before he delivered the knockout punch.

THE BRASSY SOUNDS of trombones, trumpets and tubas mixed with guitars and maracas, sending the vibrant notes and chords of traditional Mexican folk tunes across the grounds. The enticing odor of barbecued meat filled the air. Men of both Mexican and American heritage mingled with women who could be counted among the most beautiful in the world. Some were light-skinned and blond, others darker with raven tresses and matching eyes that flashed in the light from the bonfire. Above the fire pit, several goats and a lamb twirled on spits attended by servants. A picnic table not far from the house had been covered with bowls of shrimp, cream-cheese concoctions and caviar on ice. An assortment of crackers flown in from Britain and France were available on the same table, as were other more elaborate hors d'oeuvres catered by one of Tijuana's finest restaurants.

White wrought-iron benches and tables and straw gazebos were strategically placed throughout the well-tended grass of the large country estate. The sun had just gone down, dropping the temperature a few degrees and allowing those attending the party to converse more pleasantly. The attendees had divided into small groups with waiters moving between the clusters. The white-jacketed servants carried trays of champagne glasses, and took orders for beer, tequila, cognac and mixed drinks.

Scott Hix sat on the short brick wall that circled the wishing well to the side of the mansion. He watched his guests. Many were friends and business associates anxious to meet his famous friend, Ronnie Quartel. The women—the dark-skinned *señoritas,* anyway—were a mixture of the local men's mistresses and local single women who had been enticed by the chance to meet the movie star. A few were "professionals;"

Hix had placed a call earlier that day to Angelina Villa, the proprietress of Tijuana's most exclusive escort service. The American expatriate had used her service many times in the past when Quartel visited, and the movie star hadn't been disappointed yet.

Hix pulled a Havana cigar from the breast pocket of his Hawaiian shirt and held the flame of a gold lighter to the end. His eyes skirted the revelers as he twisted the tip around the fire. For the moment, things were still relatively quiet with an occasional drunken laugh the only sign that the party would eventually turn wild. But Hix had hosted enough get-togethers for his former roommate to know that is was only a matter of time before Bacchus took over. Bacchus, the Roman god of wine and revelry, seemed to travel with Ronnie Quartel wherever he went.

Hix took a pull on the cigar and let the carefully blended tobacco smoke roll around in his mouth. He looked across the grounds to where Quartel sat on one of the benches, a glass of tequila in his hand. As usual, he was the center of attention. Still dressed in the cowboy boots, pants and vest Hix suspected he had worn in the final scene of the movie, Quartel had brown-eyed, brown-skinned young women pressing their breasts against both of his arms. As he told amusing Hollywood anecdotes with the skill and timing of a well-trained comedian, other partyers—both men and women—crowded around. All wanted to get in a word that might make the American movie legend remember them.

The sight made Hix shake his head and chuckle. It was no different than it had always been—ever since their freshman year at UCLA. Quartel had always been the center of attention wherever he went, even then. Oh, it had been on a much smaller scale in those days. Fraternity and sorority parties, homecoming events, and the like. But even before he had become famous, women and men alike followed him as if he were some modern day Pied Piper.

Hix yawned. Was he jealous? No, he didn't think so. He had been the center of attention a few times in his own life, and while he couldn't say he hadn't enjoyed it, he didn't need it the way his best friend seemed to. He had watched Quartel on the few occasions when someone else stole his show, and the man either pouted or did something outrageous to get all eyes back on him.

"Let's go swimming!"

Hix heard the alcohol-influenced voice and turned in the direction from which it had come. Standing on the diving board, he saw one of the big-breasted blond starlets Quartel had brought along. He couldn't remember which one—Courtney or Leah or Tara or Errin—they all looked pretty much the same to him.

The blouse she had worn now hung open. She smiled drunkenly as all eyes turned to the pool.

The band quit playing and immediately went into a Latino version of David Rose's classic, "The Stripper." Inspired by the music, the blonde's shorts, then panties, came off to the applause of the rest of the partyers. She danced seductively for a few moments while the band finished the number, then dived into the water.

Not to be outdone, the other three starlets Quartel had brought along, as well as several of the girls from Angelina Villa's Escort Service, hurried to the pool. Clothes flew through the air as they ran. Breasts bounced and buttocks wobbled enticingly, then disappeared with splashes into the water.

Lifting the beer he had rested on the wall next to him, Hix took a sip. It had turned warm, and he set it back down. He watched the men now, bankers, attorneys and wealthy businessmen away from their wives for the evening, dash after the women. Quartel stood, the two women next to him hanging on his arms. "Hey, roomie!" he yelled across the lawn. "Wanna go swimming?"

Hix smiled and shook his head. "You go ahead," he said. "I'm a little tired."

Quartel glanced down at each of his women in turn and grinned like a cat who'd cornered a pair of mice. "I got other plans anyway," he called out. "My room ready?"

Hix nodded and raised his beer can in salute.

Quartel and the two Mexican beauties took off for the house.

One of the waiters came by and Hix replaced his warm beer with a glass of champagne, which he suspected would grow hot on the wall just as its predecessor had. His mind was still on his father, and he was in no mood for a party tonight. Deep within his soul, he wondered what was happening to him. The last several times Quartel had visited, he hadn't been able to get into the swing of things. *Maybe you're changing a little* voice somewhere in his brain suggested. *Growing up. Realizing that there has to be, or at least should be, more to life than tits and ass and alcohol.* The thought was too heavy for his present circumstances, and Hix ignored it.

He was about to taste the champagne when the odor of perfume filled his nostrils. Turning, he saw the other blonde who had come with Quartel in the mobile home. He looked up into her deep blue eyes but they were staring across the horizon, over the low hills in the distance toward the Tijuana skyline beyond.

Normandi. He remembered the unusual name from Quartel's introductions. She didn't speak, just inspected the city in the distance. Hix studied her face. The skin was smooth, the features soft, delicate.

"How far away is TJ?" she finally asked.

"Seven miles," Hix told her. "Close enough to get to when I need to. Far enough away to…to be away."

Normandi West nodded, still staring into the distance. "How about the hills?"

"A mile. Maybe a little more."

"They're beautiful," West said. "Rugged. Natural." She

wore white shorts similar to the ones the blonde on the diving board had discarded, and they framed a set of well-shaped well-tanned legs. A Mickey Mouse T-shirt was tucked into her waistband, which Hix suspected he would be able to circle with both hands. Finally, she tore her eyes from the skyline and looked down at him. "This seat taken?" she asked. Her smile was friendly, genuine and charming, but without a trace of the sexual invitation the faces his other partygoers usually displayed.

"I saved it for you," Hix said.

"If you're anything like your buddy," West said, glancing toward the house where Quartel and the two Mexican women had disappeared, "you'll be disappointed that you've wasted your time." She sat and looked at him. "Are you?"

"Am I what?"

"Like Ronnie."

Hix chuckled. "Well, I'm not gay," he said.

"I never suspected you were," West said. "You know what I mean."

Hix met her eyes. They didn't waver. "If you mean do I just assume that the fact that you sat here means I'll be in your pants in a few minutes," he said, "then, no. I'm not like Ronnie."

She laughed, the sound just slightly audible above the band and far more musical to Hix's ears. "How come you aren't in the pool?"

He shrugged. "It's my pool. I suppose I can get in it whenever I want. I'm just not in the mood."

Her smile stretched a little wider. "Courtney and Errin were talking about you earlier," West said. "They said something about engaging you in a tag-team event. later."

Hix snorted. "Never heard that expression."

"No, but I bet you can figure it out."

When he didn't reply, West looked back at the miles between the estate and Tijuana. "Are you in a bad mood tonight?" she asked. "Is something eating at you?"

Before he knew what was happening, Scott Hix found himself pouring out his heart to Normandi West. He told her about his father, the kidney dialysis, the way he suspected his father had never taken him seriously and a multitude of little things that had been on his mind for years but that he had never discussed with anyone. Occasionally, he realized how open he was being with someone he hadn't even known the day before, and that realization what snap his lips shut for a few minutes. Then she would ask a question and he'd find his mouth rattling again.

Around them, barely noticed, the party went on.

As the fire burned out and the uneaten goat and lamb over the pit began to cool, Hix looked out over the skyline. Together, he and West watched the darkness lighten as the sun began to rise on a new day. He turned back to the deep blue eyes and saw that they were looking into his now, and realized suddenly that he had never met a woman quite like her. He had felt no need to be anything other than himself with her throughout the night. She had listened to him attentively, occasionally offering opinions and advice that bespoke intelligence, kindness and concern without judgment. He felt a sudden overpowering desire to do the same for her; to let her talk to him the way he had done to her and help her with any problems she might have in her own life. He wanted to get to know her now as she knew him. He wanted to…well…he wanted to share her life. From now on.

Words like "forever," and "eternity," and even "until death do us part" suddenly danced through Scott Hix's mind at a pace that left him dizzy. He rose to his feet, reached down for West's hand, and touched her for the first time since they'd met. With their fingers interlaced, they walked slowly toward the house. When they reached the door, she turned and looked up at him, then kissed him lightly on the lips before stepping back.

"What is happening here?" Hix choked out of a throat that seemed too small for him.

West didn't break his gaze. "I don't know," she said, and her own voice seemed different somehow. "Let's just give it time."

Hix nodded. "You…" he hesitated, then went on. "Do you know where your room is?"

West nodded. She kissed him once more, again only lightly, then turned on her heel and disappeared down the hallway.

5

He had been forced to use the only pair of infrared binoculars they had during the night, and those opticals weren't good; far from the state-of-the-art surveillance equipment. He could make out only fuzzy blurs of movement which he barely identified as human beings, and at first, it had been hard to differentiate the men from the women. Then, throughout the night, he had learned to tell the difference through body language; the way women moved compared to men. And, of course, the acts in which they had engaged later in the evening had helped, too. His only major disappointment was that he couldn't specifically identify Ronnie Quartel. He thought he had been the man who appeared to be dressed like a cowboy but couldn't be sure. And it would have been nice to get a positive ID on some of the politically influential Mexican men consorting with women other than their wives. He would have liked to have known exactly who was who, doing what with whom.

It never hurt to know the sexual preferences of one's enemies for blackmail purposes later.

Jesus Hidalgo supposed, however, as he turned to look at Pablo Huertes, that the faulty night vision had also been a blessing. Huertes was an animal, pure and simple. The bandit leader had grown aroused seeing even the cloudy images of sexual acts through the night lenses, and had they been clear Hidalgo suspected he would have had to physically restrain the bandit leader from taking his men down the hills to join the orgy. He watched Huertes now in the moonlight. The bandit's back rested against a rock. He snored loudly, each exhalation sending a new mist flying from his tequila-wet mustache. Hidalgo said a quick prayer of thanks that the hills were far enough from the house that the rumbling couldn't be heard, then turned back to the Hix estate.

As the sun rose behind him, Hidalgo set down the infrared binoculars and lifted a cheap pair of Tascos. He pressed the lenses to his eyes. In the better light, he could now make out the man and woman who had sat on the wall around the well all night, ignoring the more libidinous activities going on around them. The man, he now saw, was Scott Hix himself. The woman was a blond American. Most of the others attending the party had disappeared into the house or barn but a few still lay about, passed out in various states of undress and in various lewd combinations. Hix and the woman seemed not to notice them as they continued to talk.

As Hidalgo watched, a short blond woman awoke in a pile of nude bodies. She stood, looked around her, then walked naked toward the house. Hidalgo felt a warmth in his lower abdomen as he watched her shapely buttocks jiggle in the early morning light. He turned the binoculars away. He was only human, he knew, and while he was in far more control of his natural lust than Huertes and his men, he must not let that lust cloud his judgment in the days to come.

The other members of the suborgy the blonde had just left began waking up and looking for their clothes. They, too, now disappeared into the house.

Hidalgo heard a loud belch followed by the passing of gas from the bowels of one of the men near him. He turned in disgust to see Huertes awakening. Glancing down the line of men hidden in the rocks, he saw that most wore sombreros or cheap baseball caps. Many sported crossed ammunition bandoliers on their chests. All carried rifles, and several also had pistols strapped to their sides. But even though the men were similarly dressed and armed, it was easy to distinguish Hidalgo's own *Legitimas* from Huertes's *bandidos*. The bandits were unkempt and unshaven. They smelled not only of body odor but of the massive amounts of tequila and marijuana they had indulged in throughout the night. The clothes of his own men were dirty from the excursion into the hills but it was a recent dirt. Huertes's men had accumulated their filth over a period of months, if not years, and it wasn't only ground into their skin, Hidalgo suspected it penetrated to the bone.

As he watched Huertes stretch himself awake, the *Legitima* leader again questioned his decision to allow the bandits to join him. Had he not been so short of manpower, he would never have even considered such a move. Problems were bound to arise. The bandits cared for nothing but rape, pillaging and drinking and smoking themselves out of their minds. The revolution that would do way with the feudal system in Mexico and bring to the country a true democracy of the people—a goal for which he and the other *Legitimas* were willing to sacrifice their lives—meant nothing to the bandits. To them, the revolution was nothing but a convenient conduit for more robbery and debauchery. The fact was, they would kill, steal and ravish women regardless of what government led the country. Even if the loathsome *Marxistas* in the south somehow came to power, the lives of Pablo Huertes and his men wouldn't change—they would simply adapt and move on.

Hidalgo watched Huertes's bloodshot eyes flutter open. The bandit reached up with a grimy hand and wiped sleep from the corners. "Good morning," he slurred, slowly pulling himself to his feet and bracing himself against a rock.

Hidalgo could see that the man was not only hungover, he was still partially drunk. "Get your men ready," he ordered, then turned his binoculars back to the house. In the corner of his eye, he saw the bandit leader raise his own lenses from the strap around his neck. From the barn in the distance, three Mexican women—probably from one of the many houses of prostitution Tijuana boasted—emerged. They dressed as they walked toward the house, with Hispanic men following them. The group divided near the large circular driveway, with the men getting into cars and driving away while the women continued into the mansion.

Besides Hix and the woman, the only two figures still outside now were two blond-haired women lying in the grass near the swimming pool. Fully nude and locked in each other's arms, they finally awakened and held hands as they strolled unashamedly toward the front door.

To his side, Hidalgo saw Huertes drop his binoculars to the end of the strap and leer at the house. "Yes," the bandit said. "I shall get my men ready. And it shouldn't take much encouragement if they just saw that."

Hidalgo reached to the side, grasping the ammunition belt across Huertes's chest and jerking him forward. "I've already told you," he said, pressing his nose to that of the bandit chief. "We're here for the revolution, not to satiate the loins of you and your men." He pushed the man away again as Huertes let out another belch than could have stopped a rhino in his tracks.

A mask of hatred replaced Huertes's leer. "We can do both," he said.

"We can't do both!" Hidalgo almost yelled. "And we won't do both!" He paused to regain control of himself, then said, "We're here to take custody of the American movie star and the others in order to raise money for the cause. Nothing else. Do you understand me?"

When Huertes continued to stare without answering, Hidalgo said, "Get your men ready like I told you. We'll give the people in the house one hour to get to sleep. When they are at their weakest, we will strike." He turned back to the house. Through the binoculars, he watched Scott Hix and the woman pause at the doorway. The woman kissed the American—more the kiss of a friend than of lovers. Then they disappeared inside.

Hidalgo continued to watch the house, alternately casting

glances at the men as he listened to the sound of their preparation. His own devoted revolutionaries were scattered among the bandits, and he watched them make final checks of their weapons while they, in turn, eyed Huertes's brigands. The faces of the *Legitimas* betrayed the same contempt for the uncouth desperados that Hidalgo himself felt.

Yes, trouble would arise. Probably sooner rather than later. And while his own men outnumbered the bandits, he wondered how they would fare if it came to an all-out battle.

Amorality, and the ability to kill one's fellow man without blinking an eye, it had been his observation over the years, held certain advantages when it came to warfare.

The house and the grounds lapsed into a state of silence and inactivity as the sun rose higher. A little over an hour later, Hidalgo led the men down through the rocks to the pickups and cars they had hidden in a lower valley. Pulling the camouflage sheets, grass and tree limbs from the vehicles, the men slid inside and fired up the engines. The *Legitima* leader took the passenger seat of an aging Cadillac driven by one of his lieutenants. They turned onto a road leading from the highway, then gunned the engines as they raced toward the house.

Jesus Hidalgo's mind raced as fast as the vehicles as they neared. He had divided the men into entry teams, separating Huertes's men as best he could and making sure there were more revolutionaries than bandits on each team. Such arrangements, he prayed, would eliminate or at least cut down on the abuse suffered by Hix and his guests. The American wasn't a bad man, Hidalgo knew. He had researched Scott Hix well and learned that he had come by his wealth honestly, creating jobs for Mexican laborers and paying good wages, without taking advantage of the poor.

The Cadillac and two pickups skidded to a halt by the front door as other vehicles raced around the sides of the house. Hidalgo leapt from his seat and vaulted the steps to the porch, bringing a well-worn combat boot up into the air as he neared the door, then sending the wood splintering from its hinges. His short-barreled CAR-15 in assault carry, he stopped briefly in front of a staircase, waving some of the men to his right, others to his left. He, himself, sprinted up the steps with his lieutenant, Pablo Huertes, and several other men at his heels. Behind him, he could hear the bandit leader's labored breathing and silently prayed that the man might have a heart attack.

The first door he came to was open, and through it Hidalgo could see the two blond women who had entered the house last. Still nude, they slept in each other's arms much as they had earlier on the grass by the swimming pool. Leaving a man to guard them, he took Huertes and the others and moved on. In the next bedroom, they opened the door to find Jose Cervantes, the mayor of Tijuana, and two more blondes. These three were awake, and amusing themselves in a way Hidalgo had never before imagined, let alone tried.

His entry team diminished further as he left guards in each successive bedroom. Hidalgo led Huertes and two remaining men to another door. Finding it locked, he kicked it in and saw the woman who had spent the night next to the well with Hix. Still fully dressed, she didn't appear to have been asleep and, having heard the noise, now cowered in a corner of the room. Hidalgo looked at the three men he had left—Pablo Huertes and two of his bandits. "Stay here with her," he ordered the two bandits. "Then bring her downstairs to the living room. We will meet there as soon as the house is secured."

The two men nodded. Hidalgo didn't like the look in their eyes.

Grabbing Huertes by the arm, Hidalgo sprinted down the hallway to the final door on the second floor. It was closed but unlocked, and when he opened it he saw it to be the master bedroom.

He also saw Scott Hix sitting on the bed aiming a sawed-off 12-gauge shotgun at his belly.

Hidalgo and Huertes both froze in their tracks, their weapons aimed back at Hix. For a moment, no one spoke. Then the American said, "Looks like a Mexican stand-off, boys. Hope you don't mind the pun."

"You will get only one of us," Hidalgo said. "The other will kill you." He was surprised when he saw no fear in Hix's eyes. In fact, the man laughed.

"No, I'm betting I can get you both," the American said. "But just in case I'm wrong, I'll let you decide which one of you wants it first."

Silence fell over the room. Then Hix said, "Come on, make up your minds. I haven't got all day—I'd like to get some sleep."

Before he could respond, Hidalgo heard a scream from somewhere behind him. Instantly a change came over Hix's face. Suddenly, the confidence that had been almost a death wish was gone.

And Jesus Hidalgo understood his new advantage.

"You will kill one of us," he agreed. "Perhaps even both. Who knows? But I promise you this. All of your guests will be killed if you do." He let it sink in. Then, for emphasis, he added, "Including the woman who just screamed. You know the one—you sat on the well with her last night."

As if to punctuate his words, another scream echoed from down the hall. It was followed by laughter and the sounds of scuffling.

Hix didn't have to be prompted further. He threw the shotgun to the carpet and raised his hands. But his eyes bore deeply into those of Jesus Hidalgo. "Go get her away from them," he said, then nodded toward Huertes. "He can watch me."

Hidalgo stared back at him. He didn't like the idea of the American giving him orders. He liked even less the fact that if he obeyed, he might look weak in Huertes's eyes. It might even set a dangerous precedent with Hix himself. But at the top of the list of things he didn't like that were currently going on was what he knew the bandits were doing to the woman they had just left.

Taking two steps forward, Hidalgo brought the stock of the CAR-15 around in an arc, striking Scott Hix in the jaw. The American flew back on the bed, and Hidalgo leaned over him, pressing the barrel of his rifle into Hix's throat. "*I* will be the one who gives the orders," he snarled into the man's bleeding face. "Don't forget that, gringo."

Hix stared up at him. The American's eyes betrayed neither pain nor fear.

Hidalgo stood and turned to Huertes. "Take him down to the living room," he ordered. "I'll meet you there." He sprinted back the way they had come and turned into the room where he had left the two bandits with Hix's woman. She was on the floor on her back with one of the men holding her wrists above her head. The other had worked her shorts and panties down to her ankles and was attempting to mount her.

The *Legitima* leader raised the CAR-15 and fired from the hip, sending a lone .223 round through the forehead of the man holding the woman's arms. He jerked back and slithered to the floor. The other bandit, his filthy pants unzipped, turned to see what was happening.

Hidalgo used the rifle stock again, knocking the bandit off the woman to the floor next to her. The man's eyes opened wide in horror. He scooted backwards to the wall on his ass, holding his hands up in front of him. "No!" he cried in the voice of a terrified child. "No...please, sir!"

The CAR-15 barrel swung at the man. Hidalgo's second round pierced the palm of the bandit's outstretched hand and drilled into his brain.

Jesus Hidalgo leaned over and offered the woman his hand. She frowned in confusion for several seconds, then finally took it. The *Legitima* leader helped her to her feet and said, "I'm sorry this happened, *señorita*. I gave orders that it should not. Now, please, dress yourself. You will understand, I hope, that unfortunately I can't turn my back while you do. You're my prisoner, and I can't afford to take chances."

Hidalgo forced his eyes to stay on the woman's face as she pulled up her underwear and shorts, zipped and buttoned them. He stepped behind her, prodding her lightly with the rifle barrel. They descended the stairs to the living room where the *Legitima* leader saw the others had already gathered. Hix, Mayor Cervantes, the four blond women and several of the darker-skinned prostitutes sat on the floor, their hands clasped behind their heads. Hidalgo noticed that Hix had several other bruises on his face in addition to the one he had gotten from the rifle stock. The *Legitima* glanced angrily toward Huertes.

The drunken slob grinned back.

Hix, Hidalgo suspected, could be ransomed. And Mayor Cervantes was an unexpected added dividend. But the primary object of the mission had been Ronnie Quartel, and the *Legitima* leader now saw the famous movie star semi-reclined against a wall. Quartel wore only the pair of soiled jeans Hidalgo had seen him arrive in. Two Mexican women, one wearing Quartel's shirt, the other only bra and panties, clung to him like magnets, frightened.

Jesus Hidalgo motioned the woman he had escorted into the room to a seat on the floor, and noticed that she moved automatically next to Hix. He slung the CAR-15 over his shoulder, walked to the front of the room, straightened his shoulders, and said, "Ladies and gentlemen." He shot an ironic glance toward Cervantes, then to Quartel. "Honorable mayor and revered artist of stage and screen, Mr. Ronald Quartel." His eyes now took in the rest of the room. "Guests of Mr. Scott Hix." He cleared his throat and smiled. "Congratulations. You have all just become guests of the revolution."

WHILE HE HAD taken many lives over the years, Bolan had never killed an innocent man nor had he made even the most heinous of characters suffer unnecessarily in their deaths. If a

man needed killing, he died. The Executioner was just that—
an *executioner*. He wasn't, had never been and would never be
an inflictor of torment.

But the threat of torture, he had learned over the years, often
proved invaluable.

The Executioner stared through the one-way glass that
looked into the interrogation room. Inside, alone, strapped to a
chair and staring back into the mirror side of the window he
saw the waiter who had been the last in the long line of would-
be presidential assassins. The man looked confused. Probably
trying to figure out if the mirror he saw was indeed one-sided,
and if so whether or not he was being observed.

Silently, the Executioner fingered the Derringer in his right
front pants pocket. Further examination had revealed that it was
chambered in the powerful .40 S&W caliber. And the unfired
round had proven to be a Blue Glaser. Actually rather pretty
in their gold, copper and bright royal coloring, what the Glasers
did was anything but attractive. The 115-grain round left a five-
inch barrel at 1650 feet per second. Out of the short-barreled
derringer, it would be only slightly slower. But the real destruction came from the compressed shot core within the bullet's
jacket. The construction of the round prevented breakup on
inanimate objects but disintegrated upon impact with live targets. The Glasers were designed to be safer, minimizing rico-
chet on missed shots. They were also designed to present the
most tremendous stopping power scientists had yet come up
with; after penetration, the bullet's jacket opened to release the
tiny shot hidden within. The result was similar to a small bomb
going off inside a body. The Glasers were a tremendous boon
to law enforcement and honest citizens who wanted protection.
And, like any weapon, they held no capacity for good or evil.
But as the waiter now seated in the interrogation room had
proved, they could be used for criminal purposes just like any
bullet, knife, baseball bat, bowling ball or rolling pin.

The Executioner watched the waiter through the mirror. The

assassin had attempted to use the Glasers for sinister purposes. Bolan was about to use them for good.

Turning to Captain Oliverez who stood at his side, Bolan said, "What I'm about to do won't hurt the man—at least not physically. But it would violate his constitutional rights in the U.S. Are you going to catch any heat over this?"

Oliverez grunted. "You are in Mexico," he said, and it was all that needed to be said. But Oliverez didn't stop there, just the same. "If your plan doesn't work, I have a case of Seven-Up waiting in the back room."

The Executioner didn't have to have that explained to him. One of the favorite interrogation techniques of the Mexican feds was to shake a bottle of soda pop with their thumb over the opening, then hold the neck just under the nostrils of the man being questioned. When the thumb was removed, the pressurized carbonated beverage shot into the sinuses, creating intolerable pain.

"My way will work," Bolan said. "Did your men get the items I requested?"

Oliverez nodded. He pointed toward a large cardboard carton resting against the wall.

The Executioner moved to the box and flipped open the lid. Inside, he saw roughly a dozen plastic packages of Blue Glasers. Backed by cardboard and featuring a hole at the top to hang on a display rack, each pack held six rounds. It should be more than enough.

Slipping the packages into the side pockets of his sport coat, Bolan dug deeper into the carton. He found a box of fifty sharp-nosed, full metal jacket, armor-piecing .40 caliber cartridges. These rounds were the antitheses of the Blue Glasers, designed for penetration. They would drill through the steel block of a car engine if necessary. He dropped the box into the other pocket of his sport coat.

A vinyl-covered sandbag lay at the bottom of the cardboard

carton. Not the ballistic gelatin he had ordered, but it would do.

"We didn't have the gelatin handy," Oliverez said, anticipating a question. "I suspected that speed was of more importance."

"You suspected correctly," Bolan said. He drew the empty Derringer from his pocket, flipped the loading latch and dropped two Blue Glasers into the twin barrels. "Is everybody else ready?"

Oliverez nodded.

"Then let's get started." The Executioner scooted the heavy box across the floor to a spot directly in front of the one-way mirror. He accepted a set of foam rubber earplugs that Oliverez extended, and twisted them into his ears as the captain did the same with another pair. Then, thumbing the Derringer's safety down, he aimed at the box, but let his eyes rise to the window as he pulled the trigger.

The .40 caliber Glaser exploded like a neutron bomb inside the small office. To Bolan and Oliverez, however—safe with their ear protection—it registered as a dull thud.

The man on the other side of the window jumped like a scared jackrabbit against his leather restraints.

Oliverez grinned. "That should have warmed him up," he said.

Bolan didn't answer. Lifting the box containing the sandbag, he led the way out into the hall, then into the interrogation room. The waiter was still shaking from the gunshot, and his eyes jerked up to meet the Executioner's as the door opened. "What was that?" he asked nervously.

Bolan dropped the box between the man's feet, and aimed downward. "One of these," he said, then pulled the trigger again.

Once again, the waiter jumped against his restraints. He screamed, wondering if his foot had been hit. His toes wiggled inside his shoes, and the screaming turned to a whimper as the fact that he was unharmed slowly registered in his brain.

"I'd like to ask you some questions," the Executioner said in a calm voice.

The waiter's jaw clamped shut.

"First, what is your name?"

The man frowned, obviously trying to decide whether or not this was a safe question to answer. Then, probably figuring they would identify him eventually from the fingerprints the feds had rolled before bringing him to the interrogation room, he said in a forced calm-and-collected voice, "Espinoza. Frederico Espinoza."

At his side, Bolan saw Oliverez shake his head and laugh. "Bond, James Bond," the captain mocked in a British accent.

"Well, we're off to a good start at least," the soldier said. "Now—"

He was interrupted by the door opening. A federal lieutenant in full dress uniform stepped inside holding a large set of pliers. "Where should I set these?" he asked. He worked the jaws back and forth, creating a clicking sound.

Espinoza's eyes shot to the pliers. The cool expression he had affected vanished for a moment.

Bolan smiled inwardly. Things were going about as well as could be expected. He motioned toward the table behind him, against the wall. "Just set them there for the time being," he said. "I won't need them for awhile." He looked back to Espinoza. "Maybe not at all if our friend here cooperates."

The lieutenant set the pliers on the table and left the room. Bolan continued to stare at Espinoza. "The next question is just as easy," he said. "Who hired you to kill President Fierro Blanco?"

The man's eyes flicked to the pliers for a second but he didn't respond.

Bolan reloaded the Derringer. He lifted the box hiding the sandbag and rested it in Espinoza's lap. "I'm sorry," he said.

"I didn't hear you." He fired the pistol down in direct line with the man's groin.

Espinoza screamed again and jumped.

Bolan moved to a table to the side, pulling the plastic packages of Blue Glasers from his pockets and setting them on the surface. "Captain Oliverez?" he said.

Oliverez saluted.

"If you would be so kind, would you open these for me?"

"Certainly."

At the rear of the table, the Executioner spotted a ceramic beer mug being used as a pencil holder. He dumped the writing instruments onto the floor, and set down the empty mug again. "Just dump the loose rounds in there," he said.

The door opened again and it was a federal sergeant who entered this time. The man carried a dentist's drill. Bolan nodded him toward the table, turned to look at the drill, then walked over and lifted it. The room's only electrical outlet was set in the wall above the table, and the Executioner plugged in the cord, pressed the trigger button and let the drill bit whirl and whine for a few seconds. The sound filled the room until he set it back on the table. "Looks like it works fine, sergeant," he said. "But…" The Executioner frowned at the drill, then looked across the room to the man strapped to the chair. "I'm going to need an extension cord."

The sergeant smiled and saluted. "No problem," he said as he left the room.

"Okay, where were we?" the Executioner asked, glancing up at the ceiling. "Oh yeah. You were about to tell me who hired you."

Espinoza closed his eyes tight. Bolan fired another Blue Glaser into the box. Espinoza repeated his screaming.

As the noise died down, the Executioner said, "I'm a patient man, Frederico. But you are trying my patience." He paused until Espinoza's eyes flickered open again. "By now you've figured out that there's something in the box that stops the bullets, right?''

The waiter-assassin nodded.

''That's good. You're a smart guy. There's a sandbag in the box. Not a big one, but thick enough to stop the Blue Glasers.'' He drew in a breath. ''The exact type of rounds you planned to use to blow the back of the president's head off. Am I right?''

Espinoza hesitated, then nodded.

''But what if I were to use this bullet instead?'' The Executioner reached into his pocket and produced the box of armor-piercing ammo. Slowly, he opened the end, slid off the cover and pulled one of the rounds from the plastic foam holder.

Espinoza knew his ammo. His eyes looked like saucers as he stared at the bullet.

Bolan walked over to where Oliverez was still opening the Blue Glaser packages and dumping them into the beer mug. He dropped the armor-piercing round in with the rest and said, ''Will the sand still stop this one? Well, to be honest, I don't really think so.'' He moved swiftly across the room and jammed his face close to Espinoza's. ''Do you?''

Again, the door opened and the same sergeant who had brought the drill entered with an extension cord. The man also carried a can of charcoal lighter fluid and a box of wooden matches.

''Thank you,'' Bolan said. ''Just set them down.''

Espinoza could contain his curiosity no longer. ''What are they for?'' he whispered, breathing out.

''Later,'' the Executioner said. ''After we've played my own special version of Russian Roulette.''

By now Oliverez had finished dumping the rest of the loose Glasers into the beer mug with the armor-piercing round. He lifted the mug, shook it with both hands and set it down again. Bolan walked back to the table, turned his head, reached inside and pulled out two rounds. Keeping them hidden from both himself and Espinoza, he reloaded the Derringer. "Well, let's see what the fates have in store for you, shall we?" In one swift motion, he raised the pistol and double-actioned both rounds across the room into the sandbag.

The waiter jerked twice, shrieked like a woman, and closed his eyes again. Sweat poured from his forehead onto the white jacket and his chest began to heave with silent sobs.

"You're a lucky man, Frederico," Bolan said. He gave Espinoza a few seconds to recover, then said, "You know, all of this would stop if you'd just start answering my questions."

Espinoza's head shook violently back and forth. "I can't tell you," he moaned pitifully. "They will kill me if I talk!"

Oliverez stepped forward, looked at the man in the chair, then turned to Bolan and shook his head. "I have never understood this kind of thinking," he said. "Although I frequently hear lines of dialogue such as this on television and in movies, I didn't really think any man was so stupid as to speak them in real life." He sighed and shook his head again. "Well, I suppose the drama must be played out. Señor Belasko, the next line, of course, is yours."

Bolan shrugged. "We'll kill you if you don't talk?" he said in a questioning tone.

Oliverez nodded. "Very good." He stepped away.

The Executioner looked down at Espinoza. He watched the man's terrified face as he dumped the empty brass casings from the Derringer, and reached into the beer mug again. His fingers lifted two rounds inside the container. Feeling the sharp nose on one, he let it fall again and found another of the Glasers. As he loaded the tiny gun in his hand once more, the federal lieutenant opened the door and entered carrying a black plastic body bag. The uniformed man's eyebrows rose slightly as he nodded toward the table.

Bolan returned the nod, then looked back to Espinoza. He

aimed the Derringer down at the man's lap and said, "Who hired you?"

Espinoza closed his eyes. The double-action trigger moved back with a smooth grinding sound. "Stop!" Espinoza screeched. "Stop! I'll tell you all I know!"

Bolan lowered the revolver to his side. Oliverez appeared with a glass of water and held it to Espinoza's lips. When the man had swallowed half the glass, Oliverez said, "Proceed."

The waiter took a deep breath. "I was approached last week," he said, "by a man I didn't know."

"Where?" Bolan demanded

"It was in a cantina," the man in the chair whispered. "A place I go frequently after work."

"Who was the man?"

Espinoza sighed. "He used the name Gorre. I don't know if it was his real name or a fake."

"Go on."

"He told me he had a business proposition for me, and then he bought me drinks." Espinoza shook his head for no apparent reason; maybe he was chastising himself for being stupid enough to listen and get involved in all this. Whatever the reason, he continued. "He told me the revolution was at hand. That troops were ready to move into the capital and take over as soon as they heard of the president's death. He promised me fifty-thousand pesos. Do you know how much money that is?" His eyes glazed over at the idea of such wealth.

For a moment, the Executioner felt sorry for the man. An American worker with an annual income the equivalent of fifty-thousand pesos would still qualify for food stamps. "Who did the man represent?" Bolan asked.

Espinoza looked at him with curious eyes. "I don't know," he said. "I didn't ask."

Oliverez broke in. "You expect us to believe that you agreed to assassinate the president without even knowing who was paying you?" He turned to Bolan. "Let's try the drill."

"No!" the man in the chair gasped. "For fifty-thousand pesos," he said, "I didn't care." Tears began to roll down his cheeks.

Bolan felt a mixture of remorse and anger toward the man, now. Frederico Espinoza had grown up in poverty, and it was in poverty he had expected to die. The offer of money, to most men in such a situation, was impossible to refuse. Indigence didn't excuse his behavior but it somewhat explained it. "How did you expect to get away?" he asked. "The dining hall was crawling with soldiers and feds."

Espinoza looked up at the Executioner, his face a mask of anguish. "Gorre told me that his men would be stationed within the building. He promised they would move in and take control as soon as they heard the shots."

"Frederico," Bolan said. "Didn't it occur to you that if they could get that close they could kill Fierro Blanco themselves? Without your help?"

Espinoza shook his head. "Gorre said they could get close. But not that close. He said I was the only man who could carry out the killing. That I was the only man who could save Mexico!" For a brief second, the man in the chair forgot his present circumstances and beamed with pride.

Bolan stepped back and looked at the wall. He had no doubt that Espinoza was telling the truth. The waiter was a simple man, not a complete moron but no Einstein, either. He would have been easy to persuade with the mixture of money and patriotism this "Gorre" had held in front of his nose like a carrot.

The Executioner turned back and looked at the pitiful creature before him. Bolan wouldn't kill him. But it would be a miracle if the Mexican feds didn't once they learned that he had no more information to give up. And the bottom line was, he had given up little. The Executioner didn't know any more about who was behind the assassination attempts than he had before.

Turning to Oliverez, Bolan said, "I'm through with him."

The captain nodded, opened the door and summoned the sergeant and lieutenant who had assisted in the interrogation charade. "Take him to a cell," he ordered.

The men entered, released Espinoza from his restraints and jerked him to his feet. As they dragged the quivering man into the hallway, Espinoza turned back to the room. "May I call my wife and children?" he whimpered.

Captain Juanito Oliverez let out a disgusted sigh. He looked at the lieutenant, then nodded his head.

THE SUBURBAN'S BIG ENGINE roared as Nelson navigated the vehicle across the sandy earth, dodging cactus and scraggly trees as he, James and Encizo pursued Victorio Vega. The bandit caravan had left the road as soon as they'd realized they were being followed, cutting across the desert toward a small range of rocky hills in the distance.

James had noticed Nelson glancing down at the speedometer every few minutes as they drove. Now, as the DEA man finally spoke, he realized it was actually the odometer Nelson had been interested in.

"There," Nelson said. "We're exactly ten...nope, 10.1 miles past the border. I've officially violated direct orders and I can start looking for a new job when I get back."

James watched the bandit vehicles in the distance. "Maybe we can get the woman and get back before anybody's the wiser," he said.

Nelson laughed. "Yeah, and maybe monkeys'll fly out of my butt, too," he said.

The Suburban had gained rapidly on Vega's dilapidated pickups and cars during the ten-mile chase. But the bandits had a good headstart. As the pursuit continued, James realized what Vega's strategy had to be. "They'll have horses waiting when they reach those hills," he said. "They'll abandon the vehicles."

"And we'll be left sitting on our thumbs," Nelson said. He lit a fresh cigar and jammed it between his teeth.

Encizo leaned forward from the back of the Suburban. "If we can get within firing range before they take off, we may be able to hit enough men to get horses ourselves."

"Maybe," James said. "I'd rather hit enough men that we just get the woman and go home."

Nelson drove on, the smoke from his cigar filling the Suburban. Each new mile reduced the gap separating them from the bandits. But not enough.

James turned in his seat and looked past Encizo. He saw a scoped M-16 A-2 hanging on a rack in the rear of the Suburban. "That the only rifle you got, Pug?" he asked as Nelson dodged yet another cactus.

"That's it," the former prizefighter said. "I thought this was gonna be a sight-seeing tour. I didn't realize I'd turn into Blackjack Pershing before it was over." He snorted through his nose. "Hope we have better luck."

James couldn't help but grin. He had forgotten that Nelson, besides being a champion boxer and a damn fine Navy SEAL before joining the DEA, was a serious student of military history. Blackjack Pershing's army had pursued Pancho Villa deep into Mexico close to a century before. The Mexican bandit had never been captured.

James looked over his shoulder again. "Rafe," he said. "Get that toy ready."

Encizo reached over the seat behind him and pulled the rifle onto his lap.

James drew his Beretta, checked the chamber and magazine, then slid it back into the shoulder rig under his light safari vest. He had two more mags under his right arm, and of course, the Crossada hidden under the vest across his back.

By now the Suburban was less than a mile behind the bandit convoy. Encizo rolled down the window and leaned out. In the side mirror, James saw him aim the barrel high at a forty-five degree angle. The weapon exploded, and a second later the dry sand just to the side of a pickup leapt into the air.

"Go ahead and get your jollies," Nelson said. "I may only have one rifle but there's at least fifteen magazines back there and an extra case of .223 slugs."

James saw Encizo nod silently in the mirror. The little Cuban kept the selector switch on semiauto but rapidly squeezed the trigger, sending a volley of shots arcing through the air at the escaping bandits. More sand flew around the caravan but none of the vehicles caught a round.

"Well, at least they know we're here," Nelson said.

Estimating the distance to the hills wasn't easy in the desert sun but James guessed the bandits were still three to four miles away. The distance between them, he calculated, had dropped to three-quarters of a mile. The Suburban could easily outrun any of the battered vehicles Vega's men drove, but on the rough terrain they were covering they were unable to fully capitalize on that advantage. Looking in the mirror again, he saw Encizo lower the rifle slightly. The Cuban slowed his rate of fire but continued to pump periodic rounds after the bandits.

Down the sides of the hills came two dozen horses led by three mounted men. The Suburban was still half a mile away when the sand began to fly as the battered pickups and aged cars slid to a halt at the foot of the hills. Now that the bandits had stopped, the gap began closing more quickly. But it would still be a race against the clock. If they didn't get the woman before Vega and his men disappeared into the hills with her, or at least manage to get three of the horses, they'd be stuck with no way to continue their pursuit.

Nelson cursed as only a former sailor can do, and even then only one who'd had practice. The DEA man leaned his foot on the accelerator and the Suburban sped even faster across the sand. As they neared, Encizo increased his fire, switching magazines twice and continuing. They watched the tiny antlike forms in the distance burst from the vehicles and begin mounting the horses. Barely visible, James could see a woman wearing a colorful print dress being dragged toward a horse by two men.

James calculated the distance again. "We're not going to make it," he said. "They'll shoot whatever horses they don't need and be gone before we even get there."

Encizo shook his head. "I think we're close enough I can start getting in some shots," he said. His face wrinkled tightly as he pressed his eyes to the rifle scope. "The trick is to keep from hitting the woman."

James nodded. "Don't go for the guys with her, Rafe," he said. "Just see if you can get us some horses."

A second later, the M-16 exploded again. A bandit wearing a brightly adorned sombrero lost the hat and part of his head. He fell from his horse, and the animal took off in fear.

"There's one they won't catch," Nelson said. He kept his foot on the accelerator.

"Let's hope we can," James said. His words were drowned by another .223 caliber explosion behind him. Another man fell to the ground and his horse also took off.

Encizo's next shot missed and James watched one of the two men who had forced the woman onto a horse leap onto his own steed. He grabbed the reins of the woman's mount and galloped toward the hills.

They were less than five hundred yards from the escaping men when Encizo dropped a third bandit. This horse apparently hadn't noticed the shot. He took a step or two, then lowered his head, searching the sparse ground for something to graze.

By now, the rest of the mounted bandits were charging up the hills. Encizo fired several more rounds to no effect, then pulled the M-16 back into the Suburban.

"Every second is going to count," James said. "Rafe, get the rifle and extra ammo ready to move out." He turned to Nelson. "Pug, pull to a halt about fifty yards from that horse that didn't run. I don't want to spook him, too. We'll let Encizo out to get him, and you and I'll round up the other two. Rafe, check the men you shot and see if they've got anymore rifles.''

Encizo nodded silently and began stuffing extra magazines and ammo boxes into his vest.

Nelson snorted over the cigar in his teeth. ''I feel just like Rowdy Yates,'' he said. ''Head 'em up. Move 'em out. 'Rawhide.'''

A few seconds later, the Suburban fishtailed to a halt amid a whirlwind of flying sand and pebbles. Encizo leapt out and sprinted toward the horse who stood grazing. Closer now, James could see that the animal was a medium-sized spotted mare. Nelson pulled out again, turning the truck toward the nearest horse who had spooked. In the distance, James watched the bandits disappear one by one into the cover of the hills.

A few seconds later, Nelson slowed and crept toward a horse who stood staring at the approaching vehicle. James opened his door slowly and got out. ''Easy boy,'' he said, gingerly holding out a hand. The horse, a tall black stallion, nodded as if in agreement and whinnied. Then he turned and took off across the desert.

James cursed under his breath and jumped back into the Suburban. Nelson slowly followed the galloping animal until it stopped again. James shook his head in annoyance. Each extra second it took to round up the horses was an extra second that gave Vega and his men time to get deeper into the hills. But that was only part of the problem. If they had to chase the horses all over the desert before they caught them, the animals would be too tired to pursue the bandits before they even got started.

This time, Nelson stopped a hundred yards from where the stallion had come to rest. James got out slowly and began walking toward the animal. A quick glance over his shoulder told him Encizo had experienced no similar problems with the mare. In the distance, he could see the little Cuban stroking the animal's mane.

Nelson drove toward the final horse as James cautiously approached the stallion. The animal whinnied again but didn't run. Suddenly remembering that he had a Three Musketeers candy bar with him—part of the survival pack he always carried—he reached into his vest as he walked. He unwrapped the paper and let it fall to the ground, holding the chocolate bar in front of him. "Easy boy," he said in a calm voice.

The stallion's ears pricked and his nostrils flared.

James slowed even more ten feet from the animal. "Easy boy," he said again. "I'm your friend. Got something good for you here just to prove it."

By now the odor of the chocolate was strong in the stallion's nostrils. He shook his head and stared at the candy bar. James stepped up to him and slowly extended his hand.

The horse took the Three Musketeers in one bite.

James stroked the animal's muzzle. "There, boy," he said in a soothing voice. "There you go. Lots better than those nasty old Granola bars Bolan always carries, isn't it?"

The horse whinnied its consensus. He made no protest when, a moment later, James swung into the Mexican saddle on his back.

The black Phoenix Force warrior cupped a hand over his eyes and stared off across the desert. Several hundred yards away, he could see Nelson had gotten out of the parked Suburban. Apparently his horse, a golden palomino, hadn't held the stallion's fear. The DEA man was already in the saddle.

James took off at a gallop and met Nelson halfway to where Encizo now sat in the spotted mare's saddle. He looked at the old sea dog who was obviously only partially acquainted with the equestrian arts. "You look just like Roy Rogers, Pug," he said.

Nelson fought the bridle as the palomino tried to buck. What he said would have been out of place in a church, to say the least.

Together, they rode to where Encizo was waiting. The Cuban

had gathered two rifles—an old bolt-action 30/40 Krag and a lever-action .357 Magnum Winchester carbine—and extra ammo bandoliers for both weapons. He handed the Winchester to James, the Krag to Nelson.

Calvin James slipped the .357 Magnum bandolier over his safari vest and looked up at the hills as the last bandit disappeared into the rocks. "Well, *muchachos*," he said in his best *bandido* voice. "Let's ride!"

The trio raced toward the hills.

6

The bearded man didn't like waiting. He considered it far beneath his position.

He took a seat in the living room. Crucifixes and portraits of Christ covered the scarred walls, and the furniture was worn beyond repair. The homey odor of beans and rice cooking in the next room filled the air.

The smell contrasted sharply with the screams coming from the next room.

The man with the beard glanced at his wristwatch. He hoped the ridiculous ritual taking place beyond the closed door wouldn't last much longer. The old woman considered it of extreme importance; a method by which she and her sons derived power to carry out their magic. He considered it a farce. An absurdity that, like all religion, only worked in the simple minds of simple people. He wondered, however, how the old woman and her sons rationalized the icons of Jesus in one room and the worship of Satan in the next.

Another scream sounded beyond the door and the bearded man heard chants in a tongue he didn't know. He wondered at the language. It wasn't Spanish—he was fluent in all dialects. It was none of the other several languages he spoke, either. Perhaps it was one of the many Mexican Indian tongues or some little known patois of the ancient Caribe these witches, warlocks and devil-worshippers seemed to favor. On the other hand, such fools had been known to create their own silly words from scratch just for the purposes of their ceremonies.

The bearded man sighed, glanced at his watch again and sat back against the threadbare couch. It mattered little, whatever the language was. He was curious only in an attempt to pass the time while he waited for the old woman. He tolerated her freakish eccentricities because he needed her. Her peculiarities aside, she had proven to be totally reliable and discreet. She could be trusted when others in his power structure were questionable. Therefore, there were certain parts of his plan that only she and her sons could carry out.

Glancing through the window, he saw a peasant woman walk past the house on the dirt road outside. She glanced at the small building, her eyes frightened, then made the sign of the cross over her breasts and quickened her pace.

A gurgling sound—as if someone were gargling mouthwash—drifted out of the other room and the bearded man turned back to the door and shook his head. What perversities were they performing now? What bizarre acts and painful torture were the old woman, Roberto and Santiago forcing their subject to undergo in order to strip him of his power and add it to their own? More importantly—he raised his wrist and stared at his watch once more—how long would the nonsense take?

As if to answer his question, a long bloodcurdling scream echoed through the house. It was followed by a gasp that couldn't be mistaken for anything save the final breath of a human life. The room on the other side of the door lapsed into silence, then new chants of unholy fervor filled the house. A moment later, the door opened.

Roberto and Santiago appeared carrying what could only be a body wrapped in a blanket. The burly men looked at the bearded man and smiled. Their machetes hung from their belts, the edges wet with blood. Their eyes appeared to glow as they toted their cargo into the living room.

The old woman appeared and touched Santiago on the forearm, shook her head at the front door and pointed toward the rear exit of the house. The brothers turned and hauled their cargo that way.

The bearded man saw blood drip from the blanket, leaving a trail of crimson across the dirty wooden floor as they disappeared out of the same back door he always used for his visits.

"Come," the old woman said. She stood sideways in the doorway and motioned the bearded man forward.

A few seconds later, he entered the room, again noticing the aura of evil that always permeated it. It wasn't just the terrified animal trophies mounted on the walls or the stone dagger—now coated in red—in its usual place among several blades on the coffee table. The room seemed to have a life of its own, and that life emitted its own profane wickedness.

The old woman began washing her bloodstained forearms in a metal basin on the coffee table. The bearded man watched her. Her wild eyes glowed with a new zest he hadn't seen before. Perhaps she did glean some sort of energy from her debaucheries, if only in her mind.

"Had I known you were coming," she said, drying her arms now with a dirty towel. "I would have rescheduled the sacrifice."

He shook his head. "It's all right." Then, in an effort to patronize her, he said, "Was the ritual successful?"

The old witch cackled. "They are always successful," she said. "But why do you ask? I know you don't believe in my magic."

The bearded man shrugged. "I believe in your effectiveness," he said.

She dropped the towel next to the metal basin and said, "Please, sit."

The man glanced around him. The room was soaked in blood, with no place to sit that wouldn't leave stains on his suit. "I will stand," he said.

Now it was the old woman who shrugged. Ignoring the

blood, she allowed her old bones to gingerly settle onto the couch. "You have work for me?" she asked.

He looked down at the crone and nodded. "There is a man who must die."

The old woman waited.

"The big American. Fierro Blanco's bodyguard."

The witch frowned, her face wrinkling far beyond what the bearded man would have guessed human skin capable of. "We have discussed him before. You believed him to be of no consequence."

"Yes," said the bearded man. "But that was before. He is complicating things. I suspect he is more than just a bodyguard."

"How so?"

The bearded man stared harder into the old woman's eyes. It was one of her more irritating traits—curiosity. While she might be trustworthy and closemouthed, she asked far too many questions to which she needed no answers in order to carry out his demands. "It's not important to you," he said. "But I'll tell you this. I suspect now that in addition to his bodyguard chores, he's doing a fair share of snooping through *Los Pinos*. Exactly why, I don't know."

"How do you want him killed?"

"I don't care."

The woman's wrinkled frown stretched into a wild smile. "This man is powerful?" she asked.

"Very."

The smile widened even further until it threatened to snap her aged skin. "My sons and I could gain much strength from a man like this," she said, glancing toward the bloody dagger on the table.

The bearded man shoved his hands into the pockets of his slacks. "Do as you like," he said. "But I warn you, do not take chances. Bringing him here will not be as easy as simply killing him outright. And if you fail..." he allowed his words to trail.

The meaning, however, was clear to the old woman. Slowly, the smile of anticipated pleasure faded and the bearded man saw fear creep into her eyes. She started to respond but her lips only quivered.

The sight made the bearded man smile himself—a smile he kept inside. The old woman might believe in her own witchcraft. But she also believed in the secular power she knew he wielded.

Gaining control of her speech, the witch asked, "How soon must it be done?"

"Today. Tomorrow. Yesterday would have been even better."

"I see."

The bearded man nodded. "I'm sure you do. You always do." When he pulled his hand out of his pocket it held a Mexican silver money clip. He peeled off several bills, found a dry spot amid the blood on the coffee table and set them down.

The old woman's eyes flew to the money.

Without speaking further, the bearded man turned and walked out into the living room. The door had been open during his meeting with the old woman and the house was well ventilated. So he knew it must be his imagination when the air seemed less stagnant the moment he stepped through the door. He exited through the back of the house and stopped briefly just outside.

In the moonlight, he saw Roberto and Santiago kneeling in the alley. Next to them were several stacks of objects wrapped in white butcher paper. Both men held large skinning knives as they looked up with what the bearded man could only call insane grins. The body that had been in the blanket—at least what was left of it—now lay exposed, and the bearded man could see it had once belonged to a young woman.

Her open eyes held the same terrified last look he had seen on the animals mounted inside.

GENERAL AVIA PORTILLA pulled the cheap straw sombrero from his head as he entered the taxi cab. He glanced at the multicolored round balls decorating the brim, then rested the hat in his lap as Francisco Paz got into the other side. The *Marxista* leader leaned forward. "Bosque de Chapultepec," he told the driver. He glanced across the cab to Paz. Like Portilla himself, Paz was dressed in the plain white peasant pants and shirt of the typical Mexican laborer. His sombrero, however, didn't sport the silly round balls. Paz should have been grateful, but forever arrogant, he still had balked against donning the peasant clothing. It had taken more than a little effort, then an outright threat on Portilla's part, to get him to leave the infernal swagger stick back at camp.

The leader of the *Partido Revolucionario Marxista* settled back into his seat as the cab pulled away from the curb. He let his mind glide over the events that would unfold in the next few hours. Don Juan de Fierro Blanco had decided to reschedule the speech that had been aborted due to Lopez's sniperfire and his own attempt to poison the president. The president knew that his popularity was at an all-time low, and planned to carry on in spite of the fact that he must know more assassination attempts were inevitable. Why, Portilla wondered. The man wasn't a hero. Was there more to what was going on than met the eye? Each endeavor the PRM had made to kill the bastard had been carefully orchestrated and planned. Yet each attempt had failed at the last moment, usually due to something the new American bodyguard did. It made no sense. Was Fierro Blanco's American really that good? Or was word of the projected assassinations getting back to the president in advance?

Were his attempts being purposefully sabotaged for some reason? If so, what was that reason? Could Fierro Blanco himself be somehow involved?

Portilla closed his eyes as the cab moved through the heavy Mexico City traffic. He would figure out the problem later. Right now, he had more immediate problems to handle.

The cab driver slammed the brake and honked the horn, screeching to a halt three feet in front of a trio of giggling young preteenage girls crossing the street. Portilla opened his eyes and listened to a string of curses from the front seat that accused the girls of sexual acts and preferences that were improbable at their young age. He closed his eyes again as the cab moved on toward the park.

His well-planned attacks had failed, so he had decided to try a new approach. If sniper shots and other conventional assassination attempts couldn't get Fierro Blanco, perhaps full-scale chaos could. A small smile curled his mustache upward as the cool breeze from the open window blew across his face. Until now, he had been using what he thought of as "rifle" techniques—carefully designed strategies that singled out Fierro Blanco for the kill. Today, he would shoot a "shotgun," sending thousands of pellets flying in the president's general direction and praying that at least one would find its mark.

The *Marxista* general folded his hands in his lap as they drove. What he had planned was nothing short of a full-scale riot. His men were all dressed as peasants and, in addition to them, he had contacted the leader of the Mayan Zapatista Movement. The like-minded Mayans already had an arm's-length relationship with the PRM, and they, too, would be in disguised attendance at the speech in the park. Both Mayans and *Marxistas* would appear unarmed. But beneath their blousy peasant shirts all would be carrying the Type 67 Chinese Tokarev pistols that had arrived at the compound the day before.

The men, *Marxista* and Mayan combined, numbered almost two hundred in strength. Dispersed among the crowd of the thousands expected, they would be invisible. But they were more than enough to launch a riot of angry Mexicans already pushed to the verge of violence on their own.

The cab arrived at the park and Portilla opened his eyes again. Through the windows, he could see hundreds of men and women approaching the sawhorse barriers that separated the audience from the stage. The newspapers had announced that because of the attempts on the president's life at his earlier speech, the crowds would be kept behind the barriers this time.

Portilla chuckled as he paid the driver and got out of the cab. They would stay behind the barriers all right—for awhile, at least.

Adjusting the pistol hidden in his waistband, the general of the PRM led his colonel into the throngs of men and women moving toward the barriers. He spotted two of his own men in the crowd. They ignored him, as ordered. He eyed the hundreds of police officers and military troops who had been brought in for crowd control. Armed with rifles and bayonets, Portilla had no doubt that some of his men—maybe even he himself—would die that day.

But there weren't enough soldiers or police to control the crowd once his men and the Mayans broke through the barriers. And what was a revolution without martyrs?

Pushing to the front of the crowd, Portilla and Paz took positions just beyond the barriers. A short police officer smoking a cigarette eyed him suspiciously. Portilla smiled. "There is still hope," he told the officer in a voice just loud enough to be heard over the clamor of the crowd.

The uniformed man nodded, some of the suspicion draining from his face.

Portilla laughed inwardly. How easy the fascist pigs were to deceive.

In the distance, the general could see the podium. The president hadn't yet arrived but at least two dozen uniformed feds and others in plainclothes were already in position. He reached into his pocket and produced a rumpled pack of Mexican cigarettes. Shaking one loose, Portilla jammed it between his lips. As he struck a match, he saw a tall, muscular gringo wearing a blue blazer and khaki slacks appear on the platform in the distance. The American bodyguard. He watched the big man's eyes scan the crowd, and knew with animal intuition that the bodyguard would never be fooled as easily as the police officer to whom he had just spoken.

The *Marxista* leader lit his cigarette and drew in a lung full of smoke. It didn't matter. One man couldn't control thousands. In a few minutes, the president would arrive and begin bleating his crippled words. As soon as the legitimate members of the crowd were sufficiently infuriated that their anger enabled them to be led like sheep, his men and the Mayans would go into action. The result would be total anarchy, and a bloody riot the likes of which Mexico City had never before seen.

As he stuffed the cigarettes and matches back into his pocket, Portilla decided suddenly what his particular assignment during the upcoming confusion would be. Fourteen of his best men and ten of the Mayans had already been assigned to seek out Fierro Blanco. They didn't need him.

So General Avia Portilla would move directly toward the stage and make the president's big American bodyguard his personal target.

THE EXECUTIONER had argued with all his heart and soul against the resumption of the aborted speech at the Basque de Chapultepec. It had done no good. Fierro Blanco knew his approval rating among the Mexican people was by now in the negative zone. He feared civil war any day—any moment— and he intended to carry through with the speech, even at personal risk.

But was he at personal risk, Bolan wondered as he stepped from the advance car and walked to the podium for a final check. He had still found no evidence that the president was dirty. But he had still found no evidence that the man wasn't, either. All of the assassination attempts since the Executioner's arrival had come close. But none had succeeded. Was this because Fierro Blanco himself was carefully orchestrating them in order to appear legitimate and gain the sympathy of an increasingly hostile constituency?

The answer was...Bolan didn't know.

The soldier mounted the steps to the same stage that had been set up for the last speech. At least the guards had conducted a more thorough search of the area this time—the Executioner knew they had because he himself had spearheaded it. The location of the last sniper attack had been pinpointed and permanent guards had been stationed there, and at all other spots in the vicinity that could conceivably be used as a base for concealed gunfire. Fierro Blanco, of course, was smart enough not to try to eat or drink anything during the speech other than water from the canteen Bolan carried and would personally hand to him.

But there were other ways to set up an assassination; too many to cover completely. Regardless of the method of the attempt, killing a well-guarded public official was never as enigmatic as the escape that followed. Once the perpetrator gave up the hope of getting away, the odds in his favor increased a thousandfold. And the attempts on Fierro Blanco's life were becoming increasingly desperate and kamikaze-like in the way they were carried out.

An uneasy feeling haunted the Executioner as he gazed out over the thousands already gathering to hear their president. If the collective murmur was any indication, the mood was even less supportive than it had been during the first speech. The police and military in charge of crowd control had been tripled, but that meant little. Even though they were armed, it was still a case of hundreds versus thousands and no amount of bullets or bayonets would regulate these masses if they chose to rebel.

Behind him, Bolan heard the rumble of engines and turned to see Fierro Blanco's motorcade arrive. Machine-gun toting guards hopped out of the lead vehicle and hurried to open the doors of the president's limousine. Other plainclothes bodyguards appeared from the cars that had followed and flanked the presidential limo through streets that had been temporarily closed to other vehicular traffic. All possible precautions were being taken.

The soldier shook his head. Unfortunately, there were still too many holes in the network through which a bullet, a knife or some other means of murder could slip.

Don Juan de Fierro Blanco appeared in the middle of his armed entourage with Oliverez as close as possible without becoming a Siamese twin. The president cast false smiles and generic waves at all as he moved toward the platform. He looked like a man truly worried about his safety but presenting a good front.

The Executioner studied the man as he approached. Was it a front? That was the question. Was the president truly worried or were the assassination attempts simply a ruse? True, Bolan hadn't discovered anything to prove treason on Fierro Blanco's part. But a recent unexplained occurrence was particularly suspicious.

The incident had occurred during Bolan's interrogation of Espinoza. Upon leaving the man, the Executioner had attempted to find the president in order to give the man his report. Fierro Blanco, however, had been nowhere to be found. Oliverez didn't know his whereabouts—he had been with Bolan during the interrogation—and none of the other federal bodyguards seemed to know where the president had gone. Or if they did know, they weren't talking.

Bolan sighed. It was a situation that would have been totally unacceptable in the United States. Secret Service heads would have rolled. But here in Mexico, no one except himself and Oliverez seemed concerned. And when Fierro Blanco showed up again as mysteriously as he had disappeared, General Razon—in full dress uniform, of course—at his side, the president's words to the Executioner had been simply, *"De nada."*

It was nothing. Don't worry about it.

Bolan and Oliverez had been left staring at each other in disbelief.

The Executioner moved to the other side of the president as the man reached the top of the steps. It wouldn't have been the first time a president—in Mexico or the U.S.—had kept a mistress on the side or engaged in other activities that, while not directly relating to the performance of his public duties, were of a sort that he didn't want publicized. But was that the reason for the disappearance? Some woman or minor vice that Fierro Blanco wanted kept secret? Or was there a more nefarious explanation?

Fierro Blanco took a seat behind the podium. Again, like they had two days earlier, Bolan and Oliverez dropped into chairs on each side. General Razon took the microphone and began another of his clumsy introductions featuring the word "esteemed."

The murmurs of the crowd silenced for a few moments, then returned with renewed hatred.

Razon droned on, raising his voice as the crowd's cries of disapproval grew louder. In the distance, the Executioner saw a man wearing a white peasant shirt burst through the barricade. His was quickly subdued by the rifle butts of soldiers and police, and for awhile the crowd quieted. Then another man hopped a sawhorse and sprinted forward, shouting words that were unintelligible at such a distance. This time, a soldier used his bayonet on the man and he sank to the ground like the wild boars on the hog hunt.

Silence fell over the assembled masses at the brutality of the act. Even Razon stopped speaking. Then, slowly, like some monster awakening after a short nap, the angry crowd began to roar again. Cries of "Police brutality," "Free Mexico!" and "Down with Fierro Blanco!" filled the air. A dozen men—all dressed similarly, Bolan noticed—now leapt over the barricades and sprinted toward the platform.

Which was all that it took, literally the straw that broke the camel's back. As if of one mind, the crowd suddenly moved forward, knocking the sawhorses out of the way and running over the armed soldiers and police. Shrieks, screams, threats and curses filled the air as the mass moved forward. Scattered rifle shots, mixed with pistol rounds the Executioner identified as 7.62 mms, exploded over the storm of human discord. Soldiers, policemen and members of the crowd alike began to fall.

Bolan's eyes zeroed in on another man dressed in white peasant garb shooting what appeared to be a Chinese Tokarev. He skimmed the oncoming mob and spotted two more similarly dressed men with identical pistols. Communist weapons. Hardly the kind he expected to see in Mexico.

Unless they had been brought in specifically to aid a group like the *Partido Revolucionario Marxista.*

Suddenly, the plan fell into place in the Executioner's brain. The *Marxistas,* or perhaps some other communist-backed group, had infiltrated the crowd in heavy numbers. They were spurring on the frustrated Mexicans, and at the same time they could quite possibly get Fierro Blanco in the bargain.

Bolan grabbed Blanco by the arm, ready to hustle him back to the limo and whisk the motorcade to safety. But as he spun the president, he heard gunfire break out between the platform and the cars.

And as he turned, he saw that at least two dozen of the white-clad men had penetrated the secure zone behind the podium and were now battling it out with the guards.

RAFAEL ENCIZO was waiting when James and Nelson rode up. After handing over the rifles and ammo bandoliers he'd gathered, he took the lead without being told when James shouted, "Let's ride!"

His spotted mare trotted toward the hills. The animal seemed to know the way on its own, so Encizo gave it free rein, concentrating on the ground ahead, and seeing mostly rock with sparse brown prairie grass and weeds growing through the crevices. He suspected that Nelson knew little of tracking other than what he had learned in SEAL training. The same could be said of James. Not that such training wasn't good, but it didn't make up for a childhood spent exploring the jungles of Cuba. The Phoenix Force warrior didn't know where Nelson had grown up. It was probably some suburban environment like James, the "tracks" he'd be most accustomed to were the latest spray-painted gang symbols on brick walls. While Encizo knew James, and maybe the old SEAL too, could eventually ferret out the path taken by Victorio Vega and his kidnapping bandits, he knew he could do it faster. So did James, and the black soldier had automatically fallen in behind him next to Pug Nelson.

Encizo's mare reached the foot of the hills and started automatically toward a path that disappeared upward. The Cuban let him go. The horse knew where he was headed better than Encizo did, and tracking consisted of utilizing any advantage at one's disposal. If that meant a horse that knew the way on its own, so much the better. It would make things easy.

As the mare slowed and started up the rocky incline, Encizo laughed to himself. He had yet to see a Stony Man mission in which any aspect turned out to be easy. Murphy's Law always popped up somewhere along the line, and he didn't kid himself that this would be any exception. In addition to that fact, his mare had no concept of which side he was now on.

The three horsemen reached the curve where the bandits had disappeared. Encizo slowed his mount, shifted the reins to his left hand and flipped the M-16's selector switch to full auto. For all he knew, Vega could have left men in ambush around this bend, or any of the others he knew they'd encounter as they followed the bandits through the knolls and inclines. From there, he could look for signs with one eye, but the other had better be kept open for danger.

Rounding the bend, Encizo breathed a silent sigh of relief when no gunshots broke out. Ahead he saw a stretch of perhaps twenty yards before the rocky path dipped out of sight again. His horse needed no coaxing, walking along with the gait of an animal on familiar ground. Encizo watched the hard road ahead for signs of the horses who had just passed. They were few and far between, even though it had been only minutes since the bandits made their getaway.

The slopes they were scaling seemed to grow in height as they climbed, then became steep walls on each side as the path dipped downward. Again primed for ambush, he held the M-16 braced against his side, ready to shoot a close-range volley of automatic fire from the hip should the enemy suddenly appear.

Letting the mare slow again to negotiate the steep decline, Encizo reminded himself that he was about to enter a different kind of danger zone. The human mind could endure only so much life-and-death tension. After awhile, it either relaxed or shut down completely. Carl Lyons of Able Team, a former LAPD cop, had once told him of what they called the red light syndrome in police work. The first time a rookie patrolman stopped a car, even if only for speeding, he was certain it would end in a gunfight; the rookie was ready. But with each successive automobile he stopped to find himself facing nothing more dangerous than the speeder's surly attitude, that ready edge gradually began to wear off. The officer began to relax. And with relaxation came carelessness.

The bends and dips through the rocks were similar to "red-lighted" motorists, Encizo knew. Each one that didn't hide an ambush could contribute to a sense of false security if he wasn't careful.

The mare reached the bottom of the decline and James found they were in a small canyon. It was an excellent place for an ambush, and unless he missed his guess, Vega would be aware that his pursuers had secured horses and were still on the chase. Forty yards or so ahead, the path rose again. Encizo's eyes skirted the rock walls around him as he rode.

Behind him, the soldier could hear the soft click of horseshoes against rock as James's stallion and Nelson's palomino followed. Both men rode in silence, and a quick glance over his shoulder told Encizo their eyes were as busy as his own. Nelson was looking over his own shoulder as Encizo turned. Good. Someone needed to watch their rear in case they overshot one or more of the kidnappers.

Somewhere in the distance, a horse whinnied. The mare's ears pricked and so did Encizo's. But in the strange acoustics of the rocky canyon, it was impossible to tell from exactly which direction or from just how far ahead the noise had come. It might be half a mile in front of them. Then again, it might be just beyond the next rise.

The men and horses negotiated the next climb with no more incident than the other potential traps had brought, and they found themselves facing a long open area of a hundred yards or so. Another horse—or maybe the same one—whinnied again, and this time Encizo was almost certain it came from the right side of the road. But again, it was impossible to tell from how far away the sound was.

Had the bandits left the trail? Possibly. He had to figure that sooner or later they would. If they had a hideout somewhere in these hills it wouldn't be right on the beaten path. And if they were planning an ambush, the little Cuban doubted they'd stand in the middle of the path and wait with open arms.

Looking down at the road, Encizo searched for evidence that the horses might have veered to the rocks at the side of the straightaway. The ground was hard—too hard for tracks—but the soldier knew tracks were only the most elementary of signs. For a moment, he wished Gary Manning, Phoenix Force's renowned tracker, was there. Besides his duties as an explosive expert, Manning was an expert hunter and woodsman. But Encizo knew he could wish all he wanted; it wouldn't magically transport the barrel-chested Canadian from Iran to Mexico anymore than he could call on Scotty to "beam Manning up."

The mare, stallion and palomino moved on. Encizo felt his eyes grow weary as he concentrated on the ground. He closed them for a second to clear his vision. He had barely opened them when his head jerked to the side. He pulled on the reins, stopping the mare and staring down at the ground. Behind him, he heard the other horses stop.

The Phoenix Force warrior swung his leg over the saddle and dropped to the ground. He knew James would watch the surrounding area for signs of trouble, so he gave his full attention to the spot in the rocks that had caught his eye. Just off the middle of the path, he saw several short blades of grass growing between the cracks. A small area, perhaps the size of a quarter, had been mashed flat.

Encizo squatted next to the flat spot and stared at it. In the entire world of tracking, nothing spelled "man" better than flat spots. Birds, animals, wind and weather all left their confusing autographs on the earth. But only two sources—man—or his man-made objects such as horse shoes and rifle butts—flattened the earth.

And Encizo, James and Nelson were following both sources.

The Cuban continued to study the smashed grass and the flat spot in the small amount of dirt surrounding it. Then, rising to his feet, he placed his shoe as close to the sign as he could. Taking a step past the spot, he turned and looked back at it. He had flattened the area where his boot had been, but not as firmly as the original spot next to it.

The sign had been made by an animal exerting far more weight per square inch than any man. An animal like a horse.

James finally broke the silence, whispering, "Find something?"

Encizo nodded silently. The soldier looked back to where he had seen the first sign, drawing a mental line forward. Returning to his horse, he swung back into the saddle and guided the animal off the path and over the rocks. Now that he knew where to look, he began seeing more and more signs that the horses had come this way. Overturned pebbles appeared on the invisible trail, tiny stalks of grass had been broken off. The tracks led to a new trail into another set of hills, where the Phoenix Force warrior saw a larger flattened area. Dismounting, he walked gingerly forward and saw the bent stalks of several blades of wild grass. The length of the sign was too long for a horses hoof. It had to have been a boot. At least one of the men had dismounted here.

Turning a quick 360-degrees, Encizo spotted the wet spot ten yards away. Whoever it had been that stopped had needed to urinate.

Encizo returned to his mount and swung back into the saddle. They were close, now. He couldn't explain how he knew, and he didn't know if it meant they were close to the escaping men or close to an ambush set by them. But he sensed there were other human beings near.

The new trail led into the dry mounds at a steeper angle. Lights seemed to twinkle in the hills, and the Cuban knew they had to contain deposits of alabaster. He tried to ignore the distracting sparkles from his vision but the sun refused to co-operate and they grew brighter.

Had the bandits led them to this area on purpose? Was an ambush waiting any moment now? Maneuvering the sun into an opponent's eyes was an old gunfighter's trick. Could this be Victorio Vega's personal variation of that technique?

As they neared another curve, James glanced over his shoulder and saw that James and Nelson were also squinting against the bright twinkles of light. Turning back, he shut his eyes for a second but the sparks still danced across the back of his closed lids. A feeling of impending urgency overcame him and he was about to turn and motion for the other two men to split up, taking a circular route through the rocks and meeting him some place ahead.

Before he could do so, they had rounded the curve. Suddenly, the entire hill ahead seemed to be completely made of alabaster. His eyes rebelled as if he'd just looked up at the sun.

Then Encizo heard the distinct clicks of a single action Colt revolver's hammer cocking. A split second later, the cold steel barrel of the gun pressed against his temple. Turning, he saw the shadowy figure of a man.

"Don't move again or I'll shoot you, *hombre*," the shadow said with a craggy voice that had drunk too much tequila and smoked too many cigarettes over the years. "But allow me to welcome you to Blind Man's Canyon. I, Victorio Vega, will be your host."

Bolan switched his grip from the president's arm to the back
of the man's neck. He pulled the man forward and with a quick
sweep of the foot, knocked his feet from under him and followed him to the ground.

Two shots flew over the spot where Bolan and the president
had stood only a second before.

"Stay down!" the Executioner ordered. With Fierro Blanco
still under him and shielded by his body, Bolan drew the Desert
Eagle from the hip holster under his jacket. The man who had
fired the rounds was a virtual giant, standing a good six and a
half feet tall and stretching the very seams of his peasant garb.
But his size also made an excellent target.

And he wasn't big enough to stop .44 Magnum bullets.

The Executioner fired once, riding the Desert Eagle's heavy
recoil and pulling the trigger again as soon as the gun fell back
into position. Both rounds splattered into the white peasant shirt
and drilled out the man's back, leaving tunnels of destruction
that spread scarlet across his back and chest.

Oliverez had dropped to a knee next to Bolan and Fierro
Blanco. He now fired three rounds from his Government Model
.45. The hot brass casings flew from the ejection port, the first
striking the Executioner on the neck and burning his skin. The
captain aimed again, this time hitting a gunner ten feet away,
who dropped his Tokarev and fell to the ground.

Between the stage and the presidential motorcade, the guards
continued to battle the attackers. On the other side of the po-

dium, the angry crowd made their way closer, slowed only slightly by the police and soldiers.

The Executioner fired again, scalping another of the men in white peasant dress. The identical clothing the men wore hadn't looked out of place mixed into the crowd. But now that they had drawn Bolan's attention, it became obvious that they had been purposefully outfitted for the riot. Whoever was behind the scheme—and considering the communist weapons they sported, he still had to place his money on the *Marxistas*—had bought a truckload of typical Mexican work clothes and passed them out. The men had probably changed straight from terrorist cammo into their current attire.

Another man, sporting a black beard and long hair, aimed his Tokarev toward the Executioner. Bolan swung the Desert Eagle his way and released a point-shot round that caught him dead center in the sternum. The man's knees buckled and he crossed himself on the way to meet his maker. Next to him, the Executioner heard Oliverez's .45 pistol again. Then the captain shouted, "Belasko! We've got to get the president to the car! There are far too many of them!"

The Executioner nodded in response, at the same time double-tapping a pair of Magnum rounds into another white shirt. Without looking down, he grabbed Fierro Blanco under the arm and jerked him to his feet. "Let's go, Mr. President," he said.

With Oliverez on Fierro Blanco's other arm, Bolan hurried down the steps toward the cars. He and the captain fired as they jogged the president forward. For his part, the Mexican leader was reluctant. He didn't know whether to follow the men into what looked like the very eye of the storm, drop to the ground or run in the opposite direction. His resistance to each tug by the Executioner brought that observation home to Bolan.

Turning to Oliverez, Bolan shouted, "Cover me!" then swept the president's feet from under him once again.

Fierro Blanco landed faceup on the grass, a look of shock on his bearded face. Bolan dropped over him, again using his body as a shield. "I can't fight the enemy and you at the same time, Mr. President," he said. "If you don't come with me willingly, I'll have to knock you out and carry you. And if I do that, it's going to be pretty damn hard to shoot."

The shock on Fierro Blanco's face became terror. "But—"

"You'll just have to trust me," Bolan said. He fired another two rounds from the Desert Eagle, shoved a fresh magazine into the grip and jerked the man back to his feet.

Fierro Blanco didn't resist this time as Bolan and Oliverez towed him forward. Both men fired with their free hands as they ran. Bolan dropped a Mexican who had traded his Tokarev for one of the downed guard's M-16s. The man died on his feet with two .44 Magnum hollowpoint slugs in his chest.

The Executioner and Oliverez moved Fierro Blanco on. The thickest fighting was still in front of them. Around the presidential vehicles, it had become true close quarters combat. Several soldiers had joined the bodyguards and slashed and jabbed with the bayonets on their rifles. The bodyguards fired point-blank contact rounds into the men in white, sending sprays of residual blood shooting back over their heads and shoulders. The rioters, in turn, continued to fire their Tokarevs until the pistols ran dry, then either used them as clubs or picked up the weapons of the dead.

Bolan raised the Desert Eagle to shoulder level and squeezed the trigger four times. His shots downed two men just in front of the president's limo but they had been meant more to clear a path than kill the enemy. The cover fire worked, and two more of the peasant-clad rioters dived away from the car door.

A sound not unlike angry bees whizzed past the Executioner's ears. But he had heard the sound too many times in the past to mistake it for insects. Spinning as he ran, he saw that the first members of the angry crowd had reached the speaker's platform. A man in peasant whites stood just in front of the podium holding another of the Tokarevs. In addition to the peasant shirt and trousers, he wore a cheap straw sombrero that sported gaudy round balls on the brim. As the Executioner continued to hurry Fierro Blanco toward the limo, the man raised the sights of his pistol to his eyes.

Bolan snapped a shot that missed the gunman but ruined his aim. The Tokarev's 7.62 mm bullet flew wide. Another shot from the Executioner sent the gunner's colorful hat flying from his head. The man took cover on the floor of the platform. Whether or not he had been wounded, Bolan couldn't tell.

But killing more of the men in white was of secondary importance now. The soldier's primary goal was to get Fierro Blanco into the limo and safely away. "Cover our rear!" he yelled at Oliverez, and saw the captain pivot smoothly on the balls of his feet, switch his pistol to the opposite hand and resume his grip on the president's arm. Oliverez snapped off more rounds as he ran backward.

A man with a Tokarev stepped into their path five feet from the limousine's door. Bolan didn't break stride. Raising the Desert Eagle, he pulled the trigger, hitting the man in the chest, sending him to the ground.

Bolan swept him to the side with a kick, dropped Fierro Blanco's arm, and jerked the rear door open. "Take the wheel!" he yelled at Oliverez as he threw the president into the backseat.

A bullet struck the armored limo. The soldier whirled to see that the same man who had worn the colorful sombrero had risen to his feet again on the platform. Another Tokarev round missed the Executioner by inches before Bolan emptied the Desert Eagle, driving the terrorist to the platform floor again.

With no time to reload, the Executioner tossed the big hand cannon into the limo and drew the Beretta 93-R. Thumbing the selector to 3-round burst mode, he pulled the trigger, let up and pulled again, laying a steady stream of cover fire while Oliverez rounded the hood of the vehicle and slid into the driver's seat. The sound-suppressed 9 mm slugs went unheard beneath the clamor of the other guns. But they did their job, just the same.

Three more rioters in white fell bleeding to the well-tended lawn of Bosque de Chapultepec.

The limousine's engine roared to life behind him. Bolan fired a final triburst, then ducked into the backseat next to Fierro Blanco. As the limo's tires screeched away from the curb, he saw the man on the stage rise a third time and empty his To-karev after the speeding vehicle. The rounds struck the limo's protective armor and ricochetted off.

A few seconds later, Oliverez had driven them to safety two blocks from the park. Here, the people on the sidewalks stood frozen in place, staring in the direction from which the limo had come and wondering what all the racket was about. But as he turned in his seat to look back to the block just off the park, the Executioner saw the violence beginning to spread to the streets. Windows in the storefronts began shattering as bricks and other missiles were hurled through them. The mob was snowballing, picking up new momentum and participants as it went.

Not a good sign, Bolan thought and shook his head. This was the way cities that had been peaceful one minute suddenly burst into riots of gunfire, arson and looting the next. Soon, word of the riot would reach other areas of Mexico's capital. What would happen then?

The Executioner turned back to the front as Oliverez turned a corner and headed back toward *Los Pinos*. Well, he thought, the match for such a city-wide disaster had been struck. Whether it burned itself out quickly, or found fuel to make it grow into a bonfire, remained to be seen.

Oliverez turned in his seat to face Bolan. The captain's face was drained of blood, but the excitement of battle was clear in his eyes. "I have killed several men in the line of duty," he said. "But I have never been in combat like that." He glanced back to traffic, then turned again. "Have you, Belasko?"

Bolan rested his head against the back of his seat and closed his eyes for a second. Memories of wars, both foreign and domestic, official and unofficial, swept through his mind like a videotape on fast forward. But he saw no reason to go into detail with the young captain.

"Once or twice," was all the Executioner said.

BY THE TIME they reached Victorio Vega's hideout in the hills, Calvin James's pupils had returned to normal after contracting from the flashing lights at Blind Man's Canyon. Vega and his men had led them from the area, and they had spent another hour winding through the hills before reaching the camp. James, Encizo and Nelson had all been thoroughly searched and disarmed before departure. Vega himself had radiated delight as he secured the DEA's scoped M-16, as well as James's Crossada, for himself. The bandit leader seemed more fascinated by the huge custom knife than the automatic rifle, and it was now strapped onto his belt like a trophy opposite the nickel-plated Colt Single Action Army revolver. The bandit leader constantly touched the Crossada's hilt with the hand not guiding the reins of his horse and occasionally withdrew it to inspect the blade in the sunlight. "Beautiful," he said under his breath each time he looked at the steel, and his ragged mustache curled into a grin that exposed rotting teeth surrounded by gums that had never met a toothbrush.

The men's other weapons—Encizo's and James's Berettas, Nelson's SIG-Sauer and the Winchester and Krag—had been distributed among Vega's top lieutenants. A grossly fat man named Garcia had taken the Randall Model 1 fighting knife Encizo had carried as backup, and a hideously ugly bandit known as Demonio had become the proud new owner of the North American Arms .22 Magnum minirevolver found in Nelson's pants pocket. Quality weaponry was scarce on the hilly plains of Northern Mexico, and all of the bandits who had received the booty now beamed like little boys on Christmas morning.

The Phoenix Force warriors and the DEA man were defenseless, their hands bound behind their backs.

Well, Calvin James thought, not completely defenseless. The mind of a warrior had always been, and always would be, his primary weapon. Strategy always proved victorious over firepower. And unless he missed his guess, he, Encizo and Nelson each had at least twenty IQ points over Vega and the rest of his men.

He just had to hope they'd find an opportunity to put those points to use.

His horse's hooves clicked to a halt on the rocky ground. James looked to his side and saw a large, roughly built lean-to against the boulders at the edge of the clearing. The other horses stopped around his and the bandits dismounted. Vega immediately disappeared inside the lean-to, assigning other men to take charge of his prisoners.

Not far from the lean-to was a firepit, and on the other side of it James could see a similar, larger structure. Squinting against the sunlight, it became obvious that this was a storage area. Through the open front, he could see stacked boxes of beer and tequila bottles, canned food items and miscellaneous items of value that had obviously come from the victims of Vega's raids on immigrants.

Four unwashed hands jerked James from the saddle and dropped him unceremoniously on his side on the ground. "Sit up," one of the men commanded, and the Phoenix Force warrior complied, rising to a sitting position.

Garcia and Demonio began building a campfire in the pit, arguing with each other about petty details under their breaths. Firewood was scarce in these hills, and several of the men pulled thin logs and scrap lumber from their saddlebags to add to the sparse twigs collected as kindling by others. Four more men dragged Encizo and Nelson to the fire site, forming a triangle around the pit to keep the prisoners separated from one another.

The woman was situated across from James between Encizo and Nelson. For the first time, James had a chance to study her. The young wife of the dying man in the desert had the simple beauty he had seen in so many Mexican women: smooth olive skin, long coal-black hair that fell past shoulders left bare by her ungarnished cotton dress and sultry eyes like ebony marbles set deep in her forehead. To say she was lovely was an understatement. But while comeliness might have been an advantage to her so far in life, it was perhaps the worse curse she could have had in her current situation. Like them, her hands had been bound behind her back, which forced her large unrestrained breasts to jut forward at a provocative angle under the low-cut neckline of the dress. James shook his head in silent sympathy. That wasn't going to help her either.

The knife expert turned his attention to Demonio, watching the man closely as he began cutting semidry sticks into kindling with a large Mexican-style Bowie knife. How the ''demon'' had acquired his nickname was easy to see. Sometime in the distant past, the man had been in a fire. Horrid pink scar tissue covered his face, neck and arms, looking as if he had chewed bubblegum all over his flesh. His left eye—if he still had a left eye—was hidden somewhere in the mass of scar tissue, and what little hair still grew on his scalded head did so only in spots. The long unkempt black strands jutted out at irregular angles like some heavy metal singer's spikes after a hard night of drugs, sex and rock 'n' roll.

All in all, James thought, he indeed looked like a demon who might have just arisen from the fires of hell.

James continued to study Demonio as the mangled man cut sticks. The fire might have scarred the man visually but it had not affected his coordination. The big knife in Demonio's hand moved with the precision of a heart surgeon's scalpel. He had obviously practiced with the blade until it was indeed a part of him.

Finishing the kindling, Demonio strode to the center of the camp where Garcia and other men had piled the heavier wood. His steps revealed the gracefulness of an athlete or dancer with no wasted movement. He squatted easily, stuffed the kindling under the heavier logs, struck a match and then rose swiftly to his feet without effort.

James compared Demonio's movement with the huffing, puffing, clumsiness Garcia and most of the other men exhibited. The bandits obviously spent most of their time on horseback and while that exercise created its own form of endurance conditioning and coordination, it did little to facilitate poise on the ground. All of the men except Demonio were more at home in the saddle.

Calvin James continued to watch the repulsive ghoul. Demonio was the dangerous one. It was he who should be killed first when it came time for Phoenix Force and Nelson to make their move.

Demonio's lone eye filled with lust as he stared across the fire at the woman. Dusk had fallen, then given way to nighttime, and in the rising flames of the firelight he looked more like a devil than ever. Following the man's gaze, James could see that the woman's eyes were downcast. And the expression on her face was unmistakable; a mixture of terror and resignation, she knew what her fate would be. She was horrified by it. But she was also reconciled to the inevitable. Sooner or later, both she and Calvin James knew, Victorio Vega would emerge from the lean-to with rape on his mind. When the bandit leader was finished, he would pass her around to the other men. The bandits might keep her for days—maybe even weeks—performing whatever perverse atrocities their demented imaginations could conjure. When they finally tired of her, she would be sold into slavery—if anything was left to sell. If not, they would put a bullet in her brain, cut her throat or simply leave her to die a slow and lingering death in the desert.

Vega stuck his head out of the lean-to long enough to bark orders. "Hey! Where's the whiskey?"

Garcia's abundant flesh quivered as he hurried to the other lean-to and jerked a bottle from one of the cases. He jiggled back around the fire and handed it to Vega, who disappeared into the lean-to once more.

The men continued about the various chores of setting up camp. James turned to look at Encizo. Although the Cuban was staring into space, James could see the wheels turning behind his brown eyes. Encizo wouldn't have given up hope anymore than he had. He was watching and waiting; his brain taking in tiny details about the bandits that might be of use later when an opportunity for escape presented itself.

And an opportunity would present itself. James had no doubt about that—it always did. Whether he and the other two captives would recognize that opportunity and be in a position to take advantage of it when it came, remained to be seen.

The thought caused Calvin James to turn his attention to Pug Nelson. The DEA man had held up well during the hard ride through the mountains, and the twenty-or-so pounds he'd put on since James had last seen him seemed to make no difference. As he studied his old friend closer, the knife expert saw that beneath the torn white shirt and soiled gray slacks the man wore, most of the new weight was muscle. It looked as if Nelson had taken up barbells to replace the speed he had lost since leaving the ring. The aging boxer might be a little slower, but he was still strong. And Nelson's face held no less determination to escape than Encizo's. When the time came, the former Navy SEAL would be ready and willing with guns, knives or his well-trained fists.

Above the hills, James saw the sun begin to fall. Several of the men entered the storage lean-to and emerged carrying bottles of whiskey and tequila, cans of beans, frying pans and other utensils. They swigged from the bottles and passed them around as they began preparing dinner.

Demonio took a bottle of brandy Garcia handed him and moved slowly around the fire to a spot behind the woman. He stared down at her back, his lone eye gleaming with salaciousness again, then he tipped back his head and held the bottle to his lips. When he brought it down again, the bottle was almost half empty and his eye gleamed with moisture. Brandy dripped from his wet lips as he set the bottle on the ground, then suddenly bent at the waist, leaned over the woman, and cupped her breasts.

The young woman let out a shriek of both surprise and pain as he squeezed.

Demonio laughed like—well, James thought—like a demon. Garcia looked up, hearing the noise, then looked at the disfigured man. ''It will be your *cojones* roasting over this fire if you touch her before Victorio has had his chance,'' the fat bandit warned.

Demonio laughed again, but with less enthusiasm this time. He gave the woman's breasts a final squeeze, then released them and stood back.

James closed his eyes, wondering exactly what Vega had planned for them. Killing them outright would be the simplest solution, but if that had been what the bandit leader had in mind he could have done so back at Blind Man's Canyon and saved himself the trouble of bringing them all the way to camp. No, Victorio Vega had something else in mind. Something, James suspected, that would be designed to entertain both him and his troops. After all, the Phoenix Force warrior chuckled sardonically to himself, entertainment was probably pretty scarce there. He didn't see any rock concerts going on nearby, and he couldn't remember when they'd passed the last video store on their ride into camp.

When Victorio Vega emerged from the lean-to again the whites around his irises were red. By now the beans had been heated and the men squatted around the campfire, eating, burping, gossiping and passing gas as if their prisoners were nonexistent. James, Encizo, Nelson and the woman were offered nothing, while Garcia and another fat man argued over the last of the beans with Garcia winning and shoving them into his mouth like a starving child.

By the time dinner was finished a half-moon had risen high in the sky. In the distance, a pack of coyotes began to serenade the plains. Vega stood, walked to the saddlebag on his horse, and produced a large leather pouch. Returning to the campfire, he squatted next to James and pulled out a package of cigarette papers. His deft fingers rolled a cigarette, he struck a match, and a moment later the distinct smell of marijuana wafted into the air.

The bandit leader inhaled, held the smoke in his lungs for several seconds, then let it out. He turned to Calvin James and spoke in English. "Nothing like a good smoke after dinner, eh *hombre?*" he said. He held out the joint to the Phoenix Force warrior.

James shook his head.

"Are you sure?" Vega asked. "It might make you feel better before you die." He looked up at the moon and laughed—not unlike the coyotes in the distance. "You see, I'm not cruel. I'm a sensitive man who wants my guests to be happy."

James just stared at him.

"So," Vega said, his eyes moving around the fire. "You're probably all wondering why I called this meeting." He threw back his head and howled again. This time, the coyotes in the distance even answered the call. Several of the other bandits laughed sycophantically at his weak joke.

Taking another hit from his joint, Vega went on. "What to do with you...indeed, what to do with you..." he growled hoarsely as the smoke left his lungs. "With the woman—" he glanced her way "—it's obvious. But with you three—I don't know." He turned to face James head-on. "I don't like killing men of color," he said. "You're like us. Oppressed from cradle to grave, are you not?"

James's eyes narrowed. "I've never *allowed* myself to be," he said.

Vega shook his head and looked across the dancing flames to Encizo. "And you...you aren't only like us, you are one of us."

Encizo's face could only be described as one of complete repulsion. "No," he said softly. "Not in any way, shape or form. I'm damned sure not a raping, thieving, lowlife, scumbag bandit. And I'm not even Mexican. I'm Cuban."

Vega looked down at the joint in his hand and shook his head sadly. "Nor are you a well-mannered guest," he said. He looked up again, this time at Nelson. "As to you, my Anglo friend, I have no problem." His mustache curled into an evil smile. "Have you met my lieutenant, Demonio?"

Nelson hadn't spoken since they'd arrived. But now he said, "Only in a few nightmares when I was a kid." He stared across the fire, his eyes filled with hatred. "No, wait a minute. He's a movie star, right? Played the Freddy Kruger part in that string of cheap horror flicks my teenaged son likes so much?"

Even considering their current dilemma, James couldn't help but laugh.

Vega ignored the insult. "Demonio is a full-blooded Yaqui Indian," he said. "Have you studied any history of the Yaquies?"

"Oh sure," Nelson said. "Majored in Yaqui Studies when I was an undergraduate at Fuck U."

Again, Vega ignored the man but James saw the bandit tense slightly at his side. "Not so many centuries ago," the bandit leader said. "The Yaquies were one of the few tribes in North America who practiced cannibalism. Demonio, proud of his heritage as we should all be, has revived the practice to honor his ancestors."

A quick flash of horror came over Calvin James as he got a

hazy notion of where Vega was headed. But before he could sort out the outrageous idea in his mind, the bandit leader did so for him.

"We'll drink and smoke tonight," Vega said, taking another hit of the marijuana. "Then in the morning, we will play a game. You," he turned to James, then to Encizo, "and you, will be set free. You'll have no food, water or weapons. You'll get a head start before we search for you. If you can escape, and the desert doesn't kill you, you will remain free. If we catch you, we will kill you."

James stared into the mean eyes. "How long a head start do we get?" he asked.

Victorio Vega grinned, then looked across the fire to Nelson. "However long it takes Demonio to cook and eat his breakfast," he said.

SCOTT HIX WATCHED as the others were crowded into Quartel's mobile home. His old roommate looked as if he couldn't believe it was all real and would insist that the editors cut this scene from the final version of a movie. The mayor of Tijuana, Jose Cervantes, walked like a man who knew without being told that he was on his way to the gallows, and the quartet of Hollywood blondes were all whimpering. Besides himself, only the women from the TJ brothel and Normandi West seemed still to be in their right minds and not suffering from shock. He watched West as she was pushed up the steps by one of the kidnappers. Her hair was messed and her clothing in disarray. He had heard her scream, and he tried hard not to let his imagination run away with him as to the catalyst for that scream. He couldn't bear to think of any of the men hurting her—touching her. If they had or if they did, he would dedicate whatever was left of his life to making them all pay. If it took his dying breath, he would cut off all their balls, shove them down their throats and watch them choke to death.

Hix was the last to be shoved up the steps into the living

room of the mobile home. The man who had been addressed as Huertes, and who some of the others had called Pablo, jostled him forward with the barrel of a pistol. Hix moved without resistance, trying to take in all the details about the men that he could. Something might prove useful later.

Huertes forced Hix to a sitting position on the floor amid the other crowded hostages. He looked up at the filthy man, his face protesting the movement. After the leader had hit him with the rifle stock before leaving the bedroom to check on West's screams, Huertes had taken it upon himself to strike him several more times with his pistol. His jaw was swollen and he suspected that if had a mirror, he'd see at least one black eye beginning to color.

Hix stared at the man above him. Huertes's body odor could have gagged a Hell's Angel. So could that of some of the other men. Already, the American expatriate had noticed a distinct difference between the men who had kidnapped them. All were dirty from a night obviously spent in the hills on Hix's estate. But some looked as if they spent their entire life in squalor. Their dirt was permanently ground in. He had also noticed that the cleaner men didn't associate with, or have much use for, the filthmongers. This told him they came from two different "camps," and made him suspect whatever alliance had taken place was of recent institution.

A tiny smile played at the corners of Hix's lips. Division within the ranks of the enemy was always useful.

One of the "clean" men mounted the steps, walked through the living room and down the hall, before heading for the front cab. The leader, Hidalgo, followed him, taking the passenger's seat. The mobile home's engine started. Outside, Hix heard the other vehicles fire to life. A moment later, the convoy took off. Destination? He didn't have the foggiest idea.

Hix shifted slightly on the floor, trying to get his right leg under him where it wouldn't be exposed to the eyes of the kidnappers. He had sat in a chair by his bed for almost an hour, thinking of West after she had gone to her room that morning. He had been unable to sleep, alternating between happiness, confusion, excitement and fear that went beyond any trepidation he had ever experienced in his life.

By the time he had finally moved to the bed and decided to try to sleep, he'd been emotionally drained. He had just pulled the .32 caliber Seecamp from his pocket and dropped it into the drawer of the nightstand, and was checking the loads in the bedside 12-gauge Rossi coach gun—when he'd heard the commotion outside his room.

Hix shifted again, this time getting onto his side. He hadn't yet taken the Applegate-Fairbairn dagger out of his pocket when the two men burst through the bedroom door. And seeing him without a shirt, getting ready for bed, they must have assumed he was unarmed except for the Rossi. At least they had neglected to search him before taking him downstairs.

The Applegate-Fairbairn still rode in the modified right front pocket of his pants.

The motorcade left Hix's estate and started down the highway. Like the others, the American's hands had been bound in front of him with duct tape. Then more tape had been wrapped around his waist to cinch his hands tight at the belt. Now, as the mobile home drove on, Huertes and two of his fellow foul-smellers moved through the living room, taping the hostages' ankles as well.

Scott Hix looked across the room to where West was seated on the couch. Huertes had dropped to his knees in front of her. Although he was slowly wrapping tape around her ankles, his eyes were glued to the crotch of her white shorts. West knew it, but she stared over his head at the wall, her face that of a world-champion poker player.

Again, Hix felt the anger rise in his chest. If this grimy bastard, or any of the kidnappers for that matter, so much as touched her, he'd...

What? Hix asked himself as reality took over. Exactly what

did he think he would do, could do? His hands, and now his feet, were bound with duct tape. He was facing at least three dozen men armed with pistols and assault rifles, and even if he'd been able to get to it, all he had was a knife. This wasn't a movie like Quartel would star in. He wasn't the Terminator or Johnny Rambo. This was real life and there was nothing he could do if every damn one of these bastards decided to take turns with West.

At least not for the moment. Hix took a deep breath to calm himself and let it out slowly. Right now, the best thing he could do was nothing at all. The kidnappers didn't know about the dagger in his pocket, and they didn't know he was an expert in close quarters combat. They thought he was nothing but a rich American businessman and, if he was smart, he'd let them go on thinking just that until an opportunity for action presented itself.

As if to emphasize his power, Huertes finished taping West's ankles and tore the duct tape off the roll. But his eyes stayed glued to her legs. He reached up with both hands and placed his dirty palms on her bare knees. Then, slowly, his hands began to move up her legs.

West continued to stare dispassionately past the man.

Hix was about to speak. He didn't know what he was about to say, probably some stupid ineffective threat that sounded like a bad line from one of Quartel's movies. But before he could open his mouth, a man suddenly appeared from the driver's area.

"Huertes!" Hidalgo said.

Huertes's head jerked toward him.

Slowly, Hidalgo shook his head.

Muttering under his breath, Huertes stood and moved away.

Hix watched Hidalgo's face and saw the contempt he had for the dirtier man. He still hadn't figured out the strange affiliation between the two groups but he was beginning to think of them as the "dirties" and the "cleans." Hidalgo had said that Hix and the others were guests of the revolution. That made the American suspect that the cleans were one of the many rebellious groups operating in Mexico's north. Probably the *Cuidadano para Democracia Mexicana Legitima,* although there were others. If they were the *Legitimas,* Hix had to sympathize with their goals, if not their methods of obtaining them. They were fighting for democracy in fact not just in name. That he could support.

The American glanced down at the tape on his wrists. But no, he thought ironically, he didn't suppose he could exactly give his blessings to the manner in which they were trying to achieve that democracy.

The mobile home continued down the road. The kidnappers had kept them in the living room throughout the morning and much of the afternoon. Through the windows, Hix could see the sun begin to fall. The terrain outside was familiar, and he knew they were heading west. He wondered where, then supposed he'd find out soon enough.

Hidalgo moved through the living room now, stopping and speaking with each hostage individually. He asked Jose Cervantes if he was comfortable, and the mayor nodded his head. He apologized to the still-sniveling blondes and the Mexican women, and assured them no harm would come to them if they cooperated. He told Normandi West he was sorry that Huertes had touched her, and promised it wouldn't happen again.

"You guarantee that?" West said, her voice dripping with sarcasm.

Hix felt himself smiling. Not only was the woman beautiful, smart and considerate, she had guts. He suspected he was falling in love with her.

When he got to where Quartel sat in a stuffed chair across from the television, Hidalgo squatted in front of him. "You're the reason for this," he said. "It's you we were after."

Quartel nodded his head in understanding. He didn't look like the tough soldier, cop or cowboy he usually played on screen, but he wasn't cringing like a coward, either. "I figured as much," he said in a strong, if somewhat anxious, voice. "Which brings us immediately to the bottom line. How much?"

Hidalgo stood and looked down at him. "The *Cuidadano para Democracia Mexican Legitima* will require a ten- million-dollar donation to the cause," he said. "In exchange, you and the others will be released unharmed."

Hix felt himself nodding his head. So they were the CDML.

"Ten million!" Quartel almost screamed. "Nobody can pay that!"

Hidalgo looked down at him as if he were eyeing a deceptive child. "Mr. Quartel," he said. "Don't insult me. You were well researched before we chose you. Ten million dollars is exactly the amount of money you made for the movie you just completed. And you signed a contract for even more for the one you begin filming in six weeks."

Quartel drew in a long breath and let it out. "Buddy, you don't understand the way it works in Hollywood. Yeah, I signed for ten million on this last one, and twelve and a half on the next. But that doesn't mean I've got ten million dollars lying around the house, ready to stuff into a plain black briefcase!"

"Then you'll have to send someone to the bank," Hidalgo said simply. Without waiting for a reply, he moved to the end of the room, then looked back at the bound people seated around the mobile home. "I'm sorry for the inconvenience I must put you through," he said. "If it weren't necessary, I wouldn't do it." He paused, then said, "We'll be stopping soon. At that time, restroom facilities will be available to any who require them. I regret that from that point, until we reach our final destination, you will have to be blindfolded. Again, please forgive me for the inconvenience." He strode back through the living room and moved down the hall to the driver's area.

Hix watched him go. Something in the man's manner and voice made the American think he was serious. Hix believed Hidalgo when the man said he hoped no one would get hurt, and that he wouldn't have put them through all this if he didn't believe it necessary. Hidalgo struck Hix as a true believer in his cause—a man who was so intent on establishing a legitimate democracy in his homeland that he had convinced himself that his barbarous ends justified his means. Well, the American thought, as for the hundredth time he tested the tape around his wrists, a lot of evil had been perpetrated in the name of good throughout history. And given half a chance, he planned to drive the Applegate-Fairbairn knife through the kind, loving Hidalgo's windpipe.

Fifteen minutes later, the mobile home pulled off the road. The tape around the hostages' ankles was cut, and they were led down the steps. In the twilight that had fallen, Hix could see three of the other vehicles that had been at his house. He also saw an old barn and an outhouse. He remembered the crumbling structure from a leisurely Sunday afternoon drive that he, Quartel, and a case of Tecate beer, had taken several months ago. He couldn't recall the barn's exact location, but he knew they couldn't be over twenty miles from his house.

One by one, the tape around the hostages' wrists was cut and they were allowed to use the outhouse. When each returned, he or she was again bound, and this time tape was also wrapped across their eyes. By the time Hix's turn came, dusk had turned to darkness. He had a need to use the outhouse— but it was different than the needs of the others.

Once inside the tiny building, Hix checked to make sure no one was watching through the cracks in the rotting wood. Satisfied that there were no prying eyes, he slid the Applegate-Fairbairn from his pocket, and stuck the sheath down into the crotch of his underwear.

The knife created a bulge, but it wasn't as noticeable as in his pocket. He chuckled cynically under his breath. The sight reminded him of the old story about the guy who stuffed rolled socks into his pants before heading for the disco. Zipping up his jeans, he left his shirttail out this time to cover the protuberance.

Back at the mobile home, one of the men wrapped tape around his eyes, and the sore spots on his face screamed in agony. He was led up the steps, and though he couldn't be sure, he thought to the same place on the floor where he'd been earlier. He waited while the bandit retaped his ankles, and listened to the last few hostages return from the outhouse. When the mobile home pulled away again, he was determined to follow its course as best he could. He would count off seconds, and right and left turns, to determine where they went. It had been years since the U. S. Army Intelligence had trained him in such tactics, and in truth he had never been called upon to employ them in an actual situation. But Hix had no doubt he could pull it off, and be reasonably certain where he was when the blindfold finally came off.

When the sightless men and women were in place again, the mobile home moved out. Hix felt them turn left onto the road, and registered the information in his mind. They turned right again thirty counts later, and he made a mental note of that, too.

Then, suddenly, the vehicle began spinning circles. Hix bounced first right, then left, then right and left again. Gasps issued forth from the mouths of the hostages, and a woman— it sounded like one of the Tijuana prostitutes—screamed. In one of the irrational thoughts that enter the human mind at such times, he remembered a high school Saturday night many years before when he and a friend had decided to "cut doughnuts" on Main Street.

By the time the mobile home ground to a halt, Hix was thoroughly disoriented. His head spun like an oscillating fan, and his stomach felt as if he might throw up. When they started down the road again, he had no idea in which direction they were headed.

The American felt someone squat next to him. One of cleans—he detected none of the bellycurdling body odor. When the man whispered into his ear, he further identified the speaker as Hidalgo.

"You can quit counting the turns now," the leader of the *Legitimas* said. He paused for a moment, then added, "Yes, Captain Hix of United States Army Intelligence, we researched your past as well as that of your former roommate."

8

The streets around *Los Pinos* were quiet when Oliverez pulled through the gates and up to the presidential mansion. The Executioner, however, feared that such peace might be short-lived.

Bolan got out of the backseat and stared down the street as he opened the door for Don Juan de Fierro Blanco. He saw nothing out of the ordinary; nothing to indicate that violence was popping up near the presidential mansion. Which actually meant nothing. It still could. Any second.

Bolan and Oliverez again held Fierro Blanco's arms as they hustled him toward the building. The three men had ridden most of the way from the park in silence, with the Executioner holding both the reloaded Desert Eagle and the Beretta 93-R machine pistol on his lap, ready to fire out the windows if necessary. The president had spent the drive slumped in the seat, certain that snipers hid behind every corner and in every window of the buildings they passed. The man wasn't used to traveling in a lone car without escort. And the rest of the federal protection team—at least those who had survived the riot—had been too busy battling the rioters to accompany them.

Entering *Los Pinos,* Bolan and Oliverez steered the president down the hall to the elevator. A few minutes later, they were all seated in Fierro Blanco's office with the president behind his desk. Bolan studied the man's face as the president mopped sweat from his beard with a handkerchief. All along, the soldier had wondered if Fierro Blanco himself might not secretly be behind the attempts on his life in order to provide a red herring that would distract the press and public from government-sanctioned murders, drug smuggling and other atrocities. The attempted stabbing at the hog hunt, the sniper attempts, even the poisoning and Espinoza's bid with the Derringer could have all been inside jobs, set to fail at the last instant on their own if Bolan or other bodyguards didn't step in first.

But a riot that involved thousands of people, with what looked like dozens, if not hundreds, of the rioters carrying guns and firing at the president? That was pushing the setup theory a little too far in the soldier's opinion.

Fierro Blanco finished with the handkerchief and dropped it on the desk. Bolan sat silently as the president leaned forward, crossed his arms on the desk and buried his face on his wrists. Fierro Blanco's reaction didn't bespeak that of a man who knew he would escape a carefully orchestrated ploy, either. He looked more like he knew beyond any doubt that he'd been one step ahead of the Grim Reaper as he stumbled across the grass to the limo. Either he was a world-class actor deserving of an Oscar, or the sudden outbreak of violence had come as a total surprise.

Bolan crossed his legs as he watched the top of the man's head. No, the riot had been a genuine attempt to kill the man. Of that he was certain.

The president's personal physician stuck his head in the door. *"El Presidente?"* the man said.

Fierro Blanco looked up from his arms with strained eyes. "Yes?"

"May I be of service?"

The president shook his head.

"An injection, perhaps?" the doctor pressed. "I could give you something that would calm your—"

"No!" Fierro Blanco said sternly. "I'm all right. Please go."

The doctor nodded and disappeared again.

Fierro Blanco leaned forward onto his arms.

So, what did it all mean, Bolan wondered as the three men continued to sit in silence. If the riot had been a genuine effort at assassination, did that mean all the other attempts had been valid as well? Not necessarily. The soldier was reminded of the old saying, "All horses are four legged animals—but not all four-legged animals are horses." Just because a legitimate try had occurred today didn't automatically excuse the man who now sat behind his desk like a terrorized schoolboy. Fierro Blanco was still suspect in the other incidents.

Footsteps sounded in the hallway and a moment later a bodyguard came in. The man was out of breath, and his uniform shirt was in shreds. A ribbed white undershirt beneath was also torn. The knees in his pants had been ripped out, and blood—his own, that of others or more likely a mixture of both—covered him head to toe.

Fierro Blanco looked up as he entered. "Carlos..." he said, but that seemed to be all he could get out.

"Mr. President. The other men are arriving."

The president nodded. "How many were lost?" he asked in a voice that sounded sincerely concerned.

"Four dead," Carlos told him. "Fourteen injured and on their way to the hospital." He stopped to catch his breath. "At least a half-dozen men are unaccounted for."

Fierro Blanco nodded silently, then said, "And the rioters? The assassins?"

"The body count was at thirty-two when I left," the bodyguard said. "But there were more."

A fierce gleam of malice now replaced the fear on the president's face. "At least there is some good news," he said bitterly.

The guard looked at the floor. He seemed to want to speak but was hesitant.

Fierro Blanco frowned. "Go on."

"I'm afraid there is also more bad news," he said, looking up again. "Other incidents have broken out across the city. One in the central plaza, several more in the barrios. There is word that a bomb was detonated near the Basilica Guadalupe. The people are looting everywhere."

The president shook his head in disbelief. With a childlike innocence, he said simply, "But why?"

Again, the guard appeared reluctant to answer. But after a few moments, he said, "There are rumors among the lower classes. Rumors that our army fired into the crowds at the park simply because they booed your speech."

"What!" the man behind the desk demanded. "But that's not true! None of our troops opened fire until the mob had burst through the barriers and began firing themselves!"

The guard's face turned red and he shrugged his shoulders. "I know, Mr. President," he said. "I was there. But regardless of its truth, that's the story being circulated. The people are angry."

Bolan stood and walked to the window. Several blocks away, across the city, he could see flames leaping toward the sky. Some buildings had already been torched. And he had a gut-wrenching feeling it was only the beginning.

Two more of the president's personal protection team entered the office. Both men looked like they'd been through the same hell as Carlos.

"How many men do we have guarding *Los Pinos?*" Fierro Blanco asked Oliverez.

"About forty," the captain said, speaking for the first time since they'd entered the office. "Less those lost at the park."

"Is that enough?" The anger had faded and the consternation returned to the president's face again.

"Only if all goes well," Oliverez said. Anticipating the next question, he added. "But if the rioting reaches this area...no, it won't be enough."

Fierro Blanco's arm shot to the telephone receiver in front of him and jerked it from the cradle. He held it across the desk toward Oliverez and said, "Do something."

The captain calmly took the phone and tapped in numbers. A moment later, he had made arrangements for a dozen more federal police officers and six platoons of Mexican infantrymen to head for *Los Pinos*.

"How long will it take them to arrive?" Fierro Blanco asked as he took the receiver back from Oliverez and hung up.

"An hour for the police," he said. "The infantrymen, longer."

"How much longer?" The president implored the captain. He looked like a man on the verge of a nervous breakdown.

"I can't be certain. It is impossible to say."

"Where is my wife?" Fierro Blanco asked, rising from behind the desk. "My children?"

"Your wife is in the presidential suite," one of the men who had just come in said. "Your children were in school. We took the liberty of evacuating them when the fires broke out."

"Fires! What fires?" the president demanded. His hands were shaking now.

"Several fires have been set across the city," Carlos said. "It's part of the rioting and looting of which I spoke."

Bolan looked out the window again and saw flames and smoke rising in two new areas. Both were closer to *Los Pinos* than the first one he'd spotted a few minutes before. His ears picked up a dull roar through the glass and he stepped closer. The clamor rose in volume. Unlatching the lock, the Executioner slid open the window.

"What are you doing?" the overwrought voice of Don Juan de Fierro Blanco demanded to know.

Bolan didn't answer. Instead, he stuck his head out the window.

What had been a dull roar, he now recognized as the distant sound of thousands of enraged voices and stampeding feet. Still blocks away, the storm was nevertheless heading their way. As he listened, several pistol shots echoed over the blare. The drone of fire and police sirens vibrated in his ears, as well.

"We don't have time to wait for the army," the soldier said, pulling his head inside and closing the window. "You have a helicopter on the roof, right?"

The president's bottom lip now trembled. "On the... roof...yes," he whispered, his voice all but inaudible.

Bolan pointed to the phone. "Tell your people to get it ready." He turned to the other two guards. "One of you, get to the suite and get Señora de Fierro Blanco onto the roof. Now."

The shorter of the two men took off running.

As Fierro Blanco lifted the phone again, Bolan turned to the other guard who had just come in. "You mentioned taking the children out of school," he said. "Where are they now?"

"They are being brought here, Señor Belasko."

This time it was the Executioner who lifted the phone and held it out. "Get on the horn and get that changed," he ordered. "Is there some place safe they can be taken?" He looked to the president. "Some place we could meet them in the chopper?"

"We have a summer home...north of Mérida," the man choked out.

"Will it be safe there?" Bolan asked Oliverez.

The captain nodded. "It should be," he said. "It's not public knowledge that the property is owned by the president, or even that he and his family vacation there."

"Good," the soldier said. "Then it should do—at least temporarily." He gave the phone to the other guard and said, "Tell them to meet us there." He took Fierro Blanco's arm. "In the mean time—"

A blast outside the building turned all heads toward the windows. Bolan dropped the president's arm and hurried to the glass. Directly below, he saw fire spreading across the lawn. The odor of gasoline rose into the air and permeated through the window. Looking toward the street, the soldier saw the first of hundreds of furious faces sprinting toward the iron fence that surrounded *Los Pinos*.

A man standing in the middle of the street raised a bottle and held a cigarette lighter to a rag stuffed into the neck.

Automatic gunfire from the mansion stuttered out across the

grounds and the man fell where he stood. The Molotov cocktail exploded on top of him and he burst into flames. Rising to his feet like some specter from hell, he ran in circles for a moment, then fell back to the pavement still burning.

The sight didn't slow the mob in the slightest.

The Executioner grabbed Fierro Blanco again and scrambled him out of the office into the hall. Oliverez and the other bodyguards followed. They were joined by four more bloodsoaked officers just now returned from the park. Fierro Blanco tried to stop at the elevator but Bolan jerked him past it to the stairs. Oliverez moved ahead of them and opened the door.

Bolan half-dragged, half-shoved the Mexican president up the steps to the roof. Again, Oliverez opened the door. The Executioner pushed past Fierro Blanco, stepping out first to check for danger. Besides two men in coveralls, and a similarly dressed pilot inside the chopper, the roof was clear. Through the glass, Bolan could see Señora Fierro Blanco already seated inside.

The Executioner grabbed the president and hurried him under the whirling helicopter blades. He took a final glance around and saw that the rioters were well out of sight beneath the slope of the roof. He breathed a sigh of relief. If the *Marxistas*—and he had no doubt it was them fueling the fires of this riot as well as the one at the park—knew of the helicopter, they could have stationed snipers in a dozen places around the mansion.

Bolan pushed Fierro Blanco into the helicopter, then he, Oliverez and the others of the presidential protection team climbed aboard. The pilot revved the engine and a second later the craft began to rise into the air. Another second after that, the Executioner heard a string of gunshots ring out, and at the same time a loud *ping* sounded above his head. The helicopter engine backfired. The chopper listed right, then left, then began to pirouette madly in circles.

The pilot was no Jack Grimaldi. But he knew what to do. Expertly, he guided them out of the spin and back onto the roof. Bolan opened the door and jumped out. On top of the helicopter, he saw the amputated blades revolving to a halt.

The Executioner rushed to the edge of the roof, dropped to his knees, and peered over the side. More gunshots met his ears. What looked like thousands of enraged Mexicans had begun climbing the fence that encircled *Los Pinos*. In the middle of the mass of human flesh, several bright colors caught his eye.

The Executioner squinted down at the sombrero. He had seen it before.

Flashy decorative balls circled the brim.

RAFAEL ENCIZO KNEW his fellow Phoenix Force warrior was working on a plan of escape. He could see it written across the man's face. This pleased Encizo, because he was a firm believer that two heads were better than one. But what pleased him even more was that the head on his own shoulders already had a plan. Or at least part of a plan.

Encizo watched the men eat, drink and eye the woman. Victorio Vega was still smoking the huge joint he'd rolled earlier, and many of the other men had broken out bags of marijuana and cigarette papers or smoking pipes. The sickeningly sweet odor of the weed filled the air, and as it did, the men's voices rose in volume. Demonio seemed to be dividing his attention equally between the woman and Nelson, and Encizo couldn't decide which perversion the ghastly creature was looking forward to more, rape or cannibalism.

Nelson stared stoically into the fire. The thought of being killed and eaten seemed to have had no effect on the old SEAL. At least outwardly.

Encizo continued the project he had started an hour earlier behind his back, keeping his movements as small as possible to avoid detection. Years ago, as a child, he had read an old paperback novel by Mickey Spillane that he'd found in a Havana alley. He couldn't remember the name of the book anymore but he remembered the hero, Mike Hammer. A hard-boiled private detective on the streets of New York City, Hammer seemed to be forever getting hit over the head and tied up by gangsters. So the private detective had taken to carrying a single-edged razor blade in a slit at the back of his belt.

So had the impressionable young Rafael Encizo. For the most part in those days, the inexperienced Cuban had been defenseless against Castro's dictatorship, and the razor blade had served more as a symbol than a weapon. It had been a spiritual reminder to the child that he would someday be old enough to fight the communist megalomaniac who ruled his homeland. In truth, in all the years that he had carried the blade since, he had never been called upon to use it. He had even laughed at himself a time or two when he transferred it from belt to belt, slicing a new incision into leather or taping it to the back of nylon or web gear. The razor blade had continued to serve more as a symbol of his ongoing fight against injustice than as a useful tool.

Until now.

Encizo proceeded with his small inconspicuous sawing movements as the men continued to drink and smoke. Their eyes fell more and more on the terrified woman but they made no efforts toward her. It was clear that it was Vega's call—the leader commanded the first turn and he wouldn't take it until he was ready. For that, Encizo was grateful. It gave him a little longer to work out the rest of his plan.

The Cuban has listened to Demonio and Garcia argue when they built the fire. The quarrel had turned into angry insults after Garcia had stopped the scarred monster from molesting the woman. Now, a fistfight between the two finally broke out at the side of the fire.

All heads turned that way with the other bandits whooping and hollering encouragement. Demonio's opponent was taller and outweighed him by a good sixty pounds. And even though much of the weight was lard, it appeared at first that Garcia would pummel his smaller opponent into the ground. The fat bandit landed several blows that rocked Demonio's disfigured head, but just as Rafael Encizo cut through the final strand of the rope binding his wrists, the demon landed a looping right that jarred the big man from head to toe. The momentary reprieve offered an opportunity for two things to happen simultaneously.

Demonio drew the long slender Bowie knife from the sheath on his belt.

And while the bandits waited anxiously for the next development in the fight, Encizo caught James's attention and brought one of his freed hands briefly into view. James nodded that he had seen.

The fat bandit took a step backward and cried out a protest that Encizo couldn't discern. His frightened eyes scanned the fireside for support. Finding none, he hesitantly drew a skinning blade from his pistol belt.

Demonio grinned like a fiend from hell in the firelight, and begin to slowly circle the larger man. The tip of his knife shot out suddenly and struck Garcia on the forearm.

Garcia screamed but the skinner stayed in his hand. Drops of blood began to drip from his forearm as Demonio reversed his circle. The Bowie knife shot out like lightning once more, and this time the blade slashed down across the other man's bulky torso. The ammunition bandolier crossing Garcia's chest fell to the ground.

It was clear that Demonio was merely toying with the less-skilled knife fighter, and the display brought more riotous cheers and laughter from the other men. Vega himself watched quietly with narrowed eyes and a diabolical grin. Encizo turned his own attention back to James. The other Phoenix Force warrior sat cross-legged before the fire, a good ten feet away. So close and yet so far. James's face pointed toward the knife fight but Encizo knew his fellow warrior's eyes were straining the corner of the sockets to watch him.

As Demonio continued to taunt his opponent, Encizo calculated the risks of his two options. Somehow, he had to get the razor blade to James. If he rolled that way, the movement would be large enough that it would undoubtedly draw Vega's attention from the fight. At the very least, his restraints would be checked, the razor blade discovered, and all progress so far would be lost. But if he chanced throwing the light blade, it stood a good chance of getting caught in the wind and falling too far away for James's bound hands to reach it. And even that motion might be enough to attract Vega's eyes. Still, throwing the razor blade at least stood a chance. And if it failed, at least they would be no worse off than before.

The Cuban looked back to the ongoing knife fight and saw Demonio's knife snap out and cut the gun belt from around Garcia's thick waist. He could tell by the disfigured *bandido's* face that the man was growing tired of the sport, and that the killing stroke would come soon. That would be the moment during which the other men's concentration would be most firmly on the spectacle before them. He would wait until then, then hope his throw landed close enough for James to take advantage of it.

Demonio twirled the big knife into a reverse grip, then back into a saber grip. He stepped back, laughing as Garcia took a clumsy cross-body swipe with his skinner. Compared to the graceful maneuvers of the ogre he fought, Garcia looked like a walrus lumbering down a display aisle of Waterford crystal at Tiffany's. Demonio let out a long breath of exasperation at the fat man's ineffective attempts, and as the firelight highlighted his monstrous features, Encizo saw that the end had come.

The Cuban let the hand holding the razor blade creep slowly to his side.

Demonio stepped forward with only a fraction of the speed he had displayed so far. His knife moved point-first toward Garcia's forehead.

Breathing hard, the fat man brought up his own blade to parry the thrust. A look of shock that he had been successful covered his greasy face.

As if the fast-forward button on a video machine had been

punched, Demonio's speed suddenly went into overdrive. He drew back the Bowie knife just far enough to drop below Garcia's skinner, then snapped it forward and up.

The Mexican Bowie sliced through Garcia's hanging jowls and shot into his throat. Blood burst from his severed arteries and blasted out over the men closest to the action. The bandits, including Vega, held up their arms to shield their faces from the red rain.

Encizo knew a better chance wouldn't come. So did James. The black Phoenix Force warrior turned to face him as Encizo tossed the razor blade across the rocks.

The bandits were still trying to cover themselves from the torrent of blood as the razor blade fell to the rocks just behind Calvin James. Encizo drew his hands quickly back behind his back and wrapped the severed rope around his wrist. He watched as James leaned backward and groped the ground. The soldier's fingers had to have found the sharp edge of the blade, Encizo realized as he saw James jump slightly.

By now Garcia's lifeless bulk had fallen to the ground. Most of his life's blood had drained away and his fat face looked like a cream-filled pastry. Dull eyes stared listlessly at the stars.

Vega ordered two of the men to drag the body away. The fat man's corpse took four. The unexpected entertainment now ended, the other bandits returned to their drinking and smoking. None of them seemed to care that one of their own had just been killed, and Encizo marveled at the cheap price of life on the Mexican desert.

Demonio dropped into a squat by the fire and took a large bong pipe passed to him by one of the other men. Vega looked across the flames and said, "Well done, *hombre*. He was becoming a burden anyway. But tell me…" His sight drifted to where Pug Nelson sat. "Did all that activity work up an appetite?"

The comment brought more uproarious hysterics from the bandits.

"The rest of us may starve," Vega went on. "But you, Demonio, will feast. The American, I fear, will be tough compared to Garcia. I suggest you make jerky of him.''

Another round of drunken laughter rose from the bandits. Nelson didn't respond.

Encizo watched the men drink and smoke themselves further into stupor, thankful for that small advantage. When the time came to make their move, they would be unarmed and vastly outnumbered. They'd need every edge they could get. He studiously avoided watching James now that he knew the other soldier had the razor blade. James would be busy at work on the ropes, and nothing could be gained by watching him. Much, however, could be lost if Vega or any of the other men noticed what was happening.

The Cuban turned to Nelson. The former SEAL met his eyes. Slowly, Nelson nodded that he had seen what had transpired between Encizo and James. But the boxer sat a good thirty feet away from James, and there would be no way to get the razor blade to him. Encizo and James would have to handle things themselves, and hope Nelson stayed out of harm's way.

Ten minutes later, Vega finally rose to his feet. He raised his arms over his head and stretched like a cat. The smile on his face also resembled a cat—the one who now saw the canary wearing a simple cotton dress and tied helplessly on the other side of the fire. "Perez! Gallo!" he shouted drunkenly.

They both looked up.

Vega looked across the fire to the woman and nodded his head, then jerked a thumb toward his lean-to.

The men had obviously been given similar orders in the past. Words were unnecessary. They rose quickly from the fire and grabbed the woman's arms.

Vega disappeared into the lean-to as the men dragged the screaming, biting and scratching woman toward the structure. By the time they reached the opening, her thin dress was already in shreds around her waist and her large dark-skinned breasts, wet with sweat from the heat, bounced freely in the firelight.

Encizo watched the laughing bandits throw the woman into the lean-to and return to the fire. He turned toward Calvin James. The black soldier nodded almost imperceptibly. He moved his hands behind his back just enough to show Encizo that the rope had been severed. Rather than nod this time, James shook his head, then turned back to the fire.

Encizo knew what the shake of the head meant. The ideal opportunity for escape hadn't yet presented itself. But that no longer mattered. Now that their hands were free, he and James couldn't sit by idly and allow the innocent woman to be raped. They had to try something and they had to try now.

A few seconds later, a bandit the men had called Asno walked drunkenly along the fireside. As he passed James, the soldier called quietly up to him. Asno stopped on his heels, looking down. James whispered upward, and whatever he said brought the bandit's head down closer to him.

In one smooth motion of blinding speed, Calvin James's right hand shot out from behind his back and moved across Asno's throat. For a moment, nothing appeared to have been accomplished by the gesture, and Asno remained perfectly still. Then, suddenly, blood reminiscent of that which had shot forth from Garcia's neck spewed out of a widening gap in the bandit's throat.

Encizo was about to leap to his feet but James looked over quickly and shook his head again. The Cuban froze in place, wondering what his fellow warrior's strategy might be but trusted his judgment.

Asno fell forward onto James. With his hands still behind him, James shrugged the man off to the side. Asno fell face-down onto the sandy ground.

Encizo's eyes skirted the camp. Some of the men stared at the lean-to, hungrily awaiting their turn with the woman. Others watched the flames with the glassy eyes of the drunk and stoned. None seemed to have noticed Asno's fate.

"Hey!" Calvin James called out as soon as Asno had settled on the ground. "You got a sick man over here!"

The men around the fire looked up.

"Asno, you drunken burro!" Gallo, the roosterlike man called out. "Did you piss your pants as well?"

The comment brought on new cheers.

"We should get him up before he drowns in his own vomit," slurred another.

"Let him fight the puke," said Perez. "We would see a more even battle than the one we saw between Demonio and Garcia!"

By now Encizo had figured out James's plan. He had already eliminated one of the men, and hoped the others would come to his aid, thinking him ill. That would group them closer together for when he and Encizo sprang. It was as good a plan as anyone in their present condition could have come up with. And it worked. At least partially.

Three of the men—Encizo had counted eleven around the fire now that Garcia was dead and Vega had disappeared into the lean-to with the woman—moved over to investigate Asno's condition. It was fewer than the Cuban might have hoped would be curious. But he and James would have to make the best of what they had.

"Asno, you are as well-named as Demonio!" one of the men called down as he tapped a needle-toed Mexican cowboy boot into the man's ribs. "You are a drunken ass!"

The Cuban watched him stagger slightly as he kicked the man on the ground. Like the others, he was drunk. But that in itself wasn't enough to insure victory on the part of the men from Stony Man Farm. Encizo had known many men over the years who fought better when intoxicated.

No, he and James would have to be fast and efficient when they struck. And that moment would come within seconds.

A man who had unbuttoned his shirt in the heat now fell to his knees next to Asno. Rolls of fat fell over his belt and the tails of the shirt hit the ground as he began making the braying sounds of a donkey. Then, suddenly, he stopped and his eyes widened. *"Madre de Dios!"* he yelled. "What's all this blood?"

As Encizo sprang to his feet, he saw Calvin James do the same.

THE MAN IN THE colorful sombrero looked up from the ground to meet the Executioner's eyes. In his hands was a scoped Mandragon semi-auto rifle with a 30-round helical snail magazine. The man raised the stock quickly to his shoulder and snapped a shot toward the roof of the presidential mansion.

Bolan ducked as the 7 x 57 mm Spanish Mauser round struck the stone near the top of the building and sent chips and dust flying. Staying low until he was out of the line of fire from the ground, Bolan hurried back to the downed helicopter. A woman's screams reverberated across the rooftop and he saw Fierro Blanco and his wife standing dumbfounded in the center of the roof. The screams came from the Mexican first lady. The president appeared to be in shock.

Oliverez stood in front of the Mexican leader. "Please, Mr. President," the captain pleaded. "We must—"

Bolan hadn't time for such diplomatic persuasion. He slapped Blanco across the face and said, "Wake up!"

The Mexican president turned to look at him, his eyes still glazed and withdrawn. Bolan turned to Oliverez. "There's got to be an alternate escape route," he said.

The captain nodded. "The basement," he said. "There is a tunnel." He glanced toward the edge of the roof. "But can we get there before the mob breaches the doors?"

The Executioner grabbed the president's arm for what seemed like the thousandth time that day. "If you have a better idea, I'm willing to hear it."

Oliverez shook his head.

"Then we'll have to try," Bolan said. "Take charge of the first lady." Next to the president, Señora Fierro Blanco still shrieked like a wounded cat. "And see if you can quiet her," he added. Before he could ask Oliverez the other question on his mind the captain had saluted and sprinted away. Bolan grabbed the nearest of the other bodyguards. "The tunnel in the basement," he said. "How do we get to it?"

"The elevator will take us straight down," the man said. "We can—"

"No," Bolan said. "We'll take the stairs. Do they go all the way?"

"But the elevator will be—"

"I don't have time to explain," the soldier said. He felt like cuffing the guard, too, and wondered why this man had been chosen for executive protection. Any competent officer would know elevators were never used under such conditions. But by now he was growing used to the spotty professionalism the president's guards displayed. Sometimes they behaved like well-trained specialists, other times they were like the Keystone Cops, leaving holes in the president's defense through which a rank amateur could drive a Sherman. "Do the stairs go all the way to the basement?" he repeated impatiently.

"Yes."

The Executioner grabbed Fierro Blanco and started toward the stairs. Soft sobs burped from the man's chest as he pulled him along. Señora Fierro Blanco had been screaming like a banshee ever since the chopper had been forced down to the roof, and she didn't stop now as Oliverez and several other bodyguards forced her along.

Bolan silently thanked the heavens that the children had been diverted from their course to the mansion. As short of manpower as they were, they would never have been able to take care of Fierro Blanco's daughter and twin sons. As they reached the door, he heard Oliverez speak behind him.

"Señora Fierro Blanco," the captain said. "I have explained the need for silence as we descend to the tunnel several times. Now, with all due respect, if you don't quiet down I will be forced to slap you."

The screaming stopped abruptly.

As they started down the steps, the Executioner heard gunshots below. Not outside the building this time. *Inside.*

The electricity in the mansion went off when they were halfway down the steps. The stairwell fell into semidarkness, the light from the door to the roof was the only illumination. Bolan wondered if the guard he had spoken to earlier was smart enough to make the connection between the power outage and the elevator. If the Executioner had followed his advice, they'd likely be trapped helplessly between floors right now.

Dragging the president with his left hand, Bolan held the Desert Eagle in his right. He had considered commandeering one of the guard's M-16s but all had been full-scale rifles—none of the shorter carbines. In the confines of the stairwell such a weapon would be too hard to maneuver—especially with one hand. So he had stuck to the Eagle. He would let the power of the hand cannon make up for what he traded in magazine capacity.

The landing outside the top floor of the mansion was quiet when they reached it. Bolan peered though the window into the hall. The floor was even darker than the stairwell. He saw nothing.

Starting down the next flight of stairs, the light from the door to the roof began to fade. The soldier considered pulling the Mini-Mag flashlight from his pocket but decided against it. Not yet. There was still enough light to see the steps, and while the darkness was in some ways a detriment, it might work to their advantage as well.

The next landing was as quiet as the top floor. But the sporadic gunfire continued somewhere below. Bolan moved on, his hand on Fierro Blanco's upper arm. In the darkness, he could hear the president's labored breathing as well as that of others in the party behind him. With the air-conditioning, as well as the lights, now out, the temperature in the stairwell began to rise. The smell of sweat soon filled the narrow confines.

Lower and lower they went in total darkness. The gunfire

became louder and more frequent. Spaced between the shooting the Executioner heard shouts of anger, fear, triumph and defeat. When they reached the second floor, he saw torches and flashlights through the stairwell window. Soldiers, guards and rioters raced through the hallways in pandemonium.

Other men, representing all three groups, lay in pools of blood on the floor. The flashlight beams streaked across their faces with a jumpy irregularity, creating the illusion that the Executioner was watching some macabre turn-of-the-century Hollywood horror film.

Bolan ducked beneath the window as a beam of light shot his way. He waited until it had passed, then moved the party down to the first floor. The riot was in full swing on the ground with automatic gunfire and pistol shots making *Los Pinos* sound like a war zone. But the light was better now, streaming through the window onto the steps. The Executioner turned to see the bodyguard who had wanted to use the elevator directly behind Oliverez. The man wore a light suit and tie. Even if he didn't act like one, he looked exactly like what he was—a plainclothes member of the federal protection team.

Taking a step back up from the landing, Bolan leaned past Oliverez and whispered into the guard's ear. "Take off your coat and tie and any other indication that you're one of the good guys," he ordered. "Wait until we've moved into the basement. Then go out into the hall and shout out that Fierro Blanco has been spotted on the roof heading for the helicopter."

The man nodded his understanding.

Bolan moved back to Fierro Blanco, pulling the president beneath the window in the door as they passed. As the riot continued just the other side of the door, the Executioner led the party to the basement. He ushered the president and the others out of the stairwell into a large storage room, then grabbed Oliverez. "Take over," he said. "I don't trust that idiot I left upstairs."

Oliverez's head bobbed in agreement. "He will be back in uniform tomorrow," he agreed.

"Only if he lives through this day," Bolan said. "But I want to make sure he does what I told him to do." He paused as a volley of automatic fire on the floor above drowned him out. "Where is the tunnel?"

"On the other side of the mansion," Oliverez said. "It will take a few more minutes to get there."

"Where does it lead?"

"To a safehouse about mile or so from here. There are several small electrically powered vehicles waiting just inside the tunnel. The president and his wife will be safe as soon as we reach them."

"Is there a way to seal the entrance once you're inside?" Bolan asked.

Oliverez nodded. "Yes, there is a twenty-four-hour time lock on the inside of the door. It would take more explosives than these people have to get in."

"Good," the Executioner said. "Activate it as soon as you get inside."

A deep frown of concern broke across the captain's face. "We will do so as soon as you return."

"No." Bolan shook his head. "I'm going up to make sure your man did his job. If he didn't, I'll have to do it for him. We can't take the chance."

"But you—"

"Just do it, Oliverez," the Executioner said. "If I get back down in time, fine. If not, you go on and I'll meet you at the safehouse."

"You don't even know where it is. I won't—"

"I'll find it, and yes you will," Bolan said, his voice growing firm. "Fierro Blanco placed *me* in charge. I don't enjoy pulling rank but I'm doing it now. Get the president and the others into the tunnel and activate the time lock. That's an order."

Oliverez hesitantly nodded, then saluted and turned on his heels.

Bolan moved back up the steps. He could hear the gunfire continuing as he peered through the window once more. He felt his stomach sink when he saw the guard, still wearing his coat and tie, being held against the wall by two men in white peasant garb. As he watched, one of the men jammed a Tokarev pistol into the guard's face. The other ripped open his coat to reveal the straps of a leather shoulder holster.

The Executioner cursed under his breath. The idiot might as well have worn his badge where they could see it. He watched the man who had opened the guard's coat rip a large revolver from under the bodyguard's arm.

Opening the door a crack, the soldier tried to listen around the gunfire and other uproar. By now the second man in white had found a badge case in the guard's coat and was opening it. The man with the Tokarev shoved the barrel of the gun against his prisoner's nose and said, "Where is the president?"

"On the...roof!" the guard shrieked in a voice that reminded Bolan of Josefa de Fierro Blanco's screams.

"You lie!" shouted the man with the gun. "I saw the helicopter go down myself!"

The guard trembled as a third man in white stepped forward and jammed another Tokarev into his scrotum. "Tell us the truth now!" he demanded. "Or live the rest of your life with no *cojones!*"

The guard didn't waste time. "In the basement!" he cried out like a frightened little girl. "They are taking the tunnel to the safehouse!"

His honesty got him a 7.62 mm round through the nose. Right after he lost his *cojones*.

Bolan swung the door wider and fired, sending one .44 Magnum round into each of the three men. They fell to the ground amid the general confusion, and he let the door swing shut once more. Watching through the window again, he fought the impulse to move out into the action. But he didn't know if any of the other rioters had heard what the guard had said or not. And until he did, his wisest course of action was to lie low and not draw attention to the door. One way or another, he had to give the president, his wife and the others as much time as possible to reach the tunnel. For now, that meant keeping a low profile.

Through the door, the soldier heard an unseen voice scream, "They're in the basement—there is a tunnel! I heard this man say so!" Then the rioter, wearing blue jeans and a T-shirt— one of the mob the *Marxistas* had picked up along the way— came running into Bolan's vision holding a captured M-16. He pointed to the dead bodyguard on the floor, then turned toward the doorway to the stairs. "Follow me!"

The Executioner opened the door again and leveled the Desert Eagle at the man's chest. The first round out of the chamber canceled his plans for a leadership position.

But three dozen other armed men right behind him had the same thing in mind.

They rushed the door, as Bolan pulled the trigger again.

9

Encizo had been forced to sit cross-legged on the ground so long, his legs felt as if someone had replaced the blood with starch as he bounded to his feet. Two steps in front of him, the man who had brayed like a donkey was still on his hands and knees. The Cuban ignored the stiffness in his legs, covering the two steps with one long slide. Lifting his right leg, the toe of his leather hiking boot shot straight into the bandit's face.

The kick caught the man squarely between the upper lip and nose. Bone snapped and cartilage tore under the force. The bandit's neck snapped back so violently that Encizo heard it break, too. The man fell flat onto his back, his arms stretched out to his sides and his head at a grotesque angle.

To the side of the dead man, Encizo saw James slash the razor blade across the throat of a bandit. James jumped over the man Encizo had kicked and grabbed at the third member of Vega's crew who had come to investigate Asno's fall—the tequila-drinking man who had brought his bottle with him. The man stepped back out of range, drunkenly fumbling for a pistol holstered at his waist.

Encizo turned and dropped to one knee next to a body on the ground. He jerked a single action Ruger Vaquero from the man's belt. Still kneeling, he spun again and raised the revolver to shoulder level. As the drunken bandit finally found his revolver and started to clear leather, James's left hand moved forward, trapping the weapon to the man's hip. With his right hand, the Phoenix Force warrior snatched the tequila bottle from the bandit's other side, raised it over his head and brought it down on the man's scalp.

The bottle broke off at the neck, shattering into a dozen pieces. Tequila soaked the bandit's head and neck but the blow failed to knock him out. Ducking a shoulder, James drove it into the man's sternum.

The bandit left his feet and flew into the campfire.

The alcohol soaking the bandit's hair and shirt ignited and the man screamed. While flames leaped from his head and shoulders, he jerked the trigger like some gunman from hell, firing three shots from his revolver. All three flew wild.

James took a step toward the fire as the man dropped the gun, but the weapon fell into the flames out of reach.

By now the other drunken men around the fire were on their feet scrambling for weapons. Encizo took aim with the Vaquero, cocked the hammer and sent a .45 Long Colt bullet dead center into a tall bandit's chest. As he cocked the hammer once more, he saw James bend at the waist and lift a burning log from the fire. The Cuban fired again, this time disintegrating the nose of the rooster-like bandit Vega had called Gallo. James drew back his right arm, and sent the fiery log flying. The end of the heavy stick struck Perez squarely between the eyes and thumped like a baseball bat hitting a watermelon.

Encizo fired the Ruger again, then once more, dropping a bandit dressed in black jeans and a matching shirt, followed by a squat man wearing criss-crossed bandoliers. Out of the corner of his eye, he saw James dodge a volley of return fire as he raced to Perez and recovered one of the Phoenix Force Berettas.

The return fire so far had been wild, and Encizo counted them lucky. The drunken, marijuana-saturated men had been slow to realize what was happening, then almost as slow to react. They had stumbled and staggered trying to find their weapons, then fumbled with holsters, rifle scabbards and safeties before they could operate them. Their shots were hasty and panic-stricken, and Encizo knew that was all that had saved him, James and Nelson this far.

Thinking of the DEA man now, Encizo shot a glance toward where the man had sat. Nelson was nowhere to be seen. Good. With his hands still bound, there was nothing he could contribute at this point, and getting out of the way was the best thing he could do—both for himself and the "war effort."

Only two of the eleven bandits the Cuban had counted around the camp still remained on their feet, and both suddenly disappeared into the darkness on the other side of the fire. Encizo turned toward the lean-to. Vega, of course, was still alive too. But neither he nor the woman had appeared during the few seconds the firefight had taken.

Encizo turned toward James. As he did, a round whizzed past his face far closer than the others. It would have taken him just under the ear had he not turned when he did. The Cuban dropped low, swiveling toward the direction from which the shot had come. Another bullet sailed over his head a split second after he'd ducked.

Encizo fell to the ground and rolled behind the boulders to the rear of the area where he'd been seated. In the darkness, he wondered if he actually had cover. He thought he did—at least from the gunshots of the man who had just fired. But what about the other one? And where was Pug Nelson? Was he even still alive?

Movement ten feet to his side sent the Ruger swinging that way. The hammer already cocked, Encizo's finger curled around the trigger as he spotted a dark silhouette. He was about to squeeze when a familiar voice whispered, "Rafe!"

The Cuban lowered the Vaquero as James crawled across the rocks to his side. "I count just two, plus Vega."

Encizo nodded in the moonlight. "You seen Pug?"

James's shadow shook its head.

Somewhere to their rear, a twig snapped.

James leaned in closer. "They're circling behind us," he whispered. "I'm going—"

"No," Encizo whispered back. "Watch the front. They may have split up." He turned and began belly-crawling over the rocks.

The coyotes in the distance had heard the gunfire, and they now sang an aroused medley to accompany the Cuban as he crawled. He reached the edge of the boulders and stopped, quietly hauling himself to his feet. The man or men in the darkness might be just out of sight two feet away. If they had separated, as he suspected, fine. But if he was wrong, and the men had stayed close together, the muzzle-flash of his Vaquero would give him away to whichever one he didn't shoot first. Transferring the Ruger to his left hand, he reached behind his belt for the Randall Model 1. He found only an empty belt. Cursing whichever bandit now had his blade, he switched the Vaquero back to his strong side and pressed his body against the boulder.

He could hear nothing on the other side of the rock. But somehow he sensed a human presence. Then, suddenly, two familiar odors wafted around the edge of the large boulder against his side: tequila and marijuana. Whoever was on the other side of the rock was doing a good job remaining silent. But he couldn't hold his breath forever, and probably hadn't even thought to try.

Encizo slowly lowered himself to one knee. If the man or men just beyond the rocks suspected he was there, they'd be waiting. But they'd expect him to round the boulder on foot, and be preparing to shoot either head or chest level. Encizo couldn't be certain exactly how close his enemy was. But he planned to roll, and if he struck the man, that roll should hit the bandit low and take his feet out from under him.

In the distance, the coyotes quit howling and began to bark. Encizo took a deep breath, let it out, then rolled from cover into the open, his single action six gun ready.

The Cuban had planned to come to a halt on his side, the Vaquero aimed overhead. But halfway through the roll, his back struck something that halted him. A shriek of surprise issued forth behind him, followed by a foul-smelling burp. Encizo cursed himself for not thinking his plan through to the next step; searching for all the things that could potentially go wrong. He had not even considered the possibility that the bandit, too, might be on his knees.

The Cuban rolled away from the man behind him and came up in a sitting position. The other man did the same. Sitting with their legs outstretched, toe to toe on the ground, they looked into each other's eyes in the moonlight for a long split second. Then Encizo fired.

The Vaquero bucked in his hand as another .45 Colt shot from the barrel. The big slug caught the bandit dead center between the eyes, and drilled through his brain stem, ending all muscle movement, voluntary or involuntary. The bandit fell backward into the sand.

James rolled away from the muzzle-flash signature in case the other man was nearby. Cocking the Vaquero again, he realized he had now fired five times and wondered how the weapon had been loaded. Single action revolvers like Colts and the Colt clones were traditionally carried with the hammer down on an empty chamber to prevent accidental discharges. But the Rugers, such as the Vaquero he now held, had a transfer bar that made them safe to carry fully loaded. Some men still followed the old tradition, however, dropping only five rounds into the six gun to add an extra measure of safety.

Did he have a shot left, or was he holding an empty weapon? Encizo had no idea, and this wasn't the time to open the loading gate to try to find out.

When no rounds flew toward him, the Cuban's suspicions that the remaining two men had divided were confirmed. Cautiously, he rose to his feet and made his way back through the rocks to where he and James had been. But his fellow Phoenix Force warrior was no longer there.

A moment later, he saw why.

James stood at the edge of the boulders, his Beretta aimed toward the lean-to. Vega had finally emerged. He stood behind the woman who was now fully nude. The bandit leader had one arm wrapped around her throat. With his other, he jammed the nickel-plated Colt into her ear. The hammer of the Colt was cocked.

The woman's mouth was frozen open in a silent scream.

Encizo froze in his tracks, hoping he was still far enough back in the shadows of the rocks that Vega hadn't seen him. "Throw down your gun!" he heard Vega order James.

"Not a chance," James replied.

"I don't intend to play games with you," Vega shouted. "Throw it down or I will kill her at the count of three."

Encizo's hopes that Vega hadn't seen him were short-lived. The leader's eyes flickered past James and he shouted, "You! Cuban! Step forward and throw down your gun or I will kill her on the spot!"

Encizo stepped into the firelight. But he kept the Vaquero firmly in his grip and aimed at Vega and his captive.

Vega's attention returned to James. "One..." he said.

James didn't move.

"Two..."

There was another long pause, then James tossed the Beretta in front of him to the ground.

Vega laughed. He seemed for the moment to have forgotten that Encizo still held the Ruger. The Cuban then thanked the heavens once more for tequila and marijuana. Neither was enough to win the fight for the men from Stony Man Farm. But it was still causing at least momentary lapses in Vega's concentration.

"You are weak, you Americans," the bandit called out. "You're willing to give up your lives for a whore such as this?"

When neither Phoenix Force men answered, he went on. "I'm afraid I lied to you, *amigos*," he said. "I *do* wish to play a game with you." He looked into the darkness on the other side of the fire. "Demonio!" he shouted.

The monstrously scarred man stepped into the firelight. Pug

Nelson stumbled in front of him. The DEA man had somehow freed his hands, but Demonio's Bowie knife was pressed into his throat.

"I enjoy watching Demonio at work," Vega said. "But Garcia was hardly a match." He grinned evilly. "I'll make you a new deal. If one of you can defeat Demonio with a knife, I'll let you all go free."

"How are we to know that?" James asked. "You're the one holding the gun."

Vega looked past him to Encizo, and the Cuban saw he hadn't been forgotten as he'd hoped. "Your friend still has his gun," he said. "I'll let him keep it throughout the match."

Encizo glanced down at the Vaquero, again wondering if all the chambers were empty.

James turned to face him. The black soldier grinned. "You got to do the tracking," he said. "Guess it's my turn to have fun, now."

Encizo nodded. While Vega hadn't specified Demonio's opponent, there was no question as to which of them would face him. Encizo didn't waste time offering to take James's place. Like his fellow warrior had just said, tracking was within the Cuban's realm of expertise. Edged weapons fell into his. Encizo felt no shame at letting his partner take the risk—that was how things were done by the men of Phoenix Force. Each man had his specialties, and he performed them without question when circumstances demanded.

A grin crossed the Cuban's face for a moment. Besides, he'd bet his bottom dollar on Calvin James against any blade-man he'd ever come across. The grin faded. Then again, a knife fight was ruled by a fickle mistress. Anything could happen. And he had already seen the prowess Demonio exhibited with his Mexican Bowie.

Demonio pushed Nelson forward, hooked a foot around the man's leg and sent him sprawling awkwardly to the ground. The DEA agent looked up at the disfigured man and said, "When this is over, I don't think there's gonna be enough of your burned-up hide to even stand. But just in case there is, maybe you'd like to go a round or two with bare knuckles. What do you think of that idea?''

Demonio threw back his head and laughed.

"You! Cuban!" Vega yelled to Encizo. "Come here by the fire and join your friend."

Encizo made his way to the fireside, the Vaquero still aimed in Vega's direction. But the man was well hidden behind the beautiful nude woman, and he had no shot. Not at this distance. He took a seat next to Nelson on the sandy ground.

His eyes glued to Encizo, Vega quickly shifted the Colt to his left hand and jammed the barrel into the woman's other ear. It occurred to Encizo, as the bandit drew the Crossada from the sheath on his belt, that he had never even learned the woman's name. Not that it mattered. If he was to die tonight trying to save an innocent human being, so be it. Her name made no difference.

Vega drew back his arm and threw the huge knife around the woman, through the flames of the campfire, toward James. The ten-inch spear-point blade burrowed into the sand an inch from his feet. James leaned and withdrew it from the sand.

Then the Phoenix Force warrior stepped forward to meet the devil.

FIRING THROUGH THE doorway to the stairwell, the Executioner emptied the Desert Eagle into the oncoming rioters. As the last round left the barrel, he reached under his jacket with his left hand, grabbing the Beretta 93-R. By the time the Desert Eagle had fallen from the recoil, he had thumbed the Beretta's selector switch to 3-round burst and a trio of 9 mms were chasing the .44 Magnum slugs.

Five men fell to the Israeli pistol. Three more to the Italian-made select-fire. It was enough to slow even the hardiest men rushing the door, and they took cover around corners on the ground floor.

Bolan took advantage of the respite to shove a fresh magazine up the grips of the Desert Eagle. He waited as the thundering sound of the gunfire began to die in his ears. But when the voice hidden somewhere in the hall spoke, it still sounded to the Executioner as if its owner was somewhere far away and speaking from inside a steel drum.

"You!" the voice called out. "We saw you, and you are alone! Come out with your hands above your head!"

"No thanks," Bolan called back. He wasn't usually much for small talk during a gunfight, or at any other time for that matter. But the longer he kept the men storming the presidential mansion busy, the longer Oliverez had to get Fierro Blanco and the others into the tunnel.

"We are many!" the voice returned. "If you don't come out we will kill you!"

"Yeah, well, we'll see," the Executioner said. "You were eight more thirty seconds ago, and you couldn't get it done then."

His answer came in the form of a volley of fire from one of the captured M-16s. The .223 rounds struck the wall in front of where he crouched, sending cement chips and dust flying through the hall but doing no damage. Seeing no targets for return fire, the Executioner wasted no rounds.

"This is your final chance!" the voice called out again.

"Give me a little time to think about it," Bolan called back. He glanced to his watch again. He didn't know exactly how far away the tunnel in the basement below was, or how long it would take the people heading for it to get there. But he knew each second he stalled was another in their favor.

"We won't wait any longer!"

"I need some time," Bolan said. He had pinpointed the voice around a corner just to his right. Now, as he peered from behind cover though the doorway, he saw a straw sombrero edging around the barrier. He wasn't surprised to see that the brim was decorated with a brightly colored fringe of balls.

"We grow impatient!" screamed the man in the hat.

Bolan knew that the only reason the man was even trying to

make a deal was that he had seen how many had already fallen to the Executioner's guns. The *Marxista*-led rioters might outnumber him, but his situation still wasn't all that bad. The door was narrow, making it easy to defend. Until he ran out of ammo, which wouldn't be soon, they'd have a hell of a time getting past him to the basement.

"How much time do you need?" the man called out, convincing Bolan even further that the man recognized his weak bargaining position.

"Give me until the twelfth."

"What? What do you mean? The twelfth of what?"

"The twelfth of never," Bolan said, and fired a 3-round burst at the hat.

The 9 mm hollowpoint slugs stripped two of the colored balls from the straw and made a mess out of the rest of the brim. The man under the hat ducked back around the corner.

A massive volley of fire answered the Executioner's shots, striking the concrete in front of him again and driving him down, but again doing no harm. Silence fell over the ground floor of the mansion once more as the noise dissipated. Bolan watched through the door, waiting. Suddenly, a thought raced through his mind. *Los Pinos* was a big place. It had to have more than one set of stairs.

Did the rioters know that? Had the man in the sombrero already sent men that way, staying behind with the rest of these gunmen to stall Bolan as he was trying to stall them?

The Executioner didn't know. But he couldn't afford to take the chance. Leaning slightly around the doorway, he emptied the Beretta into the hall, then turned and headed down the steps. The echos from the blasts would cover his footsteps, giving him an additional few seconds before the *Marxistas* and their newfound fellow dissidents realized he had fled. He reached the halfway landing and turned the corner, dropping the empty magazine from the Beretta and shoving a fresh 15-round mag into the butt. Still running, he held the Desert Eagle with three fingers as he pulled back the slide of the 93-R to chamber the first round.

Bolan reached the basement and sprinted into the storage room where he'd left Oliverez, then raced to an open door in the opposite wall. The captain had said the tunnel was on the other side of the mansion, but he didn't know where. The basement was a labyrinth of twisting tunnels and rooms, and he had no idea where he was going.

Passing through the door, Bolan found himself in a narrow hallway that ended fifty feet away. Four doors were set in the wall between him and the brick wall ahead. He stopped, listening, smelling, trying to sense which way Oliverez had led the others.

Through the second door on his right, he heard footsteps running in the distance. The president and the others? Or the *Marxistas?* He didn't know but it didn't matter. Regardless of which group was making the noise, that's where he needed to be.

Taking off again, the Executioner sprinted into a room stacked to the ceiling with rest-room and kitchen supplies. Two other doors set off this storage area, but the footsteps were louder now and his choice was clear. Without breaking stride, he dashed through the opening to his right and turned toward the noise.

Twenty feet away, he saw two dozen armed men sprinting down the hall directly toward him. Most of them wore white peasant outfits.

The Executioner came to an abrupt halt. Raising the Desert Eagle, he fired two rounds. Out of the corner of his eye he saw an alcove on the other side of the hall, with the mansion's air-conditioning unit set inside the recess. Raising the Beretta next to the Eagle, he pulled both triggers as he ducked into the niche and jammed between the unit and the brick wall.

With barely enough room to squeeze his arm around the corner, Bolan double-tapped another pair of .44 Magnum slugs into the still surprised *Marxistas* and their pick-up rioters. Four of the two dozen already lay dead on the tile floor. The new hollowpoint bullets added another to the count. The Executioner jerked his arm back to cover.

The other men in the hallway turned and ran back the way they'd come. The Executioner got three more before they disappeared around a corner.

Bolan knew he had no time to waste. The *Marxistas* had been running toward him when he stumbled upon them, which meant the tunnel had to be somewhere behind where he now stood. That was, of course, if the rioters knew where they were headed any better than he did. He reloaded the Desert Eagle, glanced around the corner, fired two more rounds down the deserted hall to keep the men hidden, then darted out and raced away.

He'd have to hope the *Marxistas* knew where they were going. He had to stay between them and the escaping presidential party, and the direction in which the rioters had been headed was the only reference he had. The thought brought a grim smile to the soldier's face as he ran. He couldn't remember for sure, but he suspected this might well be the first time in his long career that he hoped a terrorist group had good intelligence information.

Reaching an intersecting hall, Bolan stopped. He strained his ears but could hear nothing. He turned toward the direction from which he'd come, extending the Beretta in front of him while he pondered the dilemma in case the *Marxistas* chose this moment to break cover and resume their pursuit.

Bolan stared up one hall and down the other. Which way had Oliverez gone? He had no idea. He was about to just pick a direction and go with it—any action was better than none—when a flash of gold in the middle of the floor to his left caught his eye. With a final glance back toward the hiding *Marxistas*, he sprinted to the source of the reflection. He reached down, lifting the object to his eyes in the dim lighting.

In his hand he saw a federal badge. Across the top it read, *Capitano*.

Bolan dropped the badge into his pocket and ran on. Behind him, he heard footsteps pounding down the halls. The men he had surprised had gotten over their shock, realized he was alone and were now racing forward.

Reaching another intersection, Bolan scanned the floor both ways. He saw what he sought to his right this time. Turning that way, he sprinted on, scooping the white card from the floor without breaking stride. He glanced at it as he ran and saw exactly what he expected to see—a federal commission card bearing Oliverez's picture and name. He dropped it into his pocket with the badge.

The footsteps behind him were closer now, and Bolan heard them turn the corner into the same hallway he was in. He twisted at the waist, firing a 3-round burst over his shoulder as he ran. The footsteps slowed for a moment, then picked up again.

When the next decision came, the hand-tooled leather holster in which Oliverez carried his .45 revolver pointed the way. The Executioner pivoted back toward the *Marxistas* as he bent to pick it up, fired another triburst round, and sped on.

The captain's empty black badge case lay in the middle of the new hallway in front of a door. Bolan scooped it up as he ran, twisted and fired again at the oncoming men. One of them dropped, but the others kept coming.

The badge case led him to a round steel door. The door was thrown back wide, and in the opening stood Captain Juanito Oliverez, his familiar Government Model .45 aimed at the Executioner. Bolan angled toward the door but as he did he heard several sets of footsteps behind him.

"Duck!" Oliverez screamed.

Bolan bent at the waist and Oliverez emptied the .45 revolver. Behind him, the Executioner heard shrieks of pain. He dived into the tunnel, spun and emptied the final rounds from both the Beretta and Desert Eagle into the men rushing the door.

Oliverez and another guard swung the heavy steel gate

closed. The captain twirled the handle of the lock and the Executioner heard the tumblers fall into place. The soft ticking of the time mechanism filled the silence in the escape tunnel.

Then fists and gun butts began to beat on the other side of the door. Bolan turned and looked down the underground shaft. Behind him, voices screamed threats and curses, but in front of him the Executioner saw President and Mrs. Don Juan de Fierro Blanco and several other guards already seated in the small electrical vehicles.

Oliverez pointed at two seats in the rear of the last car and Bolan climbed in. The captain got in after him. As the underground convoy took off, heading for the safehouse, the Executioner turned toward the man next to him. "If I'm not mistaken, I ordered you not to wait," he said.

Oliverez dropped his head in mock shame. "One of my worst faults," he said, "is the inability to remember even the most simple orders sometimes." He looked at Bolan and grinned. "I'm glad you found the way."

The Executioner pulled Oliverez's badge, badge case, commission card and holster out of his pockets and handed them to the man. "Well, Hansel," he said laughing, "leaving the trail of bread crumbs didn't hurt."

RAFAEL ENCIZO WONDERED again if the Vaquero in his hand still held a round or was empty. Seated next to Nelson, the six gun still aimed toward Vega and the woman, he watched as Demonio began to circle James as he had done with Garcia. Checking a single-action revolver was considerably harder than inspecting the double-action version or an autopistol. So far, the Cuban simply hadn't had an opportunity. And as he watched James begin to mirror Demonio's circling steps, he doubted if he would soon, either.

James held the Crossada in front of him, his elbow bent. His other arm paralleled the weapon, ready to parry or check if necessary. The Phoenix Force blade expert's feet were shoulder width apart in a classic Bowie fighting stance. Demonio's posture was similar as he circled, occasionally feinting in and out. The Mexican bandit was in no hurry. He was taking his time, waiting for his adversary to make a move. But the Phoenix Force warrior didn't comply. James was waiting out the other man, too, continuing to revolve in a counterclockwise direction.

"Action!" Vega screamed from behind the nude woman. "I want to see some action! Someone do something or I'll kill her right now!"

Demonio threw a halfhearted thrust obviously designed more to watch James's reaction than draw blood. James stepped easily out of the way. Slowly, as the two men continued to circle, the Phoenix Force warrior's knife hand began to drift out, away from his body.

Encizo held his breath as, inch by inch, the Crossada moved further out. It looked as if James's concentration was so focused on strategy that he was forgetting the most basic tactics of defense. Soon the black soldier's hand was well inside the range of Demonio's Bowie. One fast slash to the hand or wrist from the bandit would cripple James and send the Crossada tumbling to the sand. Encizo wanted to scream a warning, but feared he'd break the man's concentration even further.

Demonio saw the weakness, too. Feinting a thrust toward the abdomen, he stopped the movement halfway there and slashed cross-body at James's hand. But James's elbow shot upward, pulling his hand out of range. His wrist rolled, and the Crossada flipped over and came down in a back-cut aimed at Demonio's attack hand.

Demonio, however, was a worthy adversary. He pulled his Bowie straight back to his centerline and out of the way. The Crossada whiffed air like a batter missing a strike, but Encizo breathed a sigh of relief anyway. What had appeared to be negligence on James's part had actually been sound strategy. The drifting arm had been nothing more than bait designed to draw Demonio's own hand and arm into the Crossada's range.

"Blood!" Vega shouted. "I want to see blood!"

The circling began again. James shot suddenly forward with

a thrust. For a second, it appeared the contest was over, for Encizo saw blood shoot from Demonio's head. But the distorted man didn't fall, and as he circled on, the Cuban saw that he must have eluded the steel jab at the last possible instant. Half of his already-gnarled ear was gone, and blood poured from the wound. But the man with the Bowie didn't seem to care or even notice the wound.

On they fought, thrusting and slashing, feinting and countering. At one point James and Demonio both switched into ice-pick grips, holding their big knives with the blades extended past the little fingers rather than their thumbs. They closed upon one another in a burst of flashing steel, and the encounter was so fast and well executed it looked to Encizo like a prearranged practice drill.

Switching back to saber grips, the deadly revolutions by the campfire resumed, with the big blades twinkling in the light of the flames. Demonio appeared to be tiring, his Bowie growing heavier and slower in his hand. His breathing came harder, and his feet lost a shade of their earlier deftness. Then, suddenly, he fell to his side in the sand.

James started to step in for the kill, then suddenly hopped back as the Bowie darted forward. Demonio vaulted back to his feet with the same spryness he had exhibited earlier, and Encizo saw that his fatigue had been a charade. But what the Cuban didn't notice, at least at first, was that the hideous man's left fist was now closed.

Luckily, James did.

The Phoenix Force knife expert spun backward as the sand flew toward his eyes. Thousands of tiny grains struck the back of his neck and back, ricochetting off. With footwork that looked to Encizo like the prelude to a tae kwon do spinning back-kick, James continued to spin. But his feet stayed on the ground.

The Crossada, however, came around in an arc. James's backhand slash caught the monster in the lower abdomen, slicing through his distorted flesh and disemboweling him like a shamed samurai. The cannibal dropped to his knees, the Bowie falling to his side. His lone eye widened in astonishment as he clutched his escaping intestines with both hands, absurdly trying to stuff them back into the gaping wound. Then his one eye closed. A second later, he lay facedown in the sand.

The victorious Phoenix Force warrior turned toward where Encizo and Nelson sat, then looked at Vega and the woman. The bandit leader's revolver was still pressed tightly into her ear. "Now let her go," James ordered.

Vega laughed. "Are you serious, *hombre?*" he said.

"That was the deal," Encizo said, rising to his feet. He tried to aim over the woman at Vega but he still had no good shot. He wondered again if it would do him any good if he did. Was he holding an empty gun? "Our man won. You gave us your word."

"My word, *señor?*" he said, shaking his head in disbelief. "My word? *Hombre,* I am a *bandido.*"

The three men stood looking at each other in silence for a moment. Then, suddenly, it appeared that the lovely nude woman in Vega's grasp had finally taken all she could stand. With a scream, she twisted in his grip and grabbed his gun hand. Whether by design or luck, Encizo didn't know, but her thumb found a place between the cocked hammer and firing pin of the nickel-plated Colt.

The hammer fell, but hit flesh instead of steel. The woman shrieked again as her other hand joined the first on the gun. She held on firmly as Vega tried to rip it from her grasp. Twisting further, she stretched up and sank her teeth into the bandit's fingers to strengthen her grip.

Vega screamed in a higher pitch than she had.

Encizo, James and Nelson raced forward as the bandit leader pulled and jerked on the gun. Vega looked like a dog trying to tear a rag from his master's hand as he swung the woman into the air, then back and forth. But she was like a dog with a bone, and she hung on with the same intensity, refusing to relinquish her grip. Her teeth stayed deep in his hand, and Vega continued to shriek in both pain and frustration.

James was the closest, and he reached them first. He grasped Vega's wrist with one hand, the Colt's hammer with the other. With a violent twist that broke the man's arm, he wrenched the weapon away.

Encizo planted his feet and sighted down the Vaquero's barrel at Vega's head. But as he cocked the six gun's hammer, Nelson stepped between him and the bandit. The former Navy champion threw a left hook that would have sent Evander Holyfield to the canvas. Instead, it sent Victorio Vega to the sand.

"Kill him!" the woman shouted. Her bare foot lashed out and struck the bandit's unconscious face. "Shoot the bastard!"

James kept Vega's Colt trained on him as he knelt and slapped the bandit back to consciousness. As soon as the man's eyes opened, the Phoenix Force warrior rose back to his feet. "This lady thinks we should kill you," he said.

Vega didn't answer. He just stared at the men above him with hate-filled eyes.

"Maybe we should turn him over to the feds or something," Nelson said. His voice didn't sound like his heart was in the idea. He sounded more like he was just spouting the DEA party line out of a sense of duty.

"How about that, Vega?" Encizo asked. "Want us to take you in?" The Cuban knew how the feds handled bandits.

So did Vega. "You may as well kill me now," the bandit mumbled around his broken jaw, compliments of Nelson. "But if you will release me, I will make you rich. I have treasures hidden in these hills. Treasures my men didn't know about."

"No," pleaded the woman. "You can't—"

James held up a hand to silence her. "How about that, Rafe?" James asked. "Want to be rich?"

"All the rich people I know are unhappy," Encizo said.

"How about you, Pug?"

Nelson grinned. He found another cigar in his shirt pocket. It was broken in half but he shoved the bigger piece into his mouth and struck a match. "Wouldn't mind giving it a try someday," he said. "But I figure if we let this son of a bitch go, he'd just take up his naughty ways again."

"Please!" the woman said. "If you won't kill him, let me do it!"

Encizo turned to look at the beautiful young woman. Her hair was a mess of tangles, and spots of sand stuck to her skin, none of which made her look any less radiant. She stood before the four men, naked to the world, but in all the excitement she seemed to have forgotten her nudity and made no effort to cover herself. Or maybe she just figured since they had already seen her, trying to cover up now didn't make much sense. In either case, it took an effort on Encizo's part to keep his eyes on her face as he spoke. "Did he hurt you?" the Cuban asked.

The woman shook her head. "He tried," she said. "But he had drunk too much and...he couldn't. It made him angry. He was about to cut my throat when the shooting started."

Encizo nodded. He handed her the Ruger Vaquero. "I'd say you've earned this privilege," he said.

Calvin James and Pug Nelson both nodded.

The woman took the gun.

The Vaquero's sixth chamber, it turned out, had been loaded.

EPILOGUE

The sun beat down on the northern Yucatán peninsula, causing the Executioner's forehead to break out in sweat. He wiped his face with the back of his hand, adjusted his sunglasses and looked out over the blue waters of the Gulf of Mexico. In the distance, cavorting in the waves, he could see a pod of dolphins. These animals, so close to humans, romped and frolicked through the sea with a peace that he himself had never known.

Bolan shifted his feet in the sand, turned and looked past a royal palm tree down the private beach. Fifty feet away, Don Juan de Fierro Blanco, his wife Josefa and their three children sat picnicking on a blanket. All wore swimsuits and did their best to grin and laugh, and be happy as they passed tortillas, potato salad and other food to one another. But there was a shade of apprehension in each smile; a hint of foreboding in every giggle. Bolan didn't have to ask why. He had only to look around him.

Close to two hundred plainclothes guards occupied space at the president's summer home on the Yucatán coast north of Mérida. Like Bolan, they wore shorts and T-shirts, or swimming trunks and terry cloth tops. But beneath the vacation clothes, the bulges of pistols could be seen, and the briefcases carried by many of the men held Uzis rather than papers. Each man had an M-16 and three hundred rounds of ammunition stored in the pool house, and sentries were posted along the perimeter of the isolated property. Two-way radios squawked on the men's belts—sometimes so loud that Fierro Blanco or one of his family had to quit speaking until the transmission was over.

The scene was anything but the quiet, restful, sequestered vacation it was supposed to be. It couldn't be. They'd be fools to lighten security with the *Marxistas* still on the warpath, in addition to all the other problems currently plaguing Mexico. The Executioner looked at the fear behind the smiling face of one of the twin boys. The sight threatened to break Bolan's heart. The kid had no idea what the problem was. He just knew there were men with guns everywhere he looked, and that meant he was in danger. He, his brother and sister didn't deserve to have to live under such conditions.

The Executioner's gaze shifted to the pasted-on smiles of the other members of the Fierro Blanco family. General Antonio de Razon was with them—in full dress uniform of course—and he smiled as well. The two hundred men on the premises wore similar expressions. Everyone knew what was going on but everyone tried to act like they didn't.

Bolan shifted the Beretta under his T-shirt and walked along the beach away from the family. It was time he checked on the sentries again. From now on, he would leave the guards in charge of nothing he could personally oversee. There were good ones all right—some of them damn fine officers. But there were too many incompetents among the ranks, too. Like the men who had let the sniper set up shop at the Basque de Chapeltepec. Or the ones who hadn't screened the guides at the hog hunt, allowed the waiter to get into the governor's dinner with a loaded firearm and let the cop with the poison almost kill the president. And he hadn't forgotten the man who had almost gotten them all killed back at *Los Pinos* by forgetting to take off his coat and tie like the Executioner had ordered.

Bolan looked back over his shoulder at the men swarming the grounds. Considering the number of federal bodyguards he was forced to deal with, there was no way he could check them all out personally. He would never know the good from the bad until it was too late.

Stopping to pick up a conch shell, Bolan tossed it up and down in his hand. Many things still bothered him about the situation in Mexico. Not the least worrisome was that he still didn't know if the president was hooked into any of the revolutionary terrorist organizations, mixed up with the drug cartels or behind the assassinations of journalists and political adversaries. Just that morning word had come in that the body of Emilio Romero, the internationally syndicated columnist, had been found.

Bolan corrected himself. *Pieces* of a body authorities suspected belonged to Romero had been found.

The Executioner dropped the conch shell back on the sand, picked up a flat rock and skipped it across the water toward the dolphins.

One of the guards had given him more disturbing news right after breakfast. Two Americans, an ex-patriot businessman named Scott Hix and his more famous friend, movie megastar Ronnie Quartel, had been abducted from Hix's home in Sonora. The rumor was that the mayor of Tijuana and several women had also been taken. So far, no ransom notes had surfaced and it was unclear just who the kidnappers were. But Bolan knew the right-wing *Cuidadano para Democracia Mexicana Legitima* had headquarters somewhere in the state of Sonora. If he were doing the investigation, it would be the *Legitimas* he looked at first.

Oliverez came walking out of the house through the door to the screened-in back porch. He wore khaki shorts and a black T-shirt, his .45 pistol stuck into his belt just behind the buckle. He started toward Fierro Blanco and his family, then spotted Bolan and angled off. The soldier stopped and waited for him. The sight of the Mexican captain made him smile. Some of the other members of the protection team might be washouts, but Juanito Oliverez was as good as they came. He was perhaps the only man in Mexico the Executioner trusted anymore.

Ten feet away, Oliverez glanced out at the sea. The dolphins had followed Bolan along the beach, and the captain stopped in his tracks and grinned like a ten-year-old boy. Then, turning to Bolan, he said, "If only we could be gentle like them, eh, *amigo?*"

Bolan chuckled with a humor he wasn't feeling at the moment. "Yeah, it would be nice. But we're not." He looked out at the dolphins again himself. "They aren't always gentle, you know. You see those beaks? They make formidable weapons. And dolphins each have between forty and sixty teeth that they aren't shy about using if you push them too far. Ask a few herring and mackerel if they think the dolphins are pacifists."

Oliverez shrugged his shoulders. "Dolphins have sex orgies—or so I've heard."

The Executioner's laughter was authentic this time. While Oliverez had proved himself to be a seasoned warrior, he still had a boyish innocence that made him refreshing to be around. He was always nice until it was time to stop being nice. Which was the way Bolan figured God had meant man to be; the way dolphins were. "I've heard the same thing," he said. "But tell me, what else have you heard?"

"About dolphins?"

Bolan waited.

Oliverez smiled. He had known what the soldier meant. "After yesterday, Mexico City is quiet again," he said. "How long will that last? Who knows. The mob at the mansion dispersed—those who didn't get killed—soon after the military arrived. But over a hundred died, many of them wearing the white peasant shirts we have grown to know and love so dearly."

"Any of them wearing a sombrero with a ball fringe?"

The captain shrugged. "Probably," he said. "Such hats are common. I will find out."

Bolan nodded. He turned and walked on along the beach toward the first of the sentry stations.

Oliverez fell in next to him "There is more word from Sonora, as well," he said.

Again, the Executioner waited.

"We were right. The *Legitimas* have announced they have Ronnie Quartel, Hix, Cervantes—he's the mayor—and several women. They promise to issue their demands soon."

The Executioner walked on in silence. He wished with all his heart that he had the men of Able Team and the rest of Phoenix Force with him in Mexico. He could only be in one place at one time, and he needed men he could trust to be in the other places.

That thought led him to James and Encizo. He hadn't spoken to them since they'd left Mexico City. And when he'd placed a call to El Paso earlier in the morning, he had learned that they'd left with the DEA agent who had been in charge prior to their arrival. That was thirty-six hours earlier. All three were considered missing.

Bolan wasn't worried. James and Encizo could take care of themselves. But he did want to talk to them as soon as possible; he needed a more in-depth view of the situation along the border.

From there his thoughts traveled to Carl "Ironman" Lyons, Hermann "Gadgets" Schwarz and Rosario "Politician" Blancanales. He wondered how their stakeout on the Russian Mafia in Alaska was going, and just how much longer they'd be tied up there. He could use the men of Able Team south of the border, too.

The first of the guard stations appeared a quarter-mile ahead but no sentries could be seen. Bolan and Oliverez walked on until they finally spotted one of the guards lying on the ground in the shade of a palm. His rifle lay across his lap and while he wasn't asleep, he might as well have been for all the good he was doing.

Oliverez cleared his throat when they were still fifty yards away. The man leaped to his feet and began pacing the area.

"You can cut it out," Bolan said as they reached the guard. "We saw you."

Oliverez sighed. "Go on back to the house," he said.

"But my tour of duty isn't over for another hour," the sentry said.

"Your tour of duty is over, *period*," Oliverez replied. "Go. Before I shoot you." His hand fell to the pistol in his belt.

The guard's eyes widened and he started to walk away. Oliverez reached out and snatched the M-16 from his hand first.

As the man walked down the beach with his head hanging in shame, the captain turned to the Executioner. "I'm afraid you have gotten a slanted view of Mexicans," he said. "My people aren't all this way."

"I know that," Bolan told him. "I work with two Hispanics on a regular basis, and there aren't any finer men around. Encizo and Blancanales. I suspect you'll meet them before all this is over."

Oliverez smiled the ten-year-old-boy smile again. "I'll look forward to it," he said. His face turned more serious. "Mexico is going through a very difficult time, Belasko. No one knows who to trust, and good law enforcement officials are hard to find. The guards are the best my country has, but even we must sometimes choose between men who we know to be honest but incompetent, and men we know are competent but dishonest."

"Neither kind will do," Bolan said. "You've got to have both in the same package."

"I pray that we will again someday," Oliverez said. "And I believe we will. I have dedicated my life to seeing that we survive."

"I'll do what I can to help," the soldier said. He reached out and took the M-16 from his friend's hands. "Go back and find another man to take this station, Juanito," he said. "Choose a good one. Competent *and* honest. I'll watch things until he gets here."

The captain saluted and turned away.

Bolan watched him go until he was out of sight along the

beach, then turned back and looked out into the Gulf again. The rolling azure water was deserted. Even the dolphins had left him now. The Executioner was alone.

But then, he always was.

James Axler

OUTLANDERS™

ARMAGEDDON AXIS

What was supposed to be the seat of power after the nuclear holocaust, a vast installation inside Mount Rushmore—is a new powerbase of destruction. Kane and his fellow exiles venture to the hot spot, where they face an old enemy conspiring to start the second wave of Armageddon.

Shadow THE EXECUTIONER®
as he battles evil for 352 pages of heart-stopping action!

SuperBolan®

#61452	DAY OF THE VULTURE	$5.50 U.S. $6.50 CAN.	☐ ☐
#61453	FLAMES OF WRATH	$5.50 U.S. $6.50 CAN.	☐ ☐
#61454	HIGH AGGRESSION	$5.50 U.S. $6.50 CAN.	☐ ☐
#61455	CODE OF BUSHIDO	$5.50 U.S. $6.50 CAN.	☐ ☐
#61456	TERROR SPIN	$5.50 U.S. $6.50 CAN.	☐ ☐

(limited quantities available on certain titles)

TOTAL AMOUNT	$
POSTAGE & HANDLING	$
($1.00 for one book, 50¢ for each additional)	
APPLICABLE TAXES*	$ _____
TOTAL PAYABLE	$ _____
(check or money order—please do not send cash)	

To order, complete this form and send it, along with a check or money order for the total above, payable to Gold Eagle Books, to: **In the U.S.:** 3010 Walden Avenue, P.O. Box 9077, Buffalo, NY 14269-9077; **In Canada:** P.O. Box 636, Fort Erie, Ontario, L2A 5X3.

Name: _____

Address: _____ City: _____

State/Prov.: _____ Zip/Postal Code: _____

*New York residents remit applicable sales taxes.
 Canadian residents remit applicable GST and provincial taxes.

GSBBACK1